IT SHOULD
BE A CRIME

Visit us at www.boldstrokesbooks.com

By the Author

truelesbianlove.com
(Aeros eBook)

IT SHOULD BE A CRIME

by

Carsen Taite

2009

IT SHOULD BE A CRIME

ISBN 10: 1-60282-086-4
ISBN 13: 978-1-60282-086-9

This Trade Paperback Original Is Published By
Bold Strokes Books, Inc.
P.O. Box 249
Valley Falls, NY 12185

First Edition: August 2009

Credits
Editors: Cindy Cresap and Stacia Seaman
Production Design: Stacia Seaman
Cover Design By Sheri (graphicartist2020@hotmail.com)

Acknowledgments

Many people contributed to the success of this book whether they know it or not. Special thanks to my fellow classmates and the professors and staff at the University of New Mexico for the excellent adventure called law school. Thanks also to my law partners, Tom Mills and Christie Williams, for introducing me to the exciting and dynamic world of criminal law. I had a blast writing the story of these two formidable women and their legal and romantic adventures. That I was able to use my day job as a research tool was a huge bonus. Extra special thanks to Christie for always being available when I needed to brainstorm creative story lines.

Brenda Adcock, Rachel Spangler, and Christie—thanks to all of you for reading the rough version and adding polish where needed.

Cindy Cresap—your guidance, strong and gentle, made this a much better book.

Stacia Seaman—your eye for detail provided the perfect polish.

Sheri—your cover designs are always amazing and this one is no exception.

Rad and Jennifer—I will always be grateful that you decided to take a chance on me. I can't imagine a more nurturing family than BSB.

Lainey—Thanks for your willingness to always stop what you're doing to accommodate my need to ask, "Does this sound right?" or "Can you help me figure out…?" I love you for always believing I can do anything and for all the sacrifices you've made so that I can realize my dreams.

Since the release of my first book, less than a year ago, I have enjoyed meeting, in person and online, many of the readers who have taken the time to give their feedback. To all of you out there, please know that your voracious appetite for more fuels the fire that keeps me writing.

Dedication

For Lainey and our happily ever after.

CHAPTER ONE

A foul odor and complete darkness were clear signs the door Morgan had walked through didn't lead to the patio. She was in the alley, and she didn't think the night could get any worse. She was wrong. As she tugged on the handle of the large metal door, she realized it was locked and she was stuck outside.

Morgan looked around, realizing she was completely alone. Empty delivery crates and broken-down cardboard boxes were stacked next to a small Dumpster. The opposite side of the narrow drive was fenced off with a short wire fence designed to discourage, but not prevent, foot traffic. She assessed her choices: walk down the long path and circle back to the front entrance of the bar, or scale the fence and scout out a cab on one of the adjacent streets. The latter option, though messier, was more appealing. Morgan glanced down at her outfit and sighed at the destruction she was about to cause. She'd dressed to impress, for all the good it had done. Her now inappropriate attire couldn't be helped. She had no desire to reenter the bar or risk being seen. She was determined the inevitable confrontation was not going to take place tonight. Not while she was in the weaker position. Absolutely not.

Morgan faced the fence with resolve. With a last look at her new shoes, she wedged her brand-new sling-back, peep-toe sandal into an opening in the wire structure. As she started to pull herself up and over she heard faint strains of disco music growing louder and louder. Glancing back over her shoulder, she saw her sworn enemy—the door—was now an inviting friend, propped wide open, and beckoning her back to the bar. She jumped off her perch and rushed back across the alley.

"Hey! Where did you come from?"

Morgan jumped at the unexpected voice. Warily, she turned toward its source. Less than two feet away, with a surprised expression on her face, was a tall, beautiful woman. Relief at rescue didn't preclude Morgan from taking a moment to appraise the alabaster skin, messily coiffed jet-black hair, and piercing blue eyes of the handsome woman standing before her. Her savior-slash-inquisitor stood almost six feet tall, her height accentuated by her lithe frame. She sported well-worn Levi's 501s and a plain black T-shirt, tight on her well-toned chest.

"Did you hear me?"

Morgan realized she was probably staring with her mouth wide open. She chided herself for thinking illicit thoughts about another woman after what she had been through that evening. Finding her voice, she replied, "Yes, I heard you. I'm sorry for staring." Thinking she shouldn't have acknowledged that last, she resolved to say only what was necessary. "I was in search of the patio, but apparently walked out the wrong door."

"Good thing I came out when I did. You ready to go back in?" The beauty took her turn appraising Morgan, and the heat of the woman's glance seared her. Morgan knew the rakish grin on the stranger's face meant her own mouth was probably hanging open again. The woman spoke. "You look ready for something, but you don't look like you're ready to go."

"Actually, I'm outside because I needed some air. This may not be the patio, but it provided what I was looking for." Suddenly Morgan wondered what this woman was doing out here. "And what are you doing out here?"

"I work here," the woman said simply. Seeing Morgan's expression, she explained. "I mean I work in the bar. I'm putting out the trash before I leave for the night."

"Oh."

"Look, I know you said you want to enjoy the fresh night air and all, but I'm about to go back in and, as I'm sure you know by now, this door is going to lock behind me. Sure you don't want to go back inside with me?" The woman smiled the invitation.

Morgan stared, lost in thought. She had no desire to reenter this place, not this night. Tina and her "friend" were probably huddled somewhere inside. Though they weren't likely to notice her, considering their complete and total rapture with each other, she wasn't going to put herself through the torment.

"Uh, I hate to rush you, but I need to get back in."

Morgan shook herself and focused on finding another way out of this mess. "I don't want to go back inside." She fought to hold back tears of frustration threatening to break through.

The woman walked closer until she was standing mere inches from Morgan. "My name is Parker. What's yours?"

"Morgan," she whispered. Parker's proximity robbed her breath.

"Nice to meet you, Morgan. You look like you're having a bad night." Parker gently slid an arm around Morgan's waist. She purred the next question. "What can I do to make it better?"

Morgan's thoughts raced. *Well, this is rich. Here I am stuck in an alley and a total stranger is flirting with me. Meanwhile, my partner of ten years is doing God knows what with a Barbie wannabe inside.* Morgan wiped her eyes and turned toward Parker, who had moved closer during the silence. She appraised her. *This woman is no Barbie, thank God. She's real-life, drop-dead-gorgeous and knows it.* Feelings replaced rational thought and Morgan settled on a plan of action designed to make the impact of the evening's events fade fast.

"I'd like you to take me somewhere. Anywhere." Morgan stared directly into Parker's eyes, willing her to understand the wide-ranging implication of the control she surrendered with her request.

Parker didn't betray an ounce of surprise. Instead she leaned in and kissed Morgan lightly on the cheek. "Wait for me here. I'll only be a moment." Heading toward the door, she glanced back only once to deliver a reassuring smile.

❖

Parker held a finger across her lips, signaling Morgan to quietly enter the house. The expansive porch was well lit, but the foyer inside was pitch black. Parker stepped carefully, leading Morgan upstairs to her room, careful not to wake any of the other occupants of the house. After crossing the threshold of her room, she flicked a switch to illuminate her destination. She guided Morgan to the love seat near her bed and then she walked to her nightstand and rummaged through the drawer until she found a pack of matches. She lit three candles grouped on the nightstand and cut the overhead light. The flames from the candles flickered shadows on the walls and, against the dancing images, Parker finally stopped to observe the beautiful woman in front of her.

Now seated, Parker realized Morgan wasn't as tall as she first appeared. Looking down at her feet, she saw delicious painted toes sheathed in spiked sandals. Morgan wore snug dark blue jeans and a cool white draped jersey halter top. Her auburn hair fell in soft waves against the creamy skin of her bare shoulders. Parker wanted nothing more than to run her hands through those tresses. Parker had met a fair share of beautiful women during her tenure at the bar, but Morgan topped the list. As she appraised her, she was tickled by a vague sense of recognition and she wondered why, if she had seen Morgan at the bar before, she hadn't made her acquaintance earlier. Determined to remedy past neglect with present intentions, she strode across the room, knelt, grasped Morgan's hands, and kissed her palms slowly, one at a time. Morgan melted into the light touches. She inched to the edge of her seat, pressing her body into Parker's advances. Encouraged by the response, Parker tucked herself between Morgan's legs and reached up to kiss the warm and welcoming lips hazily smiling down at her.

Morgan fought the urge to bolt. She couldn't remember the last time she had a one-night stand. Over a decade ago, at least. She knew Parker was acting on the undercurrent of her request to take her somewhere besides the bar, but Morgan was still reeling from having witnessed the tragic final act of her ten-year farce of a relationship. She should leave now before she further complicated the evening with her own antics.

As if she could sense Morgan's instinct to flee, Parker held her in place. Morgan slid her hands along Parker's arms, savoring the feel of her muscled limbs. She started to coax the strong arms around her, but stopped short. She didn't want to be held. She didn't want to be taken. She had lost enough control tonight.

Morgan stood and placed her hand on Parker's shoulder, signaling her to stay in place. She kicked off her sandals and balanced herself squarely so Parker's face was centered near her chest. With one arm, she pulled her skimpy top over her head, then deftly unhooked the clasp of her silk bra. Parker reached up to help her remove the barrier, but Morgan pushed her hands away. She flung the lacy undergarment down and then rubbed her swollen breasts while she watched Parker squirm. Morgan pinched her left nipple and rolled it between her fingers. Parker licked her lips. Morgan wasn't sure if she was making herself wet or if the desire in Parker's eyes was the catalyst of her arousal. Whatever the cause, she was soaking and she wanted to be touched. She motioned for Parker's hand. Parker ran her palm up the bare skin of Morgan's stomach, inching toward her aching breasts. Morgan marveled at the dual effect of her touch, both soothing and stimulating. She swooned, almost forgetting her intentions, but she reclaimed her focus and smacked Parker's hand as it grazed her ready nipple. "No, I want you inside me. Now."

"Let me take you to bed." Parker's voice was low and full of promise. "I want to feel your skin. I want to feel you against me while I make you come."

"I'll come all right, but this way." Morgan surprised herself with the forcefulness of her declaration. She shook off her hesitation and settled into the dominant role, guiding Parker's hand to the zipper of her jeans. "Inside. Now."

Parker complied, but not without testing Morgan's resolve. She took her time unzipping Morgan's jeans and when she finally slid her hand inside, she kept the barrier of Morgan's silk panties between her probing fingers and Morgan's wet center. Morgan ground against Parker's seeking fingers, slowly at first, then thrusting with mounting speed against the increasing pressure of Parker's insistent touch. The soft silken motion was a nice prelude, but she quickly craved the electric charge only skin on skin could provide. No longer able to stand the boundary between her aching clit and the feel of Parker's probing fingers, she reached down and firmly grasped Parker's hand. Force wasn't necessary. Parker's need to be where Morgan wanted her was evident by the urgency with which she slid her hand inside Morgan's panties to find her slick and ready. Morgan groaned as Parker traced a path on either side of her quivering lips. As Parker spread her open, she summoned what was left of her self-control and reached down to grasp Parker's hand once again.

"Not yet." She held Parker's hand still and met her eyes, now black with intensity. "Take off your clothes." Parker hesitated, almost as if she didn't register what Morgan asked. Morgan lowered her hand to Parker's waist and roughly tugged open a button of her 501s to accent each word. "Take. Off. Your. Clothes." Parker slowly removed her hand from Morgan's jeans and flashed a grin in response to Morgan's low moan. She stood and leaned so close Morgan could feel her breath, warm and sweet. She sucked in her own as she watched Parker raise her arms and peel her shirt away to reveal firm breasts, nipples erect and begging to be touched. Morgan drew a hard nipple into her mouth and rolled her tongue around it with increasing pressure, taking pleasure in the way Parker's strong body sagged against her as if melting at the touch. She nipped hard, then leaned back and gazed into Parker's glassy eyes. "You were talking earlier about wanting to feel some skin?"

Parker took the cue, shoving her jeans down and kicking them away. Morgan smiled at the sight of tight gray boy briefs. "Mmm, these are nice, and you certainly look hot in them." She ran a finger inside the waist band, dipping low to trace the curled hairs beneath. "But they're not skin. Lose 'em."

Parker obeyed, but she took her time, sliding the briefs slowly down and then dangling them in Morgan's face before tossing them over her shoulder. Morgan's breath caught at the sight of Parker's tightly muscled body. She was gorgeous. She stood proud and confident, as if standing around naked in front of other women was something she did every day. *Maybe she does.* For a brief moment, Morgan felt her own confidence ebb, but acted quickly to block its retreat. She slid her arms over Parker's lean hips, pulled her close, and leaned back hard. As they crushed into the cushions of the love seat, Morgan moaned with pleasure at the feel of the welcome weight.

"So, is this what you had in mind?" Parker's smile was irresistible. Morgan answered by kissing the corners of her mouth, then teasing her lips with light strokes of her tongue. Parker matched her movements and their dance quickly dissolved into deep, probing kisses that Morgan felt to her core. "I need to come now." The awareness that drove her to deliver the command faded into the haze of desire. Until she felt the cool air in the room skim the heat between her legs she didn't realize she was fully nude. Within moments, Parker's fingers brought her back to awareness. Morgan matched her touch for touch, unable to resist the excitement of their combined pleasure. As she writhed beneath Parker's well-toned body, she found her control in the pure physical pleasure she felt as they came together with the unbridled intimacy only strangers who never plan to meet again allow themselves to feel.

❖

Morgan woke to the realization she wasn't alone and she wasn't at home. She sighed as the events of the night before came flooding back and she realized she probably didn't have a home anymore. She rolled out of bed, determined to spend the day figuring out if she had a place to live.

She tiptoed around the room gathering clothes, doing her best to see by the shades of early morning light peaking through the blinds. The desire she still felt for the handsome woman sleeping soundly in bed did not extend to wanting to talk to her this morning, and she shrugged away the stirring sensation urging her to kiss those soft lips once more. *Too many questions*, she thought. *We've probably already exchanged more than we should.* Finally locating her missing articles of clothing, she ducked into the adjoining bathroom to dress. Emerging quietly, she blew a kiss at the sleeping beauty and whispered, "Thanks for showing this girl a good time when she needed it most."

The house was large and contained many rooms. Morgan was surprised to see all the doors were shut, but relieved to know if there were others in the house it was unlikely anyone saw her departure. She quietly slipped out the front door and walked down the street. She looked first at her watch, noting it was seven a.m. Next, she looked around, searching for a reference point since she hadn't paid an iota of attention to their destination the evening before. The nearest intersection was Abrams and Vickery. Morgan laughed. She was mere blocks away from where she had grown up. She rummaged through her bag and found her cell phone. Relieved to note remaining battery life, she dialed information and was connected with Yellow Cab, who promised to have a driver there within ten minutes.

Morgan spent the wait practicing her response to a range of reactions Tina might have to the news she had arrived in Dallas a week early. Pleasure was off the list, but surprise and dismay ranked high among her predictions. Whatever the reaction, Morgan knew she needed to spend some of the next thirty minutes coming up with a contingency plan, because she wasn't likely to be staying at the posh Preston Hollow address she was headed to now.

The cab driver arrived and, like most cabbies in Dallas, had a poor grasp of map skills for any neighborhood not in his usual path. He was eager to take her anywhere in the surrounding Greenville area, but professed to know nothing about North Dallas. Morgan managed to pull up some long-forgotten map in her head and guided him through the city toward the residence she had planned to call home.

The tall, imposing house swallowed up the lot it was sitting on and seemed to spill out into the street to consume additional terrain. The neighborhood used to be beautiful, Morgan remembered. Ranch-style houses set back from the street, well-manicured lawns and stately trees once made driving through the Preston Hollow neighborhood seem like touring a cluster of country estates. Now many of the ranch homes were teardowns replaced by McMansions, such as the one Tina had commissioned. These fake palaces made the area, in Morgan's opinion, seem cheap. *I suppose it's just as well I won't be staying long*, she thought.

Tina was sitting at the kitchen table nursing a steaming cup of coffee. She looked up at the sound of Morgan's entrance. Morgan read fatigue and the blur of hangover behind the surprise Tina expressed at her arrival.

"Honey! When did you get here? Why didn't you call and let me know you were coming?"

Morgan recalled stowing her luggage in the guest room closet when she arrived yesterday afternoon. She realized Tina didn't have any idea she had been in the house the day before.

"Actually, Tina, I got here yesterday. I wrapped things up quicker than I expected and I thought I'd surprise you by coming out early." Morgan watched the parade of expressions on her lover's face go from confusion to understanding to reflection. Morgan figured Tina was wondering if she'd left anything incriminating lying around.

Tina's expression settled on pleasure. "What a wonderful surprise!" She wrinkled her brow. "But wait a minute. If you got here last night, then where in the world have you been?"

"Gee, Tina, I was wondering when you were going to notice

my absence. I would have explained, but since you were previously occupied I figured it didn't matter what I did with my time."

Tina's puzzled look was almost convincing. "I don't know what you're talking about."

"Is that so? Let me help you remember." Morgan was tired of the charade they had played out the last few years of their relationship, and the prospect of this confrontation held equal parts disgust and relief.

"I arrived last night in time to hear one of your new friends leave a message on the machine entreating you to join the 'gang' at Betty's for happy hour. Silly me, I thought joining you would be a great opportunity to not only surprise you, but meet all the friends you've made while you toiled away the summer getting our new home ready. So I called a cab and went out to join you. Imagine my surprise when I discovered you have been very busy this summer. From what I observed, apparently your interests haven't been confined to work and nesting."

Tina mustered a look of righteous indignation. "Morgan, I don't know what you think you saw, but—"

"Darling, don't even say it. I am clear about what I saw. You and I haven't exchanged as much physical passion in the last five years as you exchanged with the hottie on the dance floor last night. I didn't know you still had it in you."

Tina sat in silence. Morgan observed her and read her with the familiarity ten years of living together brings. Tina wasn't going to deny her actions any longer, and it didn't appear she was going to apologize for them either unless pushed to do so. Morgan no longer had the energy to push her into apologies she clearly didn't mean. Regrettably, it had taken a move clear across the country to prove what they had known all along. Their relationship was beyond repair. Neither cared enough to heal the hurt between them, and Morgan knew it was time for her to move on, and the sooner she did so, the better off she would be.

"I'm going to go check into the Palomar until I find a place. The movers should be here tomorrow. I doubt I'll be ready to have them divert what I need, so we'll have to work out arrangements. I trust you'll help make this go as smoothly as possible?" Morgan knew Tina was clear about what "this" was. The two had grown emotionally distant over the last few years, but they still had the capacity to read one another's thoughts and feelings.

"So, this is it for us? We move all the way across the fucking country and after one day you're leaving me?" The anger in her voice was clear as Tina pushed her to announce her desire.

"Yes, Tina, I'm leaving. We've both moved on. I'm sorry I ever agreed to come out here with you. I was stupid enough to think we could make a fresh start, but last night proved nothing has changed between us and it never will. We loved each other once, but we don't anymore. It's as simple as that."

"Fucking lawyers. Everything is black or white, right or wrong. Maybe I got so sick of your logical approach to everything I decided to take a walk on the wild side. Can you blame me?"

"I guess not." Morgan's tone was flat. Continuing the argument with Tina would convey she cared and would only prolong her departure. She didn't care anymore and she wanted out, now. Focusing on her goals, she strode to the guest room and retrieved her luggage. Without another word, she left the house and got into the still waiting cab. An extra twenty allowed the cabbie to overcome his frustration at being asked to head back uptown.

CHAPTER TWO

Rays of sunlight poked her in the eye. Parker flinched against the pain like a vampire whose coffin had been unceremoniously invaded during non-working hours. She didn't want to get up, but she knew she would have to crawl out of bed and shut the blinds if she wanted to get any more sleep. Idly wondering if the sunlight was having the same effect on her overnight guest, Parker glanced across the bed. The pillow was askew and the covers in disarray, circumstantial evidence of the passion of the previous evening. However, the direct evidence was nowhere to be found. Parker opened both eyes wide and searched the room for Morgan. She wasn't there.

Parker slung her body out of bed and padded, naked, to the bathroom door. It wasn't locked and she eased it open. No sign of Morgan. She pulled on a pair of boxers and a well-worn T-shirt and trotted down the stairs to the kitchen. The roomy kitchen was silent and unoccupied. Parker decided to put together a pot of coffee to fuel the start of her day. While the java brewed she reflected on the previous evening. She was surprised to find her guest gone and wondered when she made her exit. Parker Casey was usually the one who slunk out in the wee hours, long before morning snuggling became an option. As she sipped her morning dose of caffeine, Parker decided she had met her match. The realization carried a bit of a sting. From the moment she laid eyes on Morgan trapped in the alley, she'd felt attraction, strong attraction, coupled with a vague sense of recognition she couldn't place. She hadn't grouped Morgan into the category of usual conquests she met at the bar. Though their interaction had been primarily physical,

Morgan came across as more sophisticated and worldly than her usual Friday night bar fare.

"Casey, you better have made enough to share!"

Parker started at the yelling from across the room. "For crying out loud, Erin, keep it down. Some of us are still sleeping."

"I'm sure you wish you were," Erin replied, moving to fill a large cup with the steamy brew. "No one in this house got any sleep last night. I hope you had a great time."

"Give me a break, Erin. We weren't that loud, were we?"

"I'm sure it's the thin wall between our rooms. Certainly, I'm the only one in the house who could make out actual words."

Parker blushed. "Geez, Erin, if I'd known you were listening I would have given you some pointers."

"You are incorrigible. I think you should make me breakfast to help erase the trauma I've had to endure."

"I'd love to, but I actually have a lot to do today. I have an orientation session for third-year mentors and I want to pick up my books before the meeting starts." Parker searched the cabinets for sustenance as she spoke, trying to find a quick bite to eat.

Erin gave her a puzzled look. "School doesn't start for almost two weeks. What's your hurry?"

Parker shrugged. "You know me, I want to get a jump start on the reading. And I volunteered to be a mentor to a one-L." Parker referred to the slang term for first-year law students. "They all start showing up for their own orientation next week, and I need to be on hand to show my assigned newbie around."

"When's your last night at the bar?"

"I have one more weekend shift right before classes start. Then I'll call it quits until winter break. I hate to leave Irene in the lurch, but I have a lot on my plate this semester and I want to make sure I impress enough of my profs to get into the clinic of my choice in the spring."

"Irene, huh?" Erin scoffed. "I'm thinking it's the women you'll have the most trouble giving up. Like shooting fish in a barrel. Do you think you'll go through withdrawal?"

Parker threw a bagel across the room, beaning her on the nose. "Work hard, play hard—the Parker Casey way. You would do well to follow my lead." She grinned at her, grabbed the last remaining bagel, and climbed the stairs to her room to get ready for her day.

The house she shared with her two roommates was large and roomy, though old and drafty. The residence was perfect for the group of students. It was close to campus and provided enough space to give them all the room they needed to accommodate their various schedules. Erin James was the youngest of the group, a graduate student at Richards University, close to completing her master's degree in sociology. Kelsey James, Erin's older sister and Parker's best friend, was in her second year of residency at the hospital associated with the university, and the rest of the group rarely laid eyes on her. Parker was a third-year at the university's law school. When the school year started, she spent most of her time on campus. Most legal research could be done wherever a wireless connection could be found, but Parker preferred the computer cubbies at the law library to the solitude of working from home.

Excited at the prospect of the start of school, though it wasn't official for another couple of weeks, Parker hurried through her shower. She dressed in a smooth, worn pair of jeans, Skechers, and a plain navy T-shirt.

Parker slid into her '68 Mustang fastback and sped the few blocks to the law school. Blazing August heat made it too hot to walk the distance. Truth was, she loved the muscle car she had restored herself and would rather drive it than walk, no matter what the weather. While jockeying for a parking place, she contemplated the ride across town the night before with Morgan occupying the seat beside her. Parker would never have imagined that the reticent woman who sat silently during the ride to her house would have turned into a dominant sex goddess. Her clit throbbed with the memory of Morgan taking total control and she was flustered by what an amazing experience it had been to let someone else direct her in the bedroom. She was used to being in charge, and though she had been in the driver's seat in the car, it was Morgan who had taken her for a wild ride in the bedroom.

Parker finally found a space to park and walked to the library. She strode across campus with all the confidence her status as a third-year accorded her. Thinking ahead to the mentor orientation, she recalled the first time she set foot on the law school grounds. All her worldly confidence drained away. It had taken her three tries to even find the law school among the numerous buildings on campus. She was so concerned she wouldn't be able to locate it among the maze of buildings for the first day of classes, she drove by a couple of times a day in the week preceding the start of the first semester. She had spent over a decade building another career when she made the decision to return to school and get her law degree. Lacking no confidence in the outside world, she'd found all her brashness faded at the prospect of starting over in the academic world, a world filled with younger, presumably brighter, students who, having come straight out of undergraduate school, were still well acquainted with how the system worked.

Within a few weeks, Parker was in the swing of things. She quickly learned all first-year law students were pretty much in the same boat and the boat was adrift on a sea filled with lots of work and little time for anything other than school. The students divided into study groups based on their affinity for each other and how they preferred to study. Parker had a history of excelling at every new venture, and her studies were no different. Her personality and good looks were magnetic, causing other students to gravitate to her. The members of Parker's study group were the top students in her class.

Parker walked into the library and shivered from the chill of the refrigerated air. She was thankful she had chosen jeans and shoes over her preferred summer uniform of shorts and sandals. She walked directly to the largest of the private study rooms. Dr. Yolanda Ramirez, the dean, was chatting with a couple of the other third-year students who volunteered to be mentors. Dr. Ramirez glanced her way, giving her a big smile. Parker reciprocated with one of her own. She gave full credit to Dr. Ramirez for supporting her application to law school. The dean had given her valuable pointers to make sure her application made its way safely through the arduous admission process. When the dean asked her to be part of this venture, she could hardly refuse.

Dr. Ramirez greeted Parker. "I'm so glad you could make it. I think it's important to have someone on this team who has more life perspective than the average third-year student." She punctuated her gratitude with a hug.

"How could I refuse?" Parker replied. She had grown accustomed to the faculty placing extra trust in her because, at thirty-four, she was older than the average law student. As the dean rounded up the rest of the gathering group and rustled them to their seats, Parker greeted some of her classmates she'd missed over the summer. Several had worked as summer associates with the numerous large firms in downtown Dallas. The pay was amazing, and a summer associate could easily live the rest of the year off what they made during the summer months. Each firm spent significant amounts of capital trying to wine and dine their summer associates while getting to know them. The goal of this summer ritual was to allow the firm to decide if these students, usually the top of their class, would make a good fit with the firm's culture and, if so, to convince the prospects there was no place better than their firm to start their legal career.

Parker found the whole process of summer associates absurd. Her conclusion wasn't based on jealousy. At the top of her class, she had been sought after each of the prior summers by virtually every firm in Dallas, but she didn't understand why she should waste a summer being a social butterfly when she could do meaningful work. She was willing to concede that a decade spent in law enforcement likely colored her perspective, despite the disastrous ending to her chosen career. At least the hefty settlement provided her with enough cash to allow her to do the legal job of her choice without concern for money, which was a good thing since working as an intern at the nearby Tarrant County Public Defender's Office didn't pay a dime. The work did, however, seal her resolve to become a criminal defense attorney and provided her with course credit along the way.

Dr. Ramirez began by explaining when the first-years would arrive and what their schedule would be like the first couple of weeks. *Funny*, Parker reflected, *after two full years of this stuff, we have to be reminded what it's like to start.* Dr. Ramirez then asked the volunteers to be present at a social she was hosting to welcome the new students to the school. Parker glanced at her Treo and noted the social was the same night she was scheduled to work her last night at the bar. A twinge of regret that she would miss the social was rapidly replaced by a flash of glistening skin and luscious curves as she recalled how her last bar shift had ended.

❖

As the valet brought her car around, Morgan performed mental calculations in an attempt to figure out how much it would cost to stay at the Palomar for the rest of her natural life. The specifics of the mathematics failed her, but she was able to cipher enough to know she couldn't afford the luxury. Morgan had money, but not enough to burn. Years of handling high-profile cases with high-dollar retainers, combined with a savvy business sense, meant Morgan had generous savings. Managed carefully, she could live a very long time on the interest from her investments alone, but Morgan liked a little luxury now and then. As a consequence, she would keep working. Today was the first day of her new job.

Morgan had spent the last ten years with Tina Middleton, software engineer. Tina was a hot commodity in the high-tech industry and when investors approached her about a start-up in Dallas, she had jumped at the opportunity. She had spent the last six months persuading Morgan to let her follow her dream, which of course meant Morgan was supposed to drop her life and come along for the ride. Morgan finally decided maybe the change of scenery would do their relationship some good and they both planned to start over in Big D.

Morgan was no stranger to Dallas. She'd grown up here and attended school at Richards University, which was her destination this morning. When the couple decided on the move, Morgan made some calls and secured a visiting professorship at her alma mater. A former colleague, now dean of the law school, was happy to have Morgan. Morgan had spent the fifteen years since graduation building a national reputation as a criminal defense counsel working on high-profile cases often involving high-profile individuals and corporations. The last few years, she combined teaching a few classes with her law practice, years of success giving her the freedom to pick and choose her cases. She was actually looking forward to this opportunity to be in the classroom more often, especially on such familiar stomping grounds.

Morgan found a spot in the faculty parking lot. She was grateful her car arrived ahead of schedule; getting cabs in Dallas was a sketchy proposition at best. She loved the comfort of her Lexus SUV, appreciating the fact that with so many other SUVs on the road in Dallas, she didn't feel the pangs of guilt for driving such a gas guzzler she usually felt back East. She switched off the radio and left the luxury of her ride to head into the law school.

As she approached the desk in the administrative office, she smiled at a familiar sight. Edith Perkins had manned the receptionist post for decades. There she sat, looking every bit as alert and all-knowing as she had when Morgan the first-year law student asked her for directions to the registrar's office on her first day. Catching Edith's eye, she grinned as she saw the stalwart gatekeeper try to stay focused on her phone conversation, though it was obvious she was busting at the seams to greet her.

"Morgan Bradley, as I live and breathe!" Edith came around the desk to give Morgan her version of a bear hug. Edith Perkins was a tiny woman and, to Morgan's mind, ageless. She looked exactly the same as she had eighteen years ago, and Morgan figured she would look the same eighteen years into the future.

"Edith, I can't tell you how good it is to see a familiar face. I assume you know why I'm here?"

"Certainly, dear. Have a seat and I'll let Dean Ramirez know you're here. She's been barely able to contain her excitement at the prospect of landing a big celebrity to teach this semester, never mind you're also an alumna." Edith pointed to a sofa in the waiting area and walked down the hall toward the dean's office. Morgan grimaced slightly at Edith's assessment of her status. She hardly thought of herself as a celebrity. True, for the past few years she had made regular appearances on the cable network legal circuit spouting her opinions on everything from current cases in the media to Supreme Court rulings. She was a go-to legal consultant for Court TV, MSNBC, and CNN. When she wasn't hyping her own cases, she was ready and willing to provide insight to the viewing layperson about the tricks of the trade employed by her colleagues in the criminal defense bar. She was looking forward to sharing the basics with her students, though, and hoped all the glitz of TV law wouldn't get in the way of the learning experience.

Dean Yolanda Ramirez entered the waiting area, apparently so eager to greet Morgan she couldn't wait for her to be ushered back to her office. After exchanging hugs, the two women adjourned to Yolanda's office. Morgan took her time appraising the space and nodded with approval. "Why, Dean, you've done very well for yourself."

"As have you, Professor, as have you. Ray spends his evenings surfing channels to hear your sound bites. I try not to be jealous, but sometimes…"

Morgan laughed at Yolanda's reference to her husband. Raymond and Yolanda had been married forever, having met and fallen in love when they were in law school. Yolanda used to joke if they could make it through three years of brutal education, they could make it through anything, so they might as well get hitched. Morgan met Raymond working at a local firm that had recruited her upon graduation. Raymond, a partner at the firm, recognized the budding talent of the first-year associate and picked her to second chair on numerous cases. Not one to let ego get in the way of a good defense, Raymond began to turn more and more major case responsibilities over to her. Eventually, Morgan was recruited by a firm with a national presence and, at forty years old, she was one of the top criminal defense lawyers in the nation. Despite the fact it had been years since she lived in Dallas, she remained close friends with Raymond and Yolanda. In fact, she and Tina had been frequent visitors to Dallas, often staying with the Ramirezes on their weekend jaunts to shop and play in the Lone Star State.

Morgan responded to Yolanda's bait. "Seriously, Yo, like Ray has eyes for anyone but you. If I weren't a lesbian, I would be offended by the lack of attention I get from your husband."

"Speaking of attention you should be getting, how's Tina?"

"Poor segue." Morgan had confided in Yolanda part of the reason for the move to Dallas was to rekindle some sparks with Tina. Now she needed to bring her up to date on the current situation, a conversation she was dreading. "Actually, I will not be relying on Tina for any attention in the future, Yolanda. We broke up and I moved out."

"What the hell? I mean, what happened?"

"Tina found someone else to spark her flame. For all I know she found several someone elses. All I know for sure is we're done. I've been staying at the Palomar since the night after I arrived."

"So, you broke up after one night here? Wow."

"Yep, I decided to surprise her by arriving early. Turns out I was the one surprised. I showed up at a bar where she was supposed to be meeting some folks from work. She was practically having sex with another woman on the dance floor."

Yolanda wrapped her in an embrace. "You poor thing. How mortifying. What did you do?"

"Well, first I felt sorry for myself. Then I decided to go home with the best-looking woman at the bar. The next morning I did what I should have done years ago. I told Tina I'd had enough and moved out. Well, I didn't actually move out since my stuff wasn't there yet, but I moved myself into the Hotel Palomar."

"Whoa there, missy! Sandwiched in between your tale of woe,

I think I heard you say something about going home with the best-looking woman at the bar. True or not true?"

Morgan grinned. "True. Can you believe it? I was so mad at Tina and there was no way in hell I was going to spend the night at the scrubby McMansion she picked out for us. I worked off my anger in the best way I knew how."

"This old married woman wants to hear all about it, but it sounds like a tale best told over cocktails. Why don't we catch up this weekend? Ray and I are hosting a thing for all the first-years Saturday night at our place. How about brunch on Sunday? You, me, and your sordid romances?"

"It's a date. The thing on Saturday, I suppose you want faculty to attend?"

"If you don't mind, we would like to have as many of the professors as possible. It helps for the newbies to meet you all in a less imposing setting than the classroom. I realize you probably won't have any first-years in your class, but it would be nice for them to meet the big star on campus. Meeting you will give them a good memory they can reflect on when they are alumni and I am sending them endless requests to donate to the scholarship fund."

"No problem, Yo. It's not like I have anything else to do. I'll come early and help."

"Come early, dear, but the caterers have everything well in hand." Yolanda stood. "Now, please allow me to give you a personal tour of the new wing. You're going to love the new moot courtroom. It's very high tech and your office is right across the hall, so you'll be perfectly situated."

Arm in arm, they made their way toward Morgan's new office.

❖

"Two? Why two?" Parker exclaimed to Gerald Lopez, the student body president, waving the slips of paper in her hand.

"No good deed goes unpunished. It's simple. We didn't have enough mentor volunteers to assign one to each first-year, so some of you have two."

"Any particular reason I was chosen as one of the lucky ones?"

"Yeah, Casey," Gerald answered without expression. "It's your winning personality. Hell, I don't know, maybe they figured because you're older you'd have more wisdom to share."

Parker would have laughed if she thought Gerald was kidding. Truth was she thought he was an idiot. Handsome, fast talking, and popular with many of the female students, he'd needed little else to secure the election as president of the law school student body. Gerald was definitely a player and relied on attributes other than hard work and legal skill to get where he wanted to be. With his luck, he'd probably be district attorney someday. Parker grimaced at the thought.

"Fine, I'll be happy to share my sage wisdom with these two. Where do I hook up with them?"

"They'll be done with their library orientation at noon. Here's your name tag. Wait in the lobby of the library and they'll find you."

Parker looked with disdain at the plastic badge Gerald had shoved into her hand. No way was she wearing a name tag. Glancing at her watch, she saw she only had five minutes to wait. No time to grab a bite to eat. *Well*, she decided, *I'll show them the snack bar as the first stop on the grand tour.*

Parker leaned against a tall cement pillar in the library while she waited for the 1Ls to appear. Within a few minutes, they came walking toward her, a whole herd of them. They huddled together, drawing on the only comfort they knew in this strange place, the familiarity of each other. Although most of them had met only a few days ago, the relationships they formed in those first hours were the most important ones they would have for the next three years. Sharing the grueling experience of law school from start to finish would make them as close or closer to one another than many of the relationships they might have had with lovers.

Parker reflected on her reluctance to take on two mentees and decided to rise to the challenge. After two years of experience, she was well equipped to handle any situation, including showing a couple of newbies the ropes. Her grades were top-notch and her class schedule consisted of courses she was sure to ace. This was her last year in law school and she was on top of the world.

CHAPTER THREE

Yolanda threw the best parties, Morgan reflected as she glanced around the room. She knew Yolanda's desire to make the new 1Ls feel comfortable was sincere and the ambience reflected it. Many top-tier law school deans would use this opportunity to impress the new students with the power and stature of their office. Instead, Dean Yolanda Ramirez thought it was her privilege and duty to offer a warm welcome to the newbies and get to know them before the semester took off with a roar. The only hint of formality was the fact waiters circulated with platters of hors d'oeuvres.

Morgan made her way over to the bar and secured a glass of Pinot Noir from the hunky blond mixing drinks for the event. Her mind wandered to thoughts of the bartender whose bed she had occupied recently, and she wondered if Parker was working at Betty's this evening. Her thoughts stoked feelings still smoldering since their night of fiery passion. Morgan was still amazed when she recalled her every action that night, from asking Parker to take her somewhere, anywhere, to her own display of sexual aggression. She revisited the sensations, hungry to repeat them outside the virtual scene in her mind.

Put those thoughts aside, Professor, she scolded herself. The last thing she needed was to make a return visit to the scene of the end of her relationship. The night she spent with the beautiful stranger was an indiscretion, excusable at the time, but untenable if repeated. Folding away images of the tall, dark-haired bartender, Morgan swallowed a healthy dose of her pinot and charged into the growing crowd of teachers and students.

❖

Parker realized she was going to miss the smoky bar. She glanced around, glad to see the place was crowded.

"Penny for your thoughts, Casey."

"Irene, you should know by now my thoughts are worth so much more." Parker playfully punched the woman at her side. She held a large measure of genuine affection for bar owner Irene Stewart. Irene was a friend from long ago. An older, crusty dyke, she had owned the bar since the beginning of time. As an undergrad, Parker had welcomed the opportunity to work at the busy establishment and Irene became more than a boss; she was also a mentor and friend.

"You haven't taken your eyes off the crowd tonight. Lookin' for someone in particular?"

Parker reflected, not for the first time, on Irene's uncanny ability to read her thoughts. She had definitely been scouring the faces in the crowded bar, hoping to see Morgan. So far, no sign of her. Resolving to be more discreet in her search, she joked, "It's my last night for a while. I'm trying to savor every moment."

"As long as it's only moments you're savoring, we'll get through the night. It's busy already and it's only nine o'clock. I'll get Dannie to stock extra glasses and make sure we have enough ice."

Parker surveyed the room and agreed. The place was packed tonight, more so than a usual Friday night. Most of the faces in the crowd were familiar. It seemed as though everyone she knew was at the bar tonight. As she reflected, she heard the music stop and the DJ asked for the crowd's attention. Wondering at the unexpected interruption to the club's routine, she turned and started to call out for Irene. The shout died in her throat as she saw Dannie and another one of the barbacks approaching slowly, each precariously balancing an end of a large sheet cake. Parker read the top of the cake—We'll Miss You, Parker!—and lost the ability to speak. Suddenly the entire room erupted in clapping, hoots, and hollers and Irene showed up in time to wrap Parker in a big bear hug.

"I love you, kid. We wanted to make your last night special."

Parker brushed aside a tear and kissed Irene's cheek. "Aw, Irene, you didn't have to do this. You know I'll be in all the time. It's not like I'm going anywhere."

Irene wagged a finger in her face. "Yeah, we'll see. I'll let you know after I see your report card."

❖

"Professor Bradley?" At Morgan's nod, the tall, barrel-chested man offered his hand. "I'm Jim Spencer. Nice to finally meet you."

Morgan shook the proffered hand and exchanged pleasantries. "Nice to meet you as well. Student or teacher?"

Jim Spencer laughed a Santa Claus laugh, his sides shaking with genuine amusement. "You're a pistol in person, just like on TV. While Yolanda does encourage older students to apply, I'm certain she doesn't mean as old as me. I'm your go-to professor for torts, civ pro, and ethics."

Morgan smiled at him. His humor was contagious. "Ah, torts, the bane of every first-year's existence. I think I'll go stand in another part of the room. I want the newbies to like me well enough to take my classes later."

"So, you'll be sticking around? I knew you had a visiting spot, but I wasn't sure how long your term was going to last."

Morgan realized she had made the statement about her future plans without conscious decision. Wanting to give herself some wiggle room while she reflected on her future plans, she said, "Let's say I'm leaving my options open."

"Well, I'll try not to scare you away. Here alone? I think Yolanda mentioned you are in a relationship."

"And that's supposed to make me feel more comfortable? You've already checked me out?" Her tone was light and teasing.

"Hey, I believe in checking out all my options right from the start. It's good litigation strategy. Don't you think I should practice what I preach?"

"Morgan, is this man bothering you?"

They both turned toward the voice of Dean Ramirez. Jim started to bluster a reply, but Morgan found words first. "Yes, Dean, very much so. I certainly hope the rest of the faculty possesses more decorum than I have seen exhibited so far."

Jim turned to Yolanda and began his protest. "Forgive me for trying to get to know the new professor and help her become acclimated to our school. I'll leave you two and go harass some of the one-Ls. Lord knows they'll take it better." Jim reached out, grasped Morgan's hand, and brushed it against his lips. "Have a wonderful evening, madam." Smiling, he disappeared into the crowd.

Morgan spoke first. "Yo, he's incorrigible, but I like him."

"I figured you might, so I sent him over to talk to you. And I told him to be available for anything you need this semester. He's been here so long he could walk the halls blindfolded. His office is next to yours. Jim is harmless, though he puts on such a big show about acting like a letch."

"Thanks for taking such good care of me."

"It's my job, sweetie. Now, I need to mingle and I want you with me. One way to get the new kids invested in the school year is the promise of things to come. I plan to talk you into staying for a while and I want them to meet our new resident celebrity. Meeting you should inspire them to stick it out through the nasty first year so they can take fun classes like yours."

Morgan thought back to her time in this very law school and remembered the first year had been at once exciting and horrible. She pledged to do her part to help smooth the way and accompanied Yolanda on her first circuit around the room to meet a dizzying number of new students. Of course, she couldn't tell new from old very well, since this was her first time to meet any of the students present. One student in particular tried mightily to monopolize her attention. She had to catch Jim's eye from across the room, imploring him to intervene.

"Gerald, I see you've met our new professor, Professor Bradley." Jim positioned himself between Morgan and the student.

"Yes, Professor Spencer. I wanted to get her take on the recent Supreme Court opinion regarding lethal injections. I know she advocated for the appeal, but my question to her has to do with how the decision will be applied."

Jim laughed. "Gerald, let me tell you what I think is cruel and unusual punishment. It's talking about Supreme Court opinions at a cocktail party. Now, run along and mentor your new folks and leave the professor to lighter conversation."

Gerald glanced at Morgan with a puzzled look, nodded, and then made his way to the bar. As he left, Jim leaned close to Morgan, whispering, "In case you couldn't tell, he's an idiot."

"Isn't he the class president?"

"Okay, he's a popular idiot. I'm sure he wants to endear himself to you. His father is a bigwig white-collar crime lawyer in town. Gerald has the same charm as dear old dad, but his smarts aren't all there. You can bet all he knows about the opinion is what he heard on talk radio, but he figures if he can impress his father by relaying he discussed a case with you, he'll look like a smartie himself even though none of his daddy's famous white-collar clients are in fear of the needle. If you like brownnosers, he'll be one of your best."

"Hate them."

"Again, I knew I was going to like you. Now, there's a group of students over here who would love to meet the new celebrity on campus. I've already vetted them and found them to be worthy. Come with me." Offering his arm, Jim led Morgan over to a cluster of excited first-years.

❖

Parker hardly worked at all the rest of the night. Everyone at the bar wanted to either buy her a drink or take a turn on the dance floor. Irene laughed off Parker's protestations and told her to have fun. She made it clear she had only gotten Parker to work this shift as a ruse to throw her the party.

Finally, all danced out and a bit buzzed, Parker decided she need to head home. Tomorrow was Sunday, and Monday marked the start of classes. Knowing she didn't have the resiliency of her undergraduate years, she would need all day tomorrow to recover from tonight's festivities. Although steady enough to politely refuse the many offers of an escort, she knew she shouldn't be driving. Irene promised to get her car safely home and told Dannie to drive Parker home.

Once safely inside her house, Parker was suddenly ravenous. She made a beeline for the kitchen. There, standing in front of the open refrigerator, was her other roommate, Kelsey James. Kelsey, like her sister, was a fiery redhead, but the similarities stopped there. Where Erin was petite and thin, Kelsey was tall and curvy.

"Well, if isn't the elusive Dr. James. Fix me dinner?"

Kelsey smiled. "Why, Parker Casey, attorney at law. Shouldn't you rich lawyers have chefs and maids to do your bidding?"

"How about you high-powered surgeons? Where in the world is your staff?"

Both often joked about being rich someday and how all the money they would make would barely be enough to pay off all the bills they accumulated while striving to achieve their respective successes. Fact was they barely saw each other, their schedules were so different. Parker was glad to have a few minutes alone with Kelsey. The two had been fast friends for many years. Kelsey and Erin had inherited the house they shared and, while it had immeasurable sentimental value, the sisters weren't at a place in their lives where they could afford to keep it on their own. The sisters thought it was fate when Parker found herself in need of a new place to live just as Kelsey contemplated running an ad for renters. Kelsey was making a tuna sandwich and offered to make an extra for Parker. Preparing the sandwich, Kelsey asked, "So, who was the cute little girl who drove you home tonight?"

"Who? Oh, Dannie. She works at the bar. Irene decided to make tonight into a huge party in my honor and I had a little too much to drink. So Dannie drove me home."

Kelsey smiled a knowing smile. "Drove you home, huh? Did you happen to stop at her place along the way? I only got a glimpse, but I could tell she is totally into you."

Parker punched her in the arm. "Give me a break! She's, like, twelve. Besides, I don't mix dating and business."

"Please. You bring home 'dates' from the bar all the time."

"Never people I work with."

"Well, it's probably time you settled down with some cute lawyer type anyway. When are you going to bag one of your fellow students?"

"Same principle, James. School is business. I don't mix business and pleasure. It makes things too complicated."

"You're full of crap, Casey. Med students go after each other like rabbits. It's not like we have time or opportunity to meet anyone outside of our clan. Are law students too good to do each other?"

"Judging by how many at school are screwing around, the answer to your question is no. Everyone does it, but I'm not everyone. I've seen sex and what folks thought was love ruin good friendships, break up entire study groups, and tank exams for even the smartest folks. We spend too much time together as it is, we don't need to inbreed too."

"Wow, Casey. Tell me how you really feel."

"It's not a judgment thing, I swear. It's just not for me. I need to be able to focus on my goals, and having a relationship with someone who's right there in the center of all my hard work distracts me. Besides, I haven't had any trouble meeting women outside of school."

"By 'meeting' you mean picking them up, bringing them home, and rarely seeing them again, right?"

Parker shrugged. "Don't knock it till you've tried it."

❖

Morgan crawled into bed, exhausted. She snuggled into the luxurious linens and reflected on the evening. She'd actually had fun. The thing about first-year law students was they were still developing their egos and there wasn't as much know-it-all-ness to get in the way of their appreciation for a good story. Yolanda pushed her to recount a couple of tales of recent successes to the newbies and they seemed enthralled at the telling. *Great for my ego*, Morgan thought.

She glanced around the room. She knew she needed to call the real estate agent Yolanda had suggested. She didn't want to live in a hotel the rest of her life. Morgan figured the market was good enough that a house would be a good investment even if she chose not to stay in Dallas after her teaching contract was up.

The phone on the bedside table rang loudly. Morgan debated letting it ring, but the constant ringing would be as annoying as answering the call. She knew it was the hotel operator, but what message the operator was passing along was a mystery. For the past week and a half, Tina had called the hotel repeatedly, all her calls focused on mending their severed relationship. Morgan had no desire to communicate with Tina except through their respective lawyers. She realized moving to Dallas with the intent of fixing what was beyond repair had been a mistake. While she was willing to accept her own culpability in their relationship downfall, she wasn't willing to prolong the agony. Tired of listening to Tina's endless promises to change, she'd resorted to having the hotel operator screen her calls.

"Hello?"

"Good evening, Ms. Bradley. I have Ms. Yolanda Ramirez on the line. Would you like to take the call?"

"Sure, please put her through."

A moment passed while the call connected, then Yolanda's vibrant voice came through. "You weren't asleep, were you?"

"About to be. Why are you still up?"

"I had to stay up to finish talking to all the students who don't know how to tell when it's polite to leave a party. I have so many stories about how wonderful you are, but I was so busy listening to how wonderful you are I forgot to plan our brunch. Do you want to come here?"

"No way. You did your share of hosting tonight. Pick a place, my treat."

"I was hoping you would say that. Let's go to La Duni. It's not far from your hotel. I'll pick you up at eleven."

"Deal."

❖

The Latin brunch was excellent and they lingered over the best mochas in town after devouring plates of migas and a basket of Cuban pastries. Having spent the entire meal dissecting the previous evening, Yolanda finally questioned Morgan about her breakup with Tina.

"Has she been unfaithful before?"

"Yes, this wasn't the first time. But this time I finally realized what I should've known all along. I don't care enough to be mad. Hurt, yes, but angry? I think you have to truly care about someone to muster up enough feeling to get angry. The hurt stems from thinking we must have loved each other once, and it's apparent neither one of us cares enough about each other to show some respect by breaking off the relationship. Going on like we are, pretending our problems will go away on their own, is plain crazy and I'm relieved we're putting an end to it."

"So, you're done?"

"Completely. I had my lawyer get in touch with her lawyer last week. We never mingled our finances, so all I want is to facilitate the return of some of my personal things. She owns the monstrosity of a house and I don't want any part of it." Morgan noted worry creep across her face. "What's on your mind, Yo?"

"Frankly, I'm concerned about how I'm going to keep you here. The only reason you came in the first place was because of Tina."

"True, I agreed to the move because I thought it would give us a fresh start, but despite what happened, I'm here now and I don't plan on going anywhere. I sold the house back East. Maybe I need a fresh start on my own, and I may as well get it here."

"Not worried about running into Tina?"

"Like I said, Yo, I don't care. I can't seem to conjure up much feeling about her right now. Seeing her is like seeing a stranger. Sad, huh?"

Yolanda paused before her next question, as if cautious about broaching the subject. "Didn't you mention something about a good-looking woman soothing your breaking heart the night you caught Tina at the bar?"

"Leave it to you not to forget the details." Morgan smiled at the thought of waking up beside Parker after a night of wanton sex. By way of conversation, they'd shared little more than first names, but the intimacy they'd shared had been worth a thousand words. Morgan had never been with a more attentive lover. Despite the fact they were strangers, their every action had been familiar, welcome, natural. Staring across the table, she wasn't sure she had the words to convey to Yolanda the enormity of the interaction. She realized it didn't matter since she doubted she would ever see the woman from the bar again. Morgan didn't spend a lot of time in bars. She only went on that particular night to surprise Tina. *Mission accomplished*, she thought, wryly. Having been a trial attorney for most of her adult life, Morgan was discreet about her activities. She never knew if a potential juror might be lurking around the next corner.

"Morgan?"

Morgan realized she had yet to answer the initial question. She told Yolanda about how she had foolishly gotten locked out of the bar and gave up details about the bartender who rescued her. "She was gorgeous and expressed an immediate interest. I was pissed at Tina and had no desire to go home and deal with her shit, so I went home with the woman. One thing led to another and we had fantastic sex."

"Wow, you make my Saturday nights seem indubitably lame. Are you going to see her again?"

"I don't even know her last name."

"You know where she lives. How did you leave things?"

"She was fast asleep when I left, as beautiful in the sober light of morning as she was the night before."

"Sounds like someone is kicking themselves over missed future opportunities."

"How do I say this? What was perfect that evening isn't likely to be replicated. I needed the experience, needed confirmation I'm desirable. I got what I needed, end of story. No need to double-dip to try to make the experience more than it was."

Yolanda gave her a knowing smile, but didn't pursue the matter. "Fine, now you've sown your wild oats. Ready for the first day of classes tomorrow?"

"Actually, I'm looking forward to it. I have a genuinely positive outlook. After these last few months, I don't think anything could throw me off my game."

CHAPTER FOUR

"When am I going to learn I'm not as invulnerable as I was in my youth?" Parker spoke to the mirror, whose unkind reflection revealed a bleary, puffy-eyed version of her former self. She splashed cold water on her face in a futile attempt to wash away the signs of her exhaustion. She had purposefully done absolutely nothing the day before, choosing to spend the Sunday before classes began nursing her hangover in hopes its effects would fade before Monday. Unfortunately, what once took a half day to recover from, now delivered a knockout punch that set her back much longer. She stalked from the bathroom into the hallway, muttering, "Damn you, Irene."

"Hey, Casey, are you still hungover?" Erin had made the mistake yesterday of beating on Parker's door early in the morning in an attempt to rouse her for a morning run. This morning Erin was up early again, coffee in one hand, newspaper in the other.

"Why do you want to know? Have plans to run a marathon and need a companion?"

"A few miles are all I had planned. You act like I tried to get you to do an Ironman. Jeez, you're still pretty grouchy. Maybe you should head back to bed and skip the first day."

"Where's Kelsey?"

"Long gone. She's started a forty-eight-hour shift last night. Whatcha need?"

"I want medical advice or maybe a quickie surgery. Look at these bags under my eyes. I feel okay, but I look like shit."

"Vanity, vanity. What if I told you I had something to fix you right up?"

Parker grabbed Erin's arm and jokingly twisted it behind her back. "I'd say give it to me now."

Erin slapped at Parker with her free hand, playing along. "Let me go, fool, and I'll help you out. You've got to cheer up, though. This is the first day of your last year. You should be happy as a clam."

Parker pointed at her face. "Eyes, Erin. I need you to focus on fixing me up, and then I'll be cheerful."

Parker followed Erin to her room and lay on the bed as Erin directed. As Erin fumbled through the drawers in her bathroom, she called out, "If having your way with me is a cure, I want you to know you don't need any accessories. Get in here and cure away." Parker was joking. Erin was engaged to a fellow grad student and they were madly in love.

Erin emerged from the bathroom with a frosted glass jar. "You wish, Casey. Though I'm sure Bob would love it if I brought home tales of how I ravaged you while you lay helpless on my bed, I have better things to do. Now, close your eyes and lay back."

"I'm not helpless."

"Who's the one with the puffy eyes and no cure?"

Parker lay still while Erin applied moist cotton discs to her eyelids. "What are those? They smell nice."

"Cucumber eye pads. They're great, even better if they've been in the fridge, but you'll have to make do. Keep your eyes closed for fifteen minutes, and then you can get up and throw the pads away. You should look much better."

"Thanks, Erin."

"You're welcome, sweetie." Erin sat on the edge of the bed and shook the newspaper in Parker's direction. "Did you hear about Camille Burke?"

The name sounded familiar to Parker, but she couldn't quite place it. "Not sure I know who you're talking about."

"You know—the Highland Park Burkes. Camille is Lester Burke's daughter." Erin waited till Parker nodded in recognition. "Camille was murdered Friday night at the Burke mansion."

"How did she die? Was it a burglary? Right there in the house?" Parker fired off questions faster than Erin could answer.

"Slow down. I can't read that fast." Erin skimmed the paper. "The story's shy on detail."

Parker nodded. "Cops are probably holding back a lot of the facts."

"I knew her," Erin said quietly.

Parker sat up and pulled the pads off her eyes. "I'm sorry, Erin. Were you close?"

Erin shook her head. "No, not really. At least we haven't been for a while. We were in a lot of the same classes as undergrads, but lost touch when we started different graduate programs."

"What was she like?"

"Sweet girl. Quiet. Not what you'd expect coming from a filthy rich family."

Parker curled Erin into a strong hug. "Funny, no matter how much we think we know, we still have the capacity to be surprised."

❖

Morgan's first class of the day wasn't until ten thirty, but she still arrived early to review her lecture notes for Criminal Procedure. In addition to Criminal Procedure, she was teaching an Advanced Evidence practicum this semester. Two classes wasn't much, but it was what Yolanda was able to conjure up on short notice. The Advanced Evidence course was one not usually offered except when a willing professor stepped up to take it on, and she certainly qualified for the task. The practicum was a hands-on class for third-years, focusing on practical application of the legal skills they had acquired in their Evidence lecture classes. Morgan's years in the courtroom gave her plenty of footnotes to make the class colorful and interesting.

Satisfied her notes were in order, Morgan wandered from her office in search of the snack bar. The small eating venue hadn't changed much since she'd been enrolled as a student, with the exception of the addition of a few new vending machines. Steaming cup of coffee in hand, she wandered out into the common area, finding a place to take in the sights. The first-year students all invariably had a look of awe on their faces, as if they couldn't quite believe they had been welcomed into this elite society yet. Morgan knew it wouldn't take long before lines of stress would replace the surprised looks, and she didn't envy them. It was her first day too, but she'd commanded both courtrooms and classrooms before, and her fear was limited to the fact this was her alma mater and she wanted to do it justice.

❖

At the far end of the common area, Parker glanced at her watch. She spent the last thirty minutes patiently answering last-minute questions from her mentees, Henry and Nicole, but now it was time for her to head to class. She asked the two if they had anything else they needed.

Henry spoke first. "Nope. By the way, you missed quite a party at the dean's house Saturday night. The new criminal law professor, Morgan Bradley, was there. Damn, she has some great stories to tell."

Nicole chimed in. "You've probably seen her on Court TV, she does a lot of commentary. She's one of those perfect people, beautiful, smart, and articulate." Nicole's sigh conveyed her own wish to be one of "those" people.

Parker replied, "Bradley? Of course I've heard of her, but I'm a third-year, do you think I have time to watch TV? Frankly, your TV watching days are over as well." Parker stood. "I have to go. Good luck with the rest of your day. Feel free to call me if you need anything."

Parker strolled across the common area. She needed to make a quick stop at the registrar's office before heading to her next class.

❖

Morgan burned her tongue as the overly large gulp of coffee sizzled its way down her throat. She thought to herself, surely the woman crossing the room wasn't Parker? The tall, beautiful brunette strolled out of sight before Morgan could be sure, but something about the gait and carriage of the woman caught her eye and held her captive. Morgan noted that she walked with great confidence, as if she owned the place. Surely it wasn't the bartender from two weeks ago. Though cocky in her own element, she couldn't have looked similarly comfortable in this institute of higher learning. Shrugging, Morgan rose and walked back to her office to retrieve her lecture notes.

❖

\Parker reviewed the syllabus from her Advanced Legal Research class in between bites of a grilled cheese sandwich. Most of the semester's projects called for teamwork, so she'd have to figure out who in the class she wanted to work with. She knew she was often sought after by many of the other students, primarily because of her high class standing. She was on track to graduate magna cum laude, and while she could always be counted on to help her fellow students, she didn't want to do anything to put her own scores at risk. This research class involved a series of complex research assignments and would be hard enough without the added task of managing group dynamics.

"Hey, Parker, aren't you signed up for the Evidence practicum?"

Parker looked up at the tall, burly redhead standing over her. Dex Gallagher, another third-year, was one of Parker's best law school buddies. Dex, like Parker, was singularly focused on criminal law as a future career, but unlike Parker, he planned to start out working as a prosecutor. To further his goal, he had completed internships at both the local county district attorney's office and the United States Attorney for the Northern District of Texas. Though their end goals were different, their path was the same and the two had become fast friends while enrolled in all the same classes.

"Hey, Dex, I sure am." Glancing at her watch, Parker realized class would start in a few minutes. "Carry my books to class?"

"Still trying to get me to be your boyfriend after all these years?" Dex winked. "When are you going to realize I only want to be friends?"

The joke was old. The first year in school, Dex had asked Parker out on numerous occasions. Reluctant to share personal details about herself, Parker begged off with her standard excuse. She didn't want to get involved with anyone at school, too messy, too complicated. When Dex came up with a thousand reasons why it wasn't, Parker finally told Dex her sexual orientation. Dex had recovered from his unrequited attraction and channeled his passion into a devout friendship. The two had been inseparable study buddies ever since.

They made their way to class and staked claim to adjoining seats near the jury box. The classroom was one of two moot courtrooms at the school. This one was far superior, having been outfitted with cutting-edge courtroom technology. Used primarily by moot court and mock trial teams for practice, it also doubled as a classroom for practical application classes such as the Advanced Evidence class.

Dex leaned over to Parker. "Did you hear who they finally signed to teach this class?"

"No, actually, I went to see the registrar about it this morning, but I didn't get in due to a long line of first-years stalking her. I was going to tell her I didn't want to commit when they weren't even sure they had a permanent instructor. Last I heard, Professor Wilson unexpectedly quit. I don't need the hours to graduate and I can think of better things to do than take six hours from a fill-in prof."

"Quit bragging about all your extra hours. Some of us need this class. Besides, you're going to love the prof they got. Hell, she's famous."

Parker raised her eyebrows, waiting for the name.

"Oh, here she is. Better sit up straight and stop talking so you can impress the pretty new teacher."

Parker turned in her seat, looking in the direction Dex had been focused. Pretty was not an accurate description. Morgan was a knockout. Her wavy auburn hair trailed to her shoulders and her emerald green eyes swept the room in crystal focus. Her height was accentuated by stylish pumps with three-inch heels, and the hemline of her skirt showed off well-toned calves. Her suit was designer with lines both soft and sharp, blending femininity and power in its russet silk threads.

A shove to her side shook Parker from her reverie. Dex leaned close and whispered, "Close your mouth, Casey. You're starting to drool."

Parker recovered enough to whisper with jagged breath, "She's the professor?"

"Yep. Morgan Bradley," Dex responded, adding, "She's one of those hotshot attorneys who's always on Court TV, commenting on cases like Michael Jackson and Enron."

Dex was still talking, but Parker heard only "Morgan Bradley." She had certainly heard of Morgan Bradley and her high-profile cases, but she rarely watched television and wasn't sure she could have picked her out in a crowd. She had no doubt, though—the commanding presence standing a few feet away was the beautiful woman from the alley who had shared her bed for one night and lurked in her thoughts ever since. Confused and feeling strangely vulnerable herself, Parker waved off

Dex's whispered fascination with the new professor and lowered her head. Flipping through pages of her notebook, she studiously avoided looking at the woman holding court at the front of the room. Willing herself to another place, she registered little of the words spoken.

"Since this is a very hands-on class, I want us all to get to know each other. We'll be working in various combinations of groups throughout the semester. If you haven't already, you'll learn what it's like to work in teams when the stakes are the highest. And I'm not talking about your grades. I'm talking about the life and liberty of the person you've been chosen to defend or the right of the individual wronged to see the defendant brought to justice. This class will focus on evidence in criminal cases. If you want to focus on civil litigation or you want an evidence course for your transcript so you can look well-rounded to prospective employers, this is not the course for you. We'll be doing simulations of real case problems, all of them using real criminal cases as the basis for our studies. If you want a drop slip, see me after class. Now, let's go around the room and introduce ourselves."

Dex poked Parker in the side. "Wake up, darling, you're about to have to state your name, rank, and serial number."

Parker stole a sidelong glance at Dex, then at the front of the room. Morgan was faced slightly away from her, focusing on the student at the other end of their row to start the introductions. Furtive looks around the room revealed all escape possibilities were blocked by the presence of other students. In mere moments, she'd have to face the woman she'd never expected to see again. The prospect was at once titillating and formidable.

❖

Years on the courtroom stage gave Morgan the skill it took to cloak her surprise behind knowing smiles. It happened to every experienced attorney. Days of preparation were rendered useless the moment a witness took the stand and began to spin tales that were made up as they went along. In court, Morgan would have a split second to decide whether to show or hide her surprise at being caught off guard. If she had evidence in reserve she could use to impeach the witness's credibility, a show of surprise was a great effect: "Really, Mister So-and-So? Are you saying the defendant told you he killed the maid?"

She would exaggerate the question, reeling the witness in, getting them to totally commit to their answer all the while waiting to whip out a series of written statements they'd provided to law enforcement stating conclusively the defendant had never confessed. On the other hand, sometimes the witness would pop off with a response she didn't expect and had no way of disproving. On those occasions she found it was best to hold her surprise in check, never letting the jury know her composure had been seriously knocked down a notch. Glancing down the aisle past the student giving the class his name, Morgan realized she was about to face a situation requiring more composure than she had ever been called upon to use in the courtroom.

"Dex Gallagher, third-year, future U.S. Attorney for the Northern District of Texas."

"Well, nice to meet you, Mr. U.S. Attorney." Turning to Parker, Morgan felt herself pause longer than necessary before asking, "And you are?"

As Parker turned to face her, Morgan nearly choked. There was no doubt in her mind, whatever name this woman uttered, she was Parker, the mysterious woman from the bar who had already introduced herself in ways Morgan should be blushing about. Feeling the heat rise to her cheeks, she willed it away waiting to hear Parker's opening remarks.

"Hi, Professor Bradley, my name is Parker Casey. I'm a third-year, and I hope my career path is as successful as yours."

Her tone was easy and even. She didn't bat an eye. *Did I hear*, Morgan wondered, *a slight emphasis on the word "professor"?* Not ready to break the connection, Morgan asked, "You want to be a law professor?"

"I'll settle for high-powered criminal defense attorney."

"Fair enough." Morgan paused, not quite ready to break contact either. "I'll do my best to share all of my skills." *Did I really just say that? She must think I'm crazy standing up here acting like we've never met.* This disconcerted feeling was unfamiliar to her. Unaware of how much time had passed, she moved on, hastening to minimize the appearance of discomfort.

The rest of the class was a blur. Morgan went over the syllabus, divided the class into groups, and made the first assignment. Although she planned to let class out early on the first day, their freedom came far earlier than she originally intended. She remained at the front of the room as the students filed out, simultaneously hoping for and dreading an encounter with a certain dark-haired third-year. As Parker walked toward her, she nearly jumped out of her skin at a voice from behind her.

"Professor Bradley, may I ask you a question?"

Morgan reluctantly released her gaze in Parker's direction and turned toward the voice. She saw a young female student who seemed very excited to have her full attention. "Uh, sure. What can I do for you?"

"Well, I was thinking about what you said at the beginning of class and wanted to discuss whether I should stay or drop. You see…"

Morgan didn't hear the rest, focused as she was on the departing Parker. Even though she willed the connection, she was startled again when, as Parker reached the door of the classroom she turned and shot Morgan a slow, easy smile, searing in its implication. Morgan covered her surprise at the unexpected contact and returned the favor. It wasn't until that very moment Morgan knew for sure Parker remembered her, and she wondered what she was going to do with that nugget of information.

❖

Parker begged off Dex's invitation to grab a sandwich and went outside to find a place to collect her thoughts. She sprawled onto a bench and closed her eyes. Despite her show of bravado in the classroom, she was completely blown away to find the woman who had last occupied her bed was Morgan Bradley, celebrity criminal defense lawyer, popular TV commentator and, most surprising of all, her law professor. She didn't want to drop the class. She wanted it on her résumé to impress future employers. Parker felt trapped.

Eyes shut, she pictured Morgan Bradley, dressed to the nines, standing at the front of the classroom. She looked completely in her element, totally in charge. And totally hot, Parker mused. Dex would simply die if he knew the famous Morgan Bradley's body had lain naked on every stick of furniture she owned. Remembering the night they spent together, Parker corrected herself. Morgan hadn't simply lain there. She'd been a wildcat, their night of sex filled with passionate agility. Reliving the memories, Parker, eyes still closed, smiled.

"Am I interrupting anything?"

Parker recognized the voice, but recognition didn't minimize the shock of hearing it here, where she wasn't expecting to encounter Morgan. The surprise nearly caused Parker to fall off the bench.

"Um, no. Do you need something?" Realizing she sounded abrupt, Parker started again, "I mean, hi, and no, you aren't interrupting anything. Do you want to sit down?"

Morgan glanced around before she replied. "Actually, yes, I would." She looked pointedly at Parker's still sprawled form. Parker grinned sheepishly and sat upright, folding her legs underneath the bench.

Seated, Morgan turned toward Parker. "I thought we should talk." Parker merely raised her eyebrows. Morgan continued, "I'm thinking neither one of us expected to see the other again." Parker nodded. She didn't want to taint whatever Morgan had to say by interjecting her own affirmations or denials.

"And certainly neither one of us expected to see each other here, in these roles."

"Roles?" Parker asked.

"Me teacher, you student."

"Oh, yeah. Those roles."

"I had fun with you. You are pretty amazing."

Parker was surprised at the unexpected compliment. As awkward as this situation was, she actually felt very comfortable sitting an arm's length away from Morgan Bradley, famous lawyer. In fact, the only discomfort she felt was a persistent nagging need to lean over and kiss the lips of her law professor. Shaking herself out of the trance threatening to make her act on the need, she replied, "Why, thanks, Professor, you were pretty amazing yourself."

"As much as I would love to see you again, you realize we can't."

Parker didn't speak. Although she'd already had the same thoughts, her recent recollections were coloring her ability to think clearly. She knew Morgan was right, but she wished she had been the one to speak the words. Parker was used to calling the shots.

"Parker, did you hear me?"

Shrugging, she replied, "Sorry, I did hear you. I completely understand." As she spoke the words, she saw relief spread over

Morgan's face and it made her unreasonably angry. Parker wondered why it should be so easy for Morgan to decide the one night was it, especially considering she was on fire just sitting next to her. *How in the hell am I going to make it through an entire semester without exploding?* Unable to resist a dig, she felt compelled to add, "Some people are capable of keeping their personal lives private and some aren't."

Morgan raised an eyebrow, urging Parker to continue.

"Now, take me for instance. I'm perfectly capable of having hot, healthy, recreational sex with another consenting adult without letting it interfere with my professional life. You, on the other hand, may be one of those people who can't. I respect our differences."

"Oh, you do, do you?" Morgan's eyebrow was still raised and she wore a smug smile that threatened to send Parker over the edge.

Incapable of stopping, she continued. "Sure. Look, I know you are attracted to me and I know you had a great time the night we were together. But if having fun makes it too difficult for you to function professionally or should I say, professorially, I understand." As soon as the words left her mouth she wanted to take them back, but pride forced her to wait for a response. Morgan's reply immediately signaled Parker wasn't winning any points in this conversation.

"Really?" Morgan's smile turned to a scowl and she growled back, "I promise you I am capable of more than you will ever know, but that's not the issue here. This situation is simple: you're a student and I'm your instructor. Those are lines I'm not willing to cross. I don't have sex with my students." Her last words with delivered emphatically.

It was Parker's turn to to be smug. "Little late, don't you think?" She glanced down at the bench as if to invite her to vacate. Morgan, taking the hint, rose and surrendered her seat. As she walked away, she shook her head, but didn't turn back in Parker's direction. Parker waited till Morgan was out of sight before taking off herself, in the opposite direction. Her surprise at seeing Morgan again in this setting, combined with the volatility of their exchange, resulted in a raging rush of hormones. Excitement warred with wounded pride and she was confused by her mixed reactions. She wasn't used to wanting seconds from the women she chose to share her bed, but she was also used to being the one to make that decision. Morgan had beaten her to the punch, but Parker wondered if she was more upset about the timing of

Morgan's rejection or the fact Morgan had rejected her at all. She shook away the desire to answer her own question and decided to blow off an afternoon in the library in favor of a workout at the campus gym. As she walked away from the law school, she ran into Dex, who was walking toward her with several of their friends.

"Hey, Parker, ready to divvy up outlines?"

With an internal groan at his eagerness to get a jump on the new semester, Parker asked, "Now?"

"You have something better to do?"

"Actually, I was on my way to the gym."

"Great. Let's do this first and then I'll join you. You could go now on your own, but I swear we'll stick you with the worst sections."

Parker knew Dex was only half teasing. Outlining was the bane and boon of every law student's existence. The key was to split the task of producing a comprehensive outline of the text and classroom notes for each section of the syllabus among group members whose work you knew and respected. Parker, Dex, and three others had worked together to create intricate outlines since their first semester in school. The size of the group had fluctuated over the last year as the individuals pursued various electives, but when it came to core courses, they still met as a group to share their skills. This semester they were all signed up for Ethics with Dr. Spencer, who had a reputation for grueling exams. Parker weighed her options and decided the gym could wait and she agreed to join her friends.

"Fine, Dex. If you're going to threaten me. But I'm holding you to your promise—a full workout after we meet."

"Yeah, like I scare you. It's a deal."

Parker let Dex lead her to the library where he had reserved one of the small study rooms available for this purpose.

"Hi there, have you eaten?"

Morgan looked up from the papers she'd been pretending to study and flashed a weak smile at her visitor. "Hi, Jim. Actually, no. I haven't."

"Then join me. I was about to head to out for lunch."

Morgan vacillated between her desire to wallow in self-pity

over the incident with Parker and the competing desire to socialize in this new environment. The recent confrontation had robbed her of an appetite, but she realized life on campus was so much easier when you had some friends or at least acquaintances to point out all the inside information. She hated continually bugging Yolanda with questions, so she'd best buck up and make nice with Jim Spencer. He had taught at the university for so long there was likely nothing he didn't know. Morgan pushed aside lingering regret over her disturbing encounter with Parker and agreed to join him for lunch.

"Thanks, Jim. I'd love to join you."

Within twenty minutes they had walked across the street and were seated at Peggy Sue BBQ in Snyder Plaza, a unique blend of upscale shops, eclectic restaurants, and college textbook stores. Morgan glanced over the menu and remarked, "Good thing I'm not a vegetarian."

"Oops, guess I should've asked," Jim said. "I hope you like barbeque. It's kind of a prerequisite if you're going to live in Texas."

Morgan smiled. "I guess Dean Ramirez didn't tell you I grew up here. I've eaten more than my fair share of brisket and ribs over the years."

"Well then, I challenge you to a rib-eating duel. Let's order the combination rib platter and see who can eat the most!"

Laughing at his exuberance, Morgan placed her order, eschewing his challenge in favor of a brisket plate with fried okra and squash casserole. As Jim gave his order to their waitress, she sized him up. He appeared to be in his mid-fifties, with graying hair. She could tell he cared about his appearance. He wore an expensive suit, carefully tailored, definitely not off the rack. Many full-time professors opted for the "I don't need to conform to the image of workaday lawyers," which resulted in a poorly matched, ill-fitting parade of outfits. Morgan was relieved to see she wasn't the only one to buck the trend.

Morgan decided to use the time waiting for their food to gently pump Jim for information about the school, and she decided to be direct about it.

"So, Jim, tell me everything I need to know about our fine law school to make this year go as smoothly as possible."

"Ah, a lady who cuts to the chase. I like, I like." Jim cocked his head. "First, let me be direct. Do you have dinner plans for Saturday night?"

"Turnabout is fair play, I suppose. I'll be equally direct. I do not have dinner plans, but I am fresh from a breakup and have no interest in anything other than platonic friendships." Morgan decided she could be direct without full disclosure. As far as she knew, Yo was the only one on faculty who knew she was a lesbian and, while she didn't go out of her way to hide her sexual orientation, she didn't feel the need to advertise it either.

"So, you're not gay, just freshly burned?"

Though their exchange had thus far been refreshingly direct, Morgan was taken aback by the focus on her sexuality. She was used to speculation about her sexual orientation. Living in the limelight, as she had the last decade, she'd had to face the question from inquiring press minds. Somehow she'd managed to deflect, quick to point out the subject was entirely irrelevant to the issue at hand, which usually concerned one of her cases or a case on which she was asked to consult. She had declined all requests for personal interviews and, she reflected with a grimace, she and Tina had been living separate lives for so long the mere fact they shared an address didn't provide any direct evidence of an intimate relationship between them. She stared across the table attempting to assess his sincerity. Finally calculating her trust would be well placed with Jim Spencer—after all, Yo would certainly have warned her otherwise—she decided to tell him the truth.

"Yes, on top of my other reasons for not wanting to date, I'm a lesbian. Are you still buying lunch, because I'm planning on having dessert." She watched as Jim worked his way through her remark, finally deciding she was kidding with him.

"Okay, now we have the important matters settled. So, I have first-base seats to the Rangers game Saturday. Care to join me? Aren't the folks who play for your team good at catching fly balls?" Jim waited through the several seconds it took for Morgan to realize she was being teased back by an artful kidder.

"Deal. Now, you owe me some intel."

"What do you want to know about first, faculty or students?"

Morgan reflected before answering. "Students, since I'm already in the midst of dealing with them."

Jim spent the next half hour giving her the spiel on the various groups of second- and third-years she was likely to encounter in her classes. As he talked, Morgan was grateful she had accepted both the lunch invitation and Jim's overtures at friendship. He was going to be a valuable source of information, and he was harmless.

"Use Casey and Gallagher, they're both great students and they know everyone else in the school."

Morgan realized she had missed part of Jim's remarks during her musings. "Pardon?"

"Dex Gallagher and Parker Casey. They're in your trial practice seminar."

"Sorry. Yes, they are. What can you tell me about them?"

"They have a friendly rivalry to be first in their class, which drives them both to be the best students they can be. Their study group consistently gets top marks in all their classes. Plus they're both older than the average student, so they have more life experience and perspective. Personally, I find the older students refreshing."

"I know what you mean. Sometimes I can't imagine being as young and naïve as some of these kids. I think the ones who've already been out in the working world have a better shot at being successful in whatever field of law they choose to practice." She waited, hoping Jim would continue to provide detail about at least one of his favorite students. She didn't have to wait long.

"I agree. Gallagher was a DEA agent before he came to law school, which probably explains his earnest desire to be on the 'right' side of the law and order equation. Casey has an interesting background as well. You should get her to tell you more about it. Suffice it to say, she has a tendency to root for the underdog. She's worked the entire last summer at the Tarrant County public defender's office. She's not afraid to work harder than everyone else, which probably explains why she's on track to graduate top in her class."

Morgan concealed her surprise. She had made assumptions about Parker Casey and they were wrong. Apparently, Parker's skills included more than merely mixing drinks. She felt the heat of her own blush as she reflected on her personal experience with the skills of Parker Casey. Fighting away the heat of the memory, she spoke. "She seems to be very perceptive." Morgan shuddered internally at the lameness of her remark. She looked up from her plate and noticed Jim was gazing intently in her direction. "What?"

He shrugged. "You're very astute. She does have a way of sizing up a situation. You're pretty perceptive yourself, especially for someone who's been teaching here all of one day."

"Why thank you, Professor Spencer." Morgan put her fork down, sighing. "If I eat one more bite, I will surely die."

"Doubtful, but you will surely sleep through your afternoon office hours. I guess this means I don't have to buy you dessert?"

"Hell no. I will, however, take a rain check in the form of ice cream at the ball game on Saturday."

Jim stood and motioned to the cash register in the front of the restaurant. "Ice cream it is, but please don't say 'rain' in the same sentence as 'ball game.'"

Morgan smiled and accompanied him back to campus. She was grateful to have had the distraction from thinking about her confrontation with Parker Casey, though she was certain the reprieve was short-lived.

CHAPTER FIVE

In the classroom, Parker was glad for the opportunity to sit wherever she wanted. Many law school professors, too important to be bothered with the task of learning their students' names, had their students all sit in the same places for each class so they could refer to a chart rather than their memory for the appropriate appellation. Apparently, Professor Bradley didn't need the extra assistance to learn her students' names, Parker thought.

She had been simultaneously dreading and welcoming the second session of class. Following the meeting with her study group yesterday afternoon, she had retired to the gym and put herself through a rigorous two-hour workout. Her attempt to exhaust her mind with physical exertion was an utter failure, however, and she'd been able to think of little other than the striking Morgan Bradley in the hours since.

Parker glanced around for Dex. She had expected him to be in class already, especially since he had their completed first assignment with him. It had been interesting, though not hard in the least. Each pair had been assigned the task of locating a movie clip that contained an example of what they thought were excellent cross-examination techniques. Parker had to admit the assignment had been fun. Dex and Parker had descended on the local video rental store and cleaned them out of legal dramas and even comedies, since Dex lobbied hard for *My Cousin Vinny*.

Dex slid into his seat at the same moment Professor Bradley strode into the room. Today she sported a slightly more casual ensemble than the day before, but she was still impeccably groomed. The sleek, classic lines of her charcoal gray gabardine pantsuit cried out expensive tailoring and Parker idly contemplated whether Morgan had her suits custom made. Those thoughts dissolved into wondering whose hands had been lucky enough to drape fine cloth over the beautiful body standing before her now, fast followed by unbridled jealousy toward the imagined tailor. A punch in the ribs startled her out of her musings.

"Did you hear a word I said?"

Parker half turned to Dex and pretended to pay attention. "Sure, something about the DVD," she guessed.

"Uh, no. But I have the DVD right here," Dex whispered, nodding to the front of the room. "I wanted to talk to you about the study group, but it looks like we're about to get started here."

Parker followed his glance back to the front of the room. "I've got some free time after class. We can talk then."

❖

Once class started, Morgan Bradley commanded the stage. "I'm sure many of you wonder why I decided to start with cross-examination techniques." Noting several nodding heads, she continued, "It's true, most trial and evidence classes begin with what evidence is admissible and the skills involved in direct examination. Frankly, I don't have a strategic reason, but I think crossing witnesses is the most fun a lawyer can have—legally, anyway.

"Which team wants to go first?" Morgan forced herself not to look in the direction her eyes had been drawn since she walked in the room. She was having trouble deciding how to deal with the fact she and Parker were destined to spend many hours a week together in roles so very different than the ones they had occupied the night they met. Her body could not deny the force of feeling that swept through it every time she glanced Parker's way. Parker Casey possessed head-turning good looks requiring no assistance from wardrobe and makeup. Today she wore a T-shirt and jeans, the same or similar to the well-worn 501s Morgan had peeled off her the night they met. Her hair was rumpled and fell in endearing chaos to twist around her ears and collar. Morgan sighed as she felt a searing need to run her hands through Parker's thick hair and create some chaos of her own. *This is never going to work*, she thought ruefully.

Years of practice made it possible for her to hide her personal feelings and forge ahead. She called on team after team, studiously avoiding the Gallagher-Casey duo until last. When she finally ran out of other options, she turned her attention to the final pair and hoped against hope they didn't have another DVD of *My Cousin Vinny* to offer. *I know Dallas is a big city, but seriously, how many copies of the damn movie are still in existence*, she wondered.

Dex took the lead while Parker acted as AV aide to his running commentary. The clip they chose was from *A Few Good Men*, the scene where Tom Cruise's Lieutenant Kaffee tangled with Jack Nicholson's Colonel Jessup. Dex was animated in his presentation of this defense lawyer cross-examination which Morgan found amusing considering his devotion to the prosecutorial side of legal practice.

"So, what's your favorite part of this cross-examination?" Morgan directed the question to Dex since he was obviously the lead showman in this particular presentation.

"I guess it would have to be the part where Jack Nicholson gets into it with Tom Cruise and starts screaming 'You can't handle the truth.' Makes for some great high drama."

"Oh, it's definitely great drama." Turning to the class, Morgan switched back into lecture mode. "I chose this particular exercise for a reason, and I'm pleased to report the clips each of you chose demonstrated my next point perfectly." Pausing for effect, she continued, "Drama is for the movies or TV. It's the result of highly scripted dialogue designed to elicit the maximum punch. It cannot be replicated in the courtroom. Good drama in the courtroom is organic. It comes from all the pieces coming together in a way you cannot plan for because you don't control all of the elements.

"What you can do, however, is be prepared. Be prepared with knowledge and skill. When you finish with this class, you will have superior skills you can translate into any situation, in any case. You will be skilled at conducting an efficient and slaying cross-examination. If, at some point in your career, you also get to be a part of some amazing courtroom drama, consider it a bonus."

Morgan waited a moment to let her pronouncement sink in. She was aware her words disappointed some in the group who thought the hotshot lawyer was here to teach them how to attain fame and fortune in a few easy steps. Better they figure it out now, she decided. Most trials were fairly boring, and though she'd had more than her fair share of movielike moments in the courtroom, those moments were few in comparison to the hundreds of unexciting but razor-edged cross-examinations that won her cases time and time again.

❖

Parker was impressed by Morgan's honesty. She undoubtedly had an arsenal of tales to tell, all casting her in the starring role of winning criminal defense lawyer. However, instead of resorting to replays of *The Morgan Bradley Show*, she seemed genuinely interested in teaching real skills at the risk of making her accomplishments look achievable to the average lawyer.

The next hour was in lecture format and Morgan finished by handing out assignments for the next class. Parker glanced over the assignment and realized she and Dex were probably going to need to schedule a regular time to meet in addition to their usual study group meetings. This particular assignment provided a case study, complete with relevant facts and listed witnesses whose cross-examination they were to prepare. They would take the role of witness and lawyer respectively and "perform" their examinations for the rest of the class.

As the students trickled out of the classroom, Parker hung back, hoping to catch a moment alone with Morgan. Their encounter the day before had been eating away at her, and she sincerely wanted to square things between them. For all her words of bravado, she agreed with Morgan. There was no way they could repeat what happened between them. It wasn't practical, and she was sorry she'd let her pride get in the way of agreeing when Morgan brought up the issue.

As she waited, she grew increasingly frustrated at the number of other students who also seemed intent on a moment alone with Morgan. Watching Morgan patiently answer each question, Parker started to fume. She was reaching her boiling point when she felt a tap on her shoulder and she twisted around, ready to strike.

"Whoa there, don't hit me!" Dex feigned a look of fear.

Parker relaxed. A little. She wasn't used to being frustrated with Dex, but lately his timing left a lot to be desired. Parker took a deep breath and told herself there was no way Dex could possibly read her mind.

"Sorry, I'm a little tense today."

"A little? Whatcha hanging around for?"

It would seem strange if she told him she wanted to talk to the professor about the assignment since they would be working on it together, she thought. *Oh well, it's not like I'm not going to see her again soon.*

"No reason. I wasn't sure what I wanted to do next."

"How about a workout and then we can grab some dinner while we go over this assignment?"

Thinking a strenuous workout was probably the best medicine for her tension, Parker agreed.

CHAPTER SIX

M organ liked the look of the restaurant. It had the feel of being in someone's home. Someone's very well-kept, well-designed home. Paintings from local artists adorned the walls and the bar area had a cozy feel. She glanced around looking for the woman whose photo she had seen on the Internet.

"Can I help you?"

Morgan turned in the direction of the deep voice. The woman posing the question was dressed in khaki pants, an oxford cloth button-down shirt, and Doc Martens, all items signaling "uniform." Short-cropped hair and a sturdy bearing also signaled "lesbian," and Morgan vaguely remembered Yolanda mentioning the Lakeside was owned by a lesbian. Taking a chance, Morgan thrust out a hand.

"Actually, I'm supposed to be meeting someone. My name is Morgan Bradley. Is this your restaurant?"

The woman chuckled. "When things aren't running smoothly. I'm the manager, Sally Gannon. Mackenzie Lewis is the owner. Did you have an appointment to meet with her?"

"No, I'm here to meet with an Aimee Howard. I've seen her picture, though, so I'm sure I can wander around and find her."

"No need. She's out on the Dock. I'll take you to her."

Ms. Howard must be a regular, Morgan reflected as she followed Sally through the restaurant. *No wonder she picked this place, she must feel very comfortable here.*

As they stepped out onto the patio deck, Morgan's eyes immediately found the woman she was here to meet. She was every bit as beautiful as her picture, though not at all Morgan's type. Aimee Howard was a buxom blonde, curvy and soft. She was in no way fat, but she definitely did not possess the lean, athletic body type Morgan was attracted to. *And that's for the best*, Morgan decided.

Sally made the formal introductions and then left them to their privacy, promising to send a waitperson over in a few minutes to see if they needed anything. A scrumptious-looking plate of appetizers was already on the table along with a bottle of Pinot Grigio and two glasses. Aimee motioned for Morgan to take a seat and she poured her a glass of wine.

"Thanks for meeting me here. On a beautiful day like today, I think it's important to be outdoors." Aimee glanced around and added with a grin, "Well, as least as close to outdoors as you can be and still have all your creature comforts. My best friends own this place and, I must confess, it's more like home to me than my own kitchen. The food's better too," she added with a grin.

"Thank you for meeting with me in the evening," Morgan replied. "My days have been packed the last few weeks, and evenings are the only time I can seem to squeeze in personal needs."

"Well, consider me in charge of this particular personal need." Aimee handed a bulging folder to her. "I've pulled an extensive list of houses based on the sketchy parameters you e-mailed to me. Before we start looking, I'll want you to go through this list and narrow it down so I can focus on what you are looking for in a new home. I thought we could do some of the narrowing down together tonight so I can get an idea of what you're looking for."

Feeling the weight of the folder, Morgan realized she hadn't been very specific in her description of what she wanted, partly because she wasn't sure. She knew she needed to find a place to live besides the luxurious Palomar. She had fond memories from her time in law school of tree-lined East Dallas neighborhoods with wood frame houses seated on large lots. Not sure where to begin, she had followed Yolanda's suggestion to hire a realtor. Yolanda had recommended Aimee Howard, who specialized in the well-established and even historic homes located in East Dallas.

Morgan opened the folder and started sifting through the pages. "Wow, you've given me a lot of choices. Sure you want to watch me wade through all of these?"

"It'll go faster than you think. As you start looking, you'll realize there are certain things you can't live without, meaning we'll discard a bunch of these right off the top. When you think you have the list narrowed down, we'll drive the neighborhoods. Some of them you'll dismiss on sight, without even going in. We real estate folk are trained to write excellent marketing materials on the homes we have listed, but what's on that paper doesn't always measure up in real life. Kind of like pitching a case to a jury, right?"

Conceding the point, she replied, "Yeah, you're right. We're both in the marketing business, in a way. Though right now, I'm not practicing. I'm sure Yolanda told you I'm teaching at the law school."

"She did mention your new position when she gave me the details of your needs."

Morgan caught the sultry undertone and wondered what else Yolanda the matchmaker had mentioned to her.

Aimee changed the subject. "Say, did you hear the story on the news about Camille Burke? Isn't she a student at your school?"

Morgan shook her head. "I did hear the story. She was a graduate student in the art department. I only heard she had been murdered, but I've missed the follow-up stories. Apparently, the Burke family is a big contributor to the university, which is probably the only reason I heard anything about this at all."

"The news report on the radio earlier today said she'd been shot and they think the family handyman did it."

"Interesting. I don't envy his attorney. From what I hear, the Burkes are an influential bunch. They'll want his head on a platter."

"Do you miss being in private practice?"

"I enjoy teaching. It's invigorating, working with eager students who are excited about the prospect of practicing law." She realized she hadn't answered the question, but she didn't know how to answer. There were things she missed about private practice, but she was also grateful not to be running her own business while she was slowly recovering from moving across the country and breaking up with Tina.

Aimee changed her line of questioning back to real estate. "Do you have any particular reasons for wanting to live in East Dallas?"

Morgan told Aimee about growing up and going to school in the area and she listed off her favorite things about life there. Their discussion lasted through several glasses of wine and most of the appetizers on the platter between them. She found herself liking Aimee, not only for her professionalism, but also her easy way of inviting conversation. Morgan was pleased at the realization she might have herself a friend outside the law school.

Aimee interrupted their discussion to ask, "Do you know the dark-haired beauty who's staring you down, or is she a secret admirer?"

Startled at the change in topic, Morgan shook her head. "Excuse me?"

"Over there." Aimee jerked her head almost imperceptibly. "She's with the big guy with red hair. Wait a minute, she's still looking, or should I say glaring? Wait, wait, okay now, quick."

Morgan turned her head slowly, feigning a stretch. She was too slow, however, and as her gaze connected on the couple across the room, Parker squarely met her glance. Without time to compose herself, she gasped in surprise.

❖

Parker entered the restaurant and walked straight toward the wood-deck patio nicknamed the Dock by patrons of the Lakeside. As she suspected, Dex was already there making short work of an enormous gourmet hamburger. She plucked a sweet potato fry from his plate and slid into the chair across from him, munching the crispy snack.

"Thanks for waiting."

"Sorry, Parker, I was starving and you were late. Eat all the fries you want. I prefer real potatoes."

"Sweet potatoes are real potatoes, silly boy. And they're better for you, though judging by the size of the burger you're eating, you couldn't care less about your health."

Dex's only response was to smile around the edges of the bun he held up to his mouth.

Parker ordered a turkey club and then spread her papers across the table. "I've been thinking about this and I don't think she's going to have us question each other in class."

"Huh?"

"Keep up, man. I don't think she's going to have us question the person we prepared," Parker repeated. "You don't get to prepare adverse witnesses in real life, so it doesn't make sense she would have us do it in her class. I think she's going to switch things around when we get to class."

"Makes sense. So what do you suggest we do to prepare?"

"I say we spend our time brainstorming what points we want to get out of the cross-examination and then work out the narrowest questions possible to box the witness in."

"That's one way of doing it."

"You have a better plan?"

"We could walk over and ask Professor Bradley how she wants it done." Dex pointed across the room.

Parker looked in the direction he was pointing. Morgan was dressed casually and the look did nothing to diminish her beauty. She wore jeans, sandals, and a sleeveless yellow linen shirt, which showed off tan, fit arms. Her toenails were painted in a soft pearl shade and she sat with one leg tucked under the other. Everything about her bearing conveyed she was relaxed in her surroundings, having a good time, and Parker glanced away from her only long enough to take in Morgan's companion. She scowled at the blonde who was sharing wine and laughs with Morgan.

As the blonde looked up, Parker realized she was staring and hastily glanced away. Finally replying to Dex, she said, "Nah, looks like she's busy. We're smart. We can figure this out ourselves." Her easy tone didn't betray the anxiety she felt at seeing Morgan in this setting.

"Sure, Casey, whatever you think." Dex pushed aside the platter containing the remnants of his meal and started pulling out papers to begin their work. As she watched him prepare, Parker felt heat on the back of her neck. She knew someone was staring at her and she suspected it was the blonde, returning looks. She turned slowly to meet the gaze, but the eyes meeting hers were unmistakably Morgan's.

❖

"Aimee, would you excuse me for a moment?" Morgan asked, already out of her chair. Barely waiting for a nod, she walked across the patio toward the table Dex and Parker shared.

"Dex, Parker, how're you doing?"

"Great, Professor," Dex answered. "Though we'd be doing even better if we were here without an assignment to work on."

"Oh, am I working you too hard?" Morgan kept her focus on Dex Gallagher though Parker's presence pulled at her, calling out for attention.

"Well, Casey here thinks you're trying to trip us up on the assignment, lulling us into thinking we're preparing our witnesses for a cross-exam, but you actually intend to have us mix it up in class to show how you don't get to prep your adverse witnesses in the real world."

Grateful for the opportunity to focus her attention on Parker, Morgan turned to her, her heart pounding. She tried for a teasing tone as she asked, "Parker, do you think I would set you up to fail?"

Parker met her look and held it. "I think you would do whatever you felt was necessary to prove a point." The words were delivered with a calm, deliberate tone, but Morgan heard the undercurrent of anger. She didn't blame Parker. She felt the heat flaming between them, but she had no plans to ignore common sense and fuel the fire. Risking a prolonged look into the eyes turned her way, she admitted to herself the difficulty of the situation. Every moment in Parker's presence was a searing reminder of what was possible when passion reigned. For one night, Parker's undivided attention to her every need had awakened in her the want she had suppressed for years, years spent in a dead relationship where desires died of disinterest. Ignoring the voice within crying out for her not to ignore those desires any longer, Morgan pulled herself together to respond.

"Trick's on me then, since you've figured out my strategy. I suppose I now know who my best students are going to be."

Dex smiled, while Parker's face was impassive. "There was never any question," she said.

❖

"Parker Casey, what the hell are you doing here on a weeknight?"

"Back off, Irene, I swear I cleaned my room and finished all my homework." Parker's tone was jesting, but Irene knew her well enough to know not to push matters.

"Fine, girl. I suppose you're entitled to blow off some steam considering how hard you're working. Beer?"

Parker relaxed and she settled onto a barstool. "Great, thanks."

"Hey, Parker, how're ya doing?"

Parker turned to meet Dannie's enthusiastic glance and couldn't ignore the outstretched arms. Dannie was truly adorable and when she got to be a few years older, she would rule this roost. Parker knew because for years she had been the one in charge, picking who she wanted from the crowds of women who came here, all seeking something different in the same safe place. Parker hadn't had a real crush in years, but she knew what it felt like to be the object of other women's avid affections. The feeling was empowering.

Releasing Dannie from the hug, Parker replied, "I'm doing all right. How 'bout you?"

"Good, but we miss having you around. Glad you stopped by. Can I buy you a drink?"

"When you turn twenty-one you can. In the meantime, I'll buy my own, but thanks for the offer." Parker ruffled Dannie's hair and softened her words with a warm smile.

❖

Morgan was beginning to believe her second trip to the bar was a mistake. She hadn't been ready to go back to her lonely hotel room and she didn't feel like returning to her office. Aimee had asked her to stay for dinner, but Morgan detected an undercurrent of desire she didn't share, so she begged off what was likely to turn into an uncomfortable encounter.

She would have been content to nurse a drink by herself in a corner booth with the presence of others serving as a backdrop to keep her from feeling truly alone. But her plan for solitude in the sparsely populated bar was foiled when she caught sight of Parker Casey seated at the bar. Her thoughts were invaded by feelings—strong, passionate feelings, all of which were hungry for attention and determined to drive away all reason. She had only herself to blame. *You knew she works here*, she chided herself.

She watched the easy exchange between Parker and the young androgynous barback with mounting jealousy as she noted the comfortably casual way Parker touched the other woman. Morgan forced herself to look deep into her vodka tonic, willing away the exchange taking place nearby. She felt rather than saw a body slide into the leather booth beside her. Morgan took her eyes off the floating ice cubes long enough to turn and tell the unwanted presence she longed to be alone. Surprise stopped the words before they left her lips.

"Why, Professor, twice in one day! We should be more careful. People might begin to talk."

Morgan bit back a sharp retort when she noticed the teasing gleam in her eyes. Distracted as she was by the heat of Parker's presence, she knew enough to know she was being baited and she was determined to keep the upper hand. Matching Parker's tone, she replied, "Should I obtain a restraining order?"

"You may need one." Parker grabbed Morgan's hand and pulled her from the booth. Morgan amazed herself by following without resistance.

Moments later, they were standing in the alley. Morgan didn't notice the smells or trash this time. All her senses were focused on Parker's commanding presence. She felt a rush of heat as her thundering heart pushed blood fast and furious through her veins. She offered no protest as Parker pulled her into strong arms and kissed her with roaring passion. In this moment they were not teacher and student. They were once again strangers meeting in a strange place. The memory of the night they shared as strangers warmed her to this embrace. She kissed Parker with abandon, crushing her lips, melding her body against Parker's welcoming frame, willing away all the barriers between them.

Her will wasn't strong enough. She pulled away even as Parker moved closer, groaning soft words against her neck. Hearing her voice brought back the reality of their relationship. They weren't strangers meeting for the first time. They were well known to each other in positions that rendered their current embrace taboo. Morgan was torn between temptation and convention. Convention won the first round.

"I have to go." Morgan's breathing was labored.

Parker stepped closer. "No, Morgan. You don't."

"Yes. I do."

Parker placed a hand on either shoulder and gave Morgan a gentle shake. "You don't get it, do you? We're both adults. There's nothing wrong with the attraction between us. I make it a rule not to fool around with anyone at school, and if I'd met you there first, we never would have had the night we had. But it didn't work out that way, and I don't see any logic in pretending things are anything other than what they are."

"And what, pray tell, are they?"

Parker's lips delivered a complete and wordless response. Morgan ceded her last grasp at maintaining their formal roles and answered with equal passion. The deep kiss left her breathless and wanting. When Parker inclined her head in the direction of the path they had taken the night they first met, Morgan could only nod and follow.

❖

The house was exactly as she remembered it. Morgan followed Parker up the stairs again, fighting away a persistent thought. *Leave now before things get really complicated.* As if sensing her consternation, Parker turned and gathered her into a tight embrace. She kissed Morgan and her tongue teased away all doubt.

"Who was the blonde?" Parker asked.

Morgan, hazy with lust, murmured back a question. "Huh? Blonde?"

Parker smiled. "Never mind."

When they reached the room, Parker wasted no time trying to get Morgan undressed while ignoring Morgan's attempts to do the same to her. Parker was intent on being in charge this time, knowing that outside this room, in the halls of the law school, Morgan would always be the one in control.

"My turn this time."

"Your turn?" Morgan raised her eyebrow and flashed a questioning smile.

"I believe last time we were here, I let you run the show." Parker began to unbutton Morgan's shirt. "Now it's my turn."

Morgan answered by placing her hand over Parker's and pulling it to her mouth. She eased Parker's index finger into her mouth and stroked it with her tongue. Parker tried to continue unfastening Morgan's shirt with her free hand, but Morgan's warm, wet tongue drew her deeper, caressing the sensitive web of skin between her fingers. For a moment Parker forgot what she was doing, where she was. Ironically, it was Morgan's voice that drew her back into the moment.

"Okay."

"Okay?" Parker opened her eyes. Her hand was back by her side and the only evidence of Morgan's mesmerizing kisses was the cool moisture on her still slick finger.

Morgan met her glance. "Yes. I think you should run the show." She finished what Parker started, undid the last button of her shirt and slid it from her shoulders. "You're in charge."

Parker knew she wasn't, but she played the role as if it were hers. She didn't bother with the niceties of candlelight this time but relied instead on the thin shafts of streetlight through the slits of the window blinds and the trace of her own touch to view Morgan's beautiful body. Parker watched Morgan shift from one foot to the other as she stood nude at the foot of the bed while Parker, still dressed, slowly observed her every feature. She wondered if Morgan's uneasiness had as much to do with the balance of power as it did with her exposed flesh. As if in answer, Morgan reached for Parker's shirt, tugging it out of her jeans. "Take your clothes off."

"I suppose you're going to say you want to feel my skin against yours?" Parker breathed the words into Morgan's ear. Morgan responded by twisting her hand in the cloth of Parker's shirt and sliding her palm against the exposed skin. Parker's breath caught at the sudden charge of the impact. Morgan's touch was as electrifying as she remembered and she almost ceded her control. Almost.

"Well, I happen to agree." Parker gathered Morgan's hands into her own and leaned closer. "Here, let me show you." She grazed the soft skin of Morgan's neck with her lips and tongue, licking a path to her luscious earlobe where she lingered, coaxing Morgan into submission. It didn't take long. As Morgan wilted against her, Parker held her in a strong embrace before gently easing her onto the bed. Lying on her back, arms above her head, Morgan was at once vulnerable and stunning. The vulnerability threw Parker off balance for a moment, but she quickly recovered her composure. She wanted to savor this experience and she wasn't going to let the reservations Morgan had expressed earlier get in the way of the undeniable attraction she felt.

Parker pulled her shirt over her head and tossed it to the floor. She grasped Morgan's wrists and held them tight while she lowered her body just enough to let her breasts rub against the hard arousal of Morgan's nipples. Parker sucked in her breath as Morgan bucked against her, but she kept the rest of her skin just out of reach though she ached to meet Morgan's insistent pursuit. Parker slid down and rested a denim-covered thigh between Morgan's legs. She felt the heat of Morgan's yearning sear through the cloth and groaned at the sensation.

"Touch me," Morgan begged. Her eyes were dark pools of liquid, seemingly unfocused as if her sight was turned inward, observing only the sensations of her own arousal. She struggled, her body straining to connect with Parker's. Every ounce of her appeared to be humming with desire, and Parker suddenly cared less about maintaining control than about granting Morgan's request. She dipped her head and flicked her tongue against a hard nipple, teasing it to its finest point before she sucked the swollen breast into her mouth. Parker released her grip on Morgan's hands to play with Morgan's other breast, squeezing and tugging as Morgan raked her nails down the muscles on her back. Parker groaned. The mix of pain and pleasure bordered on extreme, but still she craved more.

"I want to taste you."

"Please," Morgan pleaded, so unlike the woman who had commanded their first night together. "I'm so close, I may come the second you touch me."

"No, you won't," Parker promised. She drew her fingers along Morgan's glistening sex, gently opening the soft folds of flesh. Sliding down, she lowered her head and breathed in the musky aroma of Morgan's desire. Parker blew a warm breath across Morgan's clit before drawing her into the moisture of her ready mouth. Parker reveled in the slippery heat against her tongue and the twitch of Morgan's legs elicited with each increase in pressure. She caressed Morgan with long, steady strokes, taking her to the edge and holding her there without release. When she could feel Morgan edge toward climax, she slid two fingers inside her and drew herself up along the length of Morgan's body, tasting her way back to Morgan's full, gorgeous breasts. Morgan's erect nipples welcomed her touch and Parker licked them hard while her fingers replaced the stroke of her tongue below. As she lavished Morgan's breasts, she straddled her thigh and rubbed her own wet sex down the length of Morgan's leg. Lost in the feel of the woman beneath her, she was pleasantly startled by the strong thrust of fingers between her legs. She looked up to see Morgan's hazy smile and leaned in to kiss her full, ripe lips. As they kissed, she felt Morgan's hands on her breasts, coaxing her nipples into stiff knots, then rubbing them hard against the satin palm of her hand. Parker found herself on top but not in charge. As Morgan's lips and hands explored her mouth, her breasts, and her aching center, her fervor grew and Parker gave up all pretense of command. She met Morgan's thrusts with equal fervor and, lips locked in heated frenzy, they came together in a roar.

❖

Nestled in the crook of Parker's arm, Morgan pushed the thoughts crowding her head to regions far from the present time and place. Morgan took advantage of the last shades of dusk peering through the blinds to appreciate Parker's athletic form. She shivered at the memory of their night of passion. Unlike the first night, bits and pieces of experience and knowledge added depth to their encounter. Morgan now knew Parker was intelligent as well as sexy, confident as well as cocky. She wondered how Parker felt now that she knew the woman who lay beside her had power that exceeded her ability to make her partner come.

❖

Parker watched the rise and fall of Morgan's sleeping form and, not wanting to wake her, resisted the urge to curl her body around her. She remained content instead to breathe in Morgan's scent. She was amused at her inability to look away. She'd spent years loving women but never letting herself get attached. Parker Casey's definition of love was appreciation. She appreciated beautiful women, smart women, sexy women. She knew how to convey her interest with the most subtle signals and prided herself on her ability to please without promise. Parker maintained a friendly, if passing, acquaintance with many of her sexual partners, though most of her amorous encounters were one-night stands.

Lying here in bed beside Morgan, she found herself thinking ahead. Time was too short for all the things she wanted to do, all the things she wanted to say. Morgan had taken her to the edge and Parker had been so enraptured she would have gladly plunged into the abyss if Morgan had led her there. She had never allowed herself to experience such total loss of control and she wondered why she didn't begrudge her powerlessness once Morgan touched her. Shaking her head, she decided to break the parade of thoughts marching her toward unfamiliar territory and wrapped her arms around Morgan's sleeping form. Within moments, Morgan stirred and Parker kissed her gently awake.

"Good morning."

"Morning." Morgan stretched her arms and rolled away from her. "What time is it?" Sitting up, she looked distractedly around the room.

"Don't worry. Unless you have a six a.m. class, you're not late for anything." Parker grabbed Morgan around the waist and pulled her back into the covers.

Morgan squirmed out of her grasp. "Seriously, Parker. I need to get home."

Parker pinned her down. "Seriously. Do you have a six a.m. class?"

"No."

"Then get dressed and have breakfast with me." She phrased the request as a gentle command. "Did you drive to the bar?"

Parker watched the "oh shit" expression cross her face and reached out to grab her hand. "No worries. Let's have breakfast and I'll take you to your car. You'll still have time to get to wherever you need to be today. I promise."

Pulling her hand away, Morgan remarked, "You get up earlier than most law students I know."

Parker grinned. "Are you in the habit of noticing the sleeping patterns of law students?" The frozen look on Morgan's face was a clear sign she had said the wrong thing, and she scrambled to recover. "Besides, I haven't always been a student."

"Is that so?"

"That is definitely so," Parker replied. A moment of silence passed during which Parker was at once hurt and relieved Morgan didn't press her for more detail. She took the absence of follow-up questions to mean Morgan wasn't interested in anything more than a physical relationship. The realization stung, but she pushed past it. Grabbing Morgan's hand, she pulled her from the bed. "Come on, I need coffee."

Moments later, Parker ushered Morgan into the kitchen. They were greeted by the smell of freshly brewed coffee and the sleepy Kelsey James greedily sipping from a large mug. Parker felt Morgan stiffen. She spoke to lighten the mood.

"Good morning, Doctor. You look like you could use a good night's sleep instead of the monster cup of java you're working on."

"You're so observant, Parker. I could actually use about two full days of sleep, but I'm only here to change and this is my quick salvation." Kelsey raised her eyebrows in question and nodded toward Morgan.

"Sorry, I'm impossibly rude before caffeine. Kelsey James, I'd like you to meet my…friend, Morgan Bradley. Morgan, this is one of my roommates, Kelsey James." Glancing back and forth between the two, Parker asked, "Better?"

Morgan shook Kelsey's outstretched hand, murmuring, "Nice to meet you." Despite the polite veneer, Parker sensed Morgan's desire to crawl under a rock rather than be seen so obviously dressed in clothes from the day before. She shot a look at her, willing Kelsey to get the picture and exit gracefully. She did exit, though not gracefully.

"As much as I would love to have a leisurely breakfast with you two, I better get going. Morgan, it was good to meet you. Maybe next time we'll have time to talk. I'm a great source for intel on your breakfast partner." With a wicked smile, Kelsey grabbed her mug and strode out of the room, impervious to the daggers Parker was shooting her way.

"So, you have roommates," Morgan said dryly.

"I do. Most of the time, I enjoy the company. Today, not so much."

Morgan reached across the table, placing her hand on Parker's. "She seems very nice. I'm sorry if I seemed unfriendly. I'm a little anxious about all I have to get done today. Would you mind taking me to my car now?"

Parker battled the disappointment away from her expression. She sensed Morgan's desire for a quick morning-after exit had little to do with anxiety over her schedule, but she decided not to pursue the point. "At least let me get you a cup of coffee to go?"

Morgan nodded and moments later, they were speeding away in Parker's car to the scene of their first meeting.

❖

Parker nearly jumped out of her skin before she realized the noise was nothing more than someone knocking at her bedroom door. She had been studying, or at least pretending to study, since Friday evening. Now it was Sunday afternoon and she felt as though she'd accomplished nothing other than stewing in her thoughts about Morgan. "What is it?" she called out.

The door creaked upon. "Oh, so you are in here. We've been wondering where the hell you've been the past few days." Kelsey and Erin entered the room and took up positions on Parker's bed after they pushed aside all the books strewn on the comforter.

"I've been studying."

Kelsey ventured a question. "Wanna talk?"

"Not especially, but I get the impression this isn't about what I want. You two are up to something. What is it?"

Erin started the conversation. "Kelsey tells me you had a friend over for breakfast Friday morning."

Friday seemed like forever ago, Parker thought. Here it was Sunday afternoon and she'd been able to think of little else since kissing Morgan good-bye at her car Friday morning. The fierce embrace they had shared signaled it was more than a "see you soon" good-bye. Since then she'd glided through Friday's classes, resisting the urge to walk by Morgan's office to catch a glimpse of the real person who now faded into fantasy. With the weekend almost over, she realized she hadn't been mentally present, but had instead slipped into a weird kind of walking coma which allowed her to accomplish only routine tasks while saving her from thoughts of what might have been.

"Um, Parker? Are you in there?" Erin waved a hand in front of Parker's face.

"Yeah, I'm here."

"Wanna tell us about your hot new friend? We couldn't help but notice she's a repeat customer."

Something about the connotation of the word "customer" made Parker snap. "What the hell do you mean?"

Kelsey grabbed Parker's arm and pulled her close. "Hey, tiger, calm down. We're not used to you seeing someone more than once. We were wondering if we should be reading bridal magazines." Her teasing words were delivered with a gentleness designed to soothe the bristling anger Parker held below the surface. Recognizing her attempt to defuse the situation, Parker relaxed.

"Sorry, I'm having a bad day."

"Anything we can do to help?" Erin's question was tentative.

Parker offered a half-smile. "No, I don't even know what's wrong. I feel like I'm coming out of my skin. Normally, I'd work out to get rid of this feeling, but I can't seem to muster up the energy."

"Casey, are you sure it's not the girl who's got you down?" Kelsey asked.

Parker surprised herself by replying in a muffled voice, "I don't know, maybe."

"She's beautiful. And, she seems very nice," Kelsey offered.

"Oh, she's nice and beautiful all right." Parker looked at them, then glanced away, choosing not to see their immediate reaction at her next words. "She's a nationally known criminal defense lawyer, TV commentator, and she also happens to be one of my professors."

"No way!" Kelsey punched her on the shoulder. "How in the hell did you two wind up in bed together?"

"Oh, it's over." Parker shrugged. "I mean it has to be. We never would have hooked up if we'd known what we were getting into, but we met before school started and neither of us had any idea. Conversation wasn't big on the list of things we shared the night we met." Looking up, she dared them to comment on this revelation.

They both resisted, but Parker could tell by the subtle looks they exchanged when they thought she wasn't looking that they wondered if her affair with Morgan Bradley was truly over. She knew it had to be. For Parker, who had always placed more value on the heat of the moment than the emotions she left behind, the realization was crushing.

CHAPTER SEVEN

Back East, the night air this time of year would be crisp and cool. Morgan missed the predictability of the changing seasons. Here in Dallas, the intense heat of August had boiled over into a steamy September. Green leaves clung to trees and gardeners still planted, gambling on endless sunny, warm weather since there seemed to be no cool winds in sight.

The last week of class had been as stifling as the muggy evening air. She spent hours reliving her last intimate moments with Parker, hastily saying good-bye as Parker dropped her at her car. Neither acknowledged those moments as their last, but clearly they both knew. Over the course of the last week, they resumed the roles of teacher and student and, Morgan was certain, no one suspected those boundaries had ever been pushed, let alone broken. As she walked through campus, Morgan allowed herself, for the first time, to imagine an alternate ending.

She didn't see the lights until she was at the edge of the crowd. Pausing, she took note of the bowed heads, the signs, and the flickering flames of candles in the hands of dozens of young men and women. Vaguely, she realized it was dark outside and she wondered how long and how far she had walked, lost in thought. Rather than skirt the crowd, she stopped on the edge and listened in. The handwritten signs and scattered photos clustered on a makeshift altar made it clear this gathering was in remembrance of Camille Burke, the young graduate student who had been brutally murdered in her own home.

Public displays of affection have the effect of drawing people in. Vigils for the dead are no different. Morgan imagined she wasn't the only one in this crowd who hadn't known Camille Burke in life but relished the idea of knowing her now, through others' memories and recollections. Looking in, it was possible to imagine how it would be when she was no longer alive. What would people say, what snippets of her life would they think were important, would they choose to share?

Morgan reflected on the many murder cases she had worked on over the years. Some defense attorneys refused to allow themselves any intimate connection to the victim or the victim's family, deciding that distance allowed them to exercise their skills more effectively. Morgan, on the other hand, armed herself with knowledge about the life that had been taken. Her ability to reach beyond crime scene photos and autopsy reports often enabled her to find an explanation, if not a reason, for the death. Whether the explanation helped or harmed her client was evenly divided, but knowledge was power and Morgan looked for leverage wherever she could find it.

"Did you know her?"

Morgan recognized the voice and closed her eyes as if she could choke off the tide of emotions it evoked by cutting off at least one of her senses. She turned cautiously and, steeling herself, slowly reopened her eyes. Parker looked tired, sad, far removed from the self-assured woman she had come to know. She was overwhelmed with a desire to pull her close, wrap her in her arms, and whisper comfort. But Parker stood with her arms held tightly at her sides, not inviting. Morgan shook her head. "Did you?"

"No, I was on my way to the gym. But it's a bit like a train wreck. Kind of hard to look away." Parker whispered this last, either out of respect for the crowd or a desire to keep her thoughts secret between them. Morgan couldn't tell which, but she responded by nodding, wondering what source other than grief caused Parker to look so drawn.

Words were inadequate to fill the space between them, so Morgan and Parker stood in silence with the rest of the mourners, keeping their own private vigil. An hour later, when the crowd dispersed, a glance was all that passed between them before they left to rejoin their separate worlds.

❖

Morgan was startled by the ringing of the hotel phone. Other than Yolanda, the only person to call her at the hotel was Tina. Just this week, she'd stopped having the operator screen her calls once it became apparent Tina had resigned herself to their failed relationship. It had been two weeks since she'd run into Parker at the Burke vigil. Their encounters in class had been strictly professional. However, in the late-night hours, she had been able to think of little else besides Parker's tight, beautiful body coiled around hers. As she reached for the phone, she thought *maybe.*

"This is Morgan."

"Morgan, how the hell are you?"

Morgan instantly recognized the voice of Ford Rupley, though she hadn't talked to him in almost a year. Her initial disappointment faded into happiness of a different sort. Ford Rupley was the deputy chief public defender of Dallas County. He and Morgan had attended law school together. She felt bad she hadn't contacted Ford since her return to Dallas. She kept meaning to, but it seemed the details of all her current life changes kept getting in the way of reconnecting with her past. "Ford! Sweetie! It's so good to hear your voice."

"Are you sure? I haven't heard from you since you got back to town." His tone was teasing, but Morgan recognized a shade of hurt beneath the surface.

"I'm still reeling from all the changes. I have a lot to report. Let's have dinner this week and catch up. My treat. Are you still at the PD's office?"

"How about dinner tonight, *my* treat?"

Morgan glanced down at her attire. She had planned on a cozy date with the room service menu and was dressed appropriately in silk pajamas. Much as she would have liked to catch up with Ford over dinner, she decided to gracefully postpone. She started to turn him down but was distracted by loud yelling on the other end of the phone and asked, "Where are you?"

"Lew Sterrett. Can you meet me down here?" Though it had been a while, Morgan still recalled the reference. Ford was at the Dallas County Jail.

"What the hell? You're inviting me to dine at the jail cafeteria?"

"There's someone here I want you to meet. We'll eat after. Seriously, Morgan, I'll make it worth your while. I promise."

The excited pleading in his voice triggered Morgan to react the way she always did at the prospect of taking on a new venture. Curiosity battled comfort and won. "Give me thirty minutes. I'll meet you in the lobby."

❖

The drive downtown was quick and easy since rush hour was long over. The Lew Sterrett Justice Center was located just west of downtown, directly behind the Frank Crowley Criminal Courthouse, and was the headquarters of the Dallas County jail system. As a young attorney, Morgan had logged many hours in both of these buildings. She parked in the open lot across the street from the jail and walked through the courtyard separating the jail from the courthouse. Ford was waiting outside.

"Morgan, you look fantastic! Thanks for coming."

"I assume at some point before I turn into a pumpkin, you'll let me know why you summoned me."

"Let's sit for a minute." Ford pointed to a low stone wall. "I want to talk to you about a very interesting case."

"And this case must be dealt with under dark of night?"

"I'm in the middle of a capital case. This is the only time I could meet with him. I want you to work with me on his case."

"Back up, mister. You're still at the PD's office, correct?" At Ford's nod, she continued her questions. "And I assume you've been appointed to work on this case?"

"Correct, Counselor. Now before you start lecturing me about your standard hourly rate, all I'm asking you to do is meet the guy and hear his story. Whatever you decide after you meet him is completely up to you."

Morgan knew it wouldn't be so simple. Once you knew names and faces, the intrigue got under your skin. She let several seconds tick away before deciding it already had. "Okay, what the hell else do I have to do at midnight on a Wednesday night?"

"Terrific. We don't have a lot of time, so I'll hit the highlights and you can pick up the rest as we go." In his traditional manner, Ford buzzed through the details. Toward the end, Morgan felt her head spinning as she tried to keep up.

"Luis Chavez, he's our client, was the trusted handyman for the Burke family." He paused while Morgan nodded at the familiar Highland Park name. "Camille Burke, beloved daughter, was found in her room with a gaping hole in the middle of her face, and Luis Chavez was standing over the body. Instead of waiting around to answer questions, Luis took off and hid out for a few weeks until a concerned citizen reported his location to the police. He was arrested last night. Turns out he has a record. Despite his checkered past, he's always been a great employee and he's worked for the Burkes for years."

"What's his sheet look like?"

"One felony conviction. Drug case. Possession."

"Have you met him?"

"Yes. About an hour ago."

"What does he have to say about all this?"

"Not much. He didn't kill her. Doesn't know who did."

"Lovely. Looks like you have your hands full. You'll be lucky to get a plea offer of any kind on a case involving the Burkes."

"Yeah, you're right. The odds are stacked against us." Ford looked down at his shoes.

"I guess there aren't any other witnesses?"

"I only had a moment this afternoon to glance at the police report, but it appears Camille's brother, Teddy Burke, saw Luis standing in a pool of blood next to Camille's freshly dead body. When Luis saw Teddy, he took off running."

"That's not great."

"True. It's probably a hopeless case. I should pass it off to one of my assistants." Ford shrugged, feigning nonchalance.

Morgan knew she was being played, but she couldn't resist the challenge of impossible odds. "I don't have my bar card with me." The card, issued by the state bar, was required in order to transact business at the jail and the courthouse.

Ford grinned. "I can get you in."

❖

"Sour," "dank," and "nasty" were the first words that came to Morgan's mind as she sat on the edge of a plastic chair Ford had dragged into the visitor booth. Ford occupied the round metal seat permanently affixed to the floor in what was certainly an ergonomically incorrect position in relation to the phone secured to the wall. While they waited for the deputies to escort Luis to the other side of the booth, Morgan tried to guess how many years had gone by since the county had decided to forgo simple tasks like cleaning. At this point, it would take a sandblaster to make a dent in the layers of grime that had been allowed to form on the walls, the floor, and the counter, and no doubt such extreme measures had not been included in the budget. As a result, the entire jail was rank and Morgan tried her best to avoid touching anything she didn't have to.

After what seemed like forever, a small Hispanic man entered the booth, on the other side of the Plexiglas. Nodding to Ford, he picked up the phone on his side and said hello.

"Hello, Luis. I came back because I want you to meet a colleague of mine." Ford waved a hand in Morgan's direction. "Her name is Morgan Bradley. She's an attorney and I want you to talk to her about what happened." Ford started to hand the phone to Morgan, but Luis asked him to wait.

"Is she the prosecutor?"

"No. She's a friend of mine, a lawyer. I may want her to help me on your case. Tell her what you told me." Ford indicated to Morgan they should switch seats. Morgan barely had the phone in her hand before Luis started speaking.

"I didn't kill her."

"I didn't ask, but thanks for letting me know that." Morgan met Luis's pleading eyes. "Tell me why you think you were arrested."

"I don't know." Luis sounded dejected. "I was downstairs, fixing a leak in one of the bathrooms. I heard a noise, like a gun, from above. I went upstairs to check."

Morgan urged him on. "What happened next?"

"I saw her. Miss Camille. She was lying on the floor."

"Was she dead?"

"I don't know. I guess." Luis's squeezed his eyes shut as if to shut out the memory. "There was blood everywhere."

"Did you see anyone else?"

"No. Not then. I saw a gun. I picked it up."

"Why did you pick up the gun, Luis?"

"I was scared. Whoever shot her might come back."

His tone was defensive and Morgan decided to leave the "why" questions for later and stick to the basic facts. "Then what happened?"

"Mr. Burke, he saw me."

"Where was he?"

"In the door. He looked at the gun in my hand, then he looked at me."

"What happened next?"

"I threw the gun down and I ran." As if anticipating Morgan's next question, he continued. "I was scared. I didn't know what else to do. I hid at a friend's house. They came and got me last night."

Morgan didn't need to ask to know that "they" was probably the police. "Did they ask you questions when they arrested you?"

"Yes. I told them what I'm telling you. They didn't care."

She didn't see any point in asking him more questions, especially since she didn't have the benefit of knowing the exact proof that would need to be refuted. Morgan offered what she hoped was a sympathetic smile. "No, I don't imagine they did. I can tell you this, Luis, you have a very good attorney. Mr. Rupley will do his best to fight the charge against you."

"What about you? Will you help me?"

Morgan shot Ford a pointed look before meeting Luis's pleading eyes. "I'll see what I can do."

❖

"How can you eat so much this late at night?"

"It's not late, it's early." Ford grabbed a fistful of fries off Morgan's plate to replace his own, which had been consumed within seconds of reaching the table. "Besides, I need my energy if we're going to get right to work." He grinned.

"I have class in the morning. You, by all means, should burn the midnight oil on behalf of your client. Let me know how it turns out."

His expression was pained. "Wait a minute. I was sure I had you interested enough to work with me on this one. You practically promised Luis you would work on his case."

"I did no such thing. Besides, you boxed me in a corner. What was I supposed to say to the guy?"

"Come on, Morgan. Admit it. You'd love to work with me again."

Ignoring his remark, Morgan asked, "Was there a statement in the police report from Teddy Burke?"

"I don't know yet. I've been in trial all day and I just got the summary of the report."

"Luis said he was working on the downstairs bathroom. Surely there would have been tools lying around."

"We'll have to check the police report to see if they checked. Or talk to other employees in the house at the time to see what they remember."

"What in the world do they think his motive was?"

"That's a good question."

"Who's the prosecutor?"

"Not sure. The case is in Judge Thompson's court, but I don't think it's been assigned yet. With a victim from the Burke family, I wouldn't be surprised if the elected DA gets involved." As if he could tell Morgan's resistance was fading, he pressed on. "I heard you're single now. Some extra work would be good for you. Maybe you could make some new friends." Ford placed extra emphasis on the word "friends."

"Make up your mind. Either I'm the fierce advocate battling law enforcement or the passion-hungry schoolteacher looking for a good time. I don't have the energy for both." Even as she spoke the words, she could feel herself giving in.

"Well, when you put it that way…" Ford's attention returned to his plate, but a moment later, he used his fork to wave a Eureka! in the air. "Actually, I've got a great idea. What if you could be a fierce advocate and a schoolteacher? I mean, what if we formed a defense team using the top students in your Advanced Evidence class? What better scenarios could you come up with than the real thing? You'd get to work on this case and your students would get real-life experience. Mr. Chavez would get a kick-ass defense. Justice for all!"

"No more coffee for you. Seriously, Ford. I have no idea if I could get permission to run a clinic as part of my class, let alone figure out how to fit it into the schedule. I would certainly need to run it by Yolanda." Even as she spoke, Morgan's thoughts belied her words. Something about this particular case intrigued her. She reflected on the vigil for Camille Burke she had happened upon earlier. All those students, gathered to mourn a life cut short. The crowd at the makeshift memorial was small in comparison to the number of voices that would cry out for vengeance when Luis went on trial. Maybe it was the challenge of turning a lost cause into a victory that captured her attention. Whatever it was, she was already casting a trial team from the students in her class and, knowing Parker had to be a part, wondering how in the world they would work together.

Ford shook a French fry in her direction and she set her thoughts of Parker aside to turn her attention back to him. "Yes?"

"I know you want to work on this case with me. I can see the gleam in your eyes. Will you at least ask Yolanda?"

"Was there ever any doubt?"

CHAPTER EIGHT

I s she in?" Morgan asked.
Edith nodded. "Go on back, she's never too busy for you."
Yolanda was on the phone, so Morgan waited in the doorway of
Yolanda's office and considered her approach. She was prepared for some
resistance, considering the Burkes' generosity, but she had prepared a
courtroom-worthy argument in favor of taking the Luis Chavez case,
complete with an outline of the constitutional implications. She was
ready to pitch her case when Yolanda finished up her phone call and
waved her in.

"Thanks for giving me an excuse to get off the phone." Yolanda
looked closely at her. "You look like you want something. Finally
decide your office isn't big enough?"

"No, my office is fine. I was thinking it needs more in it,
though."

Yolanda looked puzzled and then smiled. "Want to go shopping
for furniture? Please, take me away for an afternoon!"

"No, dear. I was thinking I miss work, the excitement of the
courtroom."

"Am I losing you already? We're not even to midterms. Seriously,
Morgan, what can I do to convince you to stay?"

"Oh, I'd be happy to stay. I want to work on a project, though. I
can fit it in with my class. Give them some real-life experience. I could
even pick the best of the lot to be on a trial team if you'd approve me to
work a small clinic practice for extra credit hours."

"Perfect use of your skills and a great experience for your students.
Where do I sign?"

"Don't you want to know more about the project?"

"Unless you're representing the KKK, I think we're safe." Yolanda looked closely at Morgan's face. "It isn't the KKK, is it? Now, don't give me a spiel about freedom of speech—"

Morgan interrupted her. "No, it's an indigent client. I'd be working with his public defender, Ford Rupley. The client's name is Luis Chavez." Morgan watched Yolanda's furrowed brow, knowing she was trying to place the name. She decided to help her out.

"He's the Burkes' handyman. He's charged with the murder of Camille Burke." Morgan winced at Yolanda's sharp intake of breath. "Now, before you say anything, I know the Burkes have been very generous to this university."

"Complete understatement. They're campus darlings. Lester Burke will have a coronary when he finds out the students whose education he helped fund are defending his baby girl's killer."

Morgan was poised and ready. "So the people with the money are the only ones who should reap the benefits of a good defense? And whatever happened to innocent until proven guilty? He's not a killer until a jury says he is—wait, did you say 'defending'? You mean you'll let me do this?"

Yolanda's expression was neutral. "Will you stay the year?"

"Is that a bribe?"

Yolanda smiled. "Bribery? No. Coercion, maybe. This project will require a great deal of spin on my part, but I'm already working it out in my head. Why have great teacher talent if we can't use it? This demonstrates our commitment to equality. Of course, I'll have to impose a few conditions."

Morgan sighed. She knew there would be a catch.

"Pick your top three students. They can be your trial team. The rest of the class can work on issues related to the case—motion filings, etc. Oh, and Gerald Lopez has to be one of the top three."

"You're kidding, right? Gerald is an idiot. He couldn't find his way out of a paper bag, let alone be able to navigate a courtroom. I don't even know why he's in my class. He'll never make it as a trial lawyer."

"Cool your jets, hotshot. I happen to agree with you. But Gerald's daddy is a big donor. Not a Lester Burke–size donor, but big nevertheless.

If we can make him happy by giving his baby boy a chance to show off in court, I can fade some of the heat I'll get from the trustees about Burke."

"You drive a hard bargain. Maybe you should get back into private practice. Fine, it's a deal. Now, I'm leaving before you tack on any more conditions." Morgan turned as she walked through the doorway. "Oh, Yolanda?"

"Yes?"

"I would've agreed to stay two years."

❖

An hour later, Morgan sat in her office pondering the best way to approach this project with her students. Part of her wanted to use her autocratic power and select the students she wanted to work with. Her bargain with Yolanda meant she only had two slots to work with, and Dex and Parker topped the list. Both older students, they possessed a unique perspective, and there was no question they were the top of their class. But Morgan knew she couldn't pick Parker, not without a process.

A small part of Morgan felt guilty for not confiding her affair to Yolanda. She decided a confession at this point would merely complicate matters, and since the affair was over, the complication was unnecessary.

Morgan spent the next hour devising a method to select her trial team. She wanted to make the announcement in class and select the students by the end of the week so they could begin working. She decided she would take Jim Spencer up on his offer to help her out. She would convince him and Yolanda to do the judging. Then Yolanda would be solely responsible for making sure Gerald made the team, and surely Parker's innate talents would win her a place on the team. Morgan had every confidence in Parker's talent.

❖

Dex pushed Parker along as they made their way to Morgan's office. "Come on, don't you want to find out if we made it?"

"We, huh? What if only one of us made the team?"

Dex punched her in the arm. "Not a chance. We're the two musketeers!"

Parker couldn't help but catch his infectious grin. "You dope, it's three, not two, musketeers."

Dex stopped in front of the closed office door and ran his finger over the index card taped under Morgan's nameplate. When he turned to face Parker his grin was gone.

"As usual, you're right, but you'll probably be sorry you were."

Parker pushed past him trying to get to the door. "What the hell?" She ran her finger along the posted names. "Damn, how the hell did he make it?"

"They need three musketeers?" Dex offered.

"Whatever. I can't work with him. This is going to be hard enough," Parker muttered. She wished she hadn't spoken the last words out loud, but having to work side by side with Morgan was going to be enough of a challenge without having Gerald Lopez in the mix. How in the world had he made the team, she wondered. He had the trial skills of a gnat.

"Oh, lighten up. His daddy probably bought him a place on the team. Don't worry. With our combined expertise, his ineptitude will barely be noticed."

Parked frowned. "What scares me is no one seemed to notice in the first place." She resolved to let it go, but she was having a hard time shaking the disappointment of knowing Gerald Lopez had been picked for the trial team. Maybe his father's influence did have something to do with it, which almost made it worse since it meant Morgan had succumbed to conventional pressure rather than doing what was right. Parker had had her fill of people who didn't possess the courage of their convictions. That she had had to sue her former employer, the Dallas Police Department, to make them admit they had wronged her still rankled. That she had lost a friend and lover because the other woman, her partner on the force, had refused to admit the same wrong cut Parker to the core. She knew it was naïve, but she had expected more integrity from Morgan. Wistfully, Parker realized keeping her relationship with Morgan strictly within the bounds of teacher and student was probably for the best.

❖

Morgan debated canceling the meeting. She and Ford had scheduled their first meeting with the students who would be working on the trial team for this afternoon, but he called to say he was stuck in court and to go on without him. She had spent time reviewing the bare-bones police report Ford had obtained from the prosecutor, so she was prepared to discuss the basic facts of the case and the work to be done. What she wasn't prepared for was working with Parker in such close proximity. The last few weeks in the large classroom setting had been difficult enough. She should never have gone to the bar that last time. She couldn't deny the attraction, but she certainly didn't have to put herself in the path of destruction. And there was no doubt that continuing to act on her attraction to her student would be destructive. The lack of sleep and focus she experienced now were mere precursors of the havoc she was sure to experience if she had sex with Parker again.

A knock on the door startled Morgan from her thoughts. As the students entered, she made a command decision to move the meeting from her office to the classroom. She met Gerald and Dex halfway to the door.

"It's a bit cramped in here. Let's take this to the classroom." Morgan led the way, her glance sweeping the hall, but Parker was nowhere in sight. Dex, perhaps seeing her looking around, offered, "She's on her way. She had a little bit of trouble with her baby." At Morgan's raised eyebrows, he continued, "Her car. It may as well be a baby, the way she takes care of it."

"She should junk that old thing and get some new wheels." Gerald's tone was disdainful.

Dex punched him on the arm. "You only wish you could handle a beast like that. Her Mustang could take your bright, shiny Beemer any day of the week."

Morgan felt herself start to defend Parker's method of transportation, but she bit back the words when she realized she didn't have an explanation for why she should even know what kind of car Parker drove. She did know, though, and the memory of her last ride in the Mustang was a mixture of pleasure and regret.

"I thought we were meeting in your office." Parker looked flushed and out of breath. A stray lock of hair fell across her eyes and Morgan longed to reach over and brush it away. She resisted the urge and focused her attention on the door to the classroom.

"I decided we'd have more room in here."

The group settled near the front of the class and Morgan passed around copies of the indictment and gave them a few minutes to look it over. The group already knew the case involved Camille Burke's murder. Since Camille had been a student at the school, Morgan wanted to make sure no one who tried out for the team had any conflicts about working on the defense team representing the man who was accused of murdering the young student.

"Luis Chavez was the handyman for the Burke family. He was working inside the house the night Camille was killed. He was arrested and the grand jury indicted him for murder last week. We'll be assisting the chief public defender on this case. You'll meet him tomorrow at the DA's office. We have a meeting scheduled at two o'clock to look at the evidence the prosecutor has developed in the case. The meeting tomorrow is a hunt and gather session. We're not there to talk about the facts, negotiate, or discuss the law. We'll listen, look, and walk away. Once we have seen and copied their evidence, then we'll analyze it and work out a strategy for developing our defense.

"Now, here's the deal. When I graduated from law school, I didn't know jack about the real world of criminal law except some random snippets of information I gathered working on petty crime cases at the public defender's office. The first time I was hired to be lead counsel on a murder case, I nearly threw up every day until it was over." Morgan surveyed their expectant looks. "So, even though I understand you have all worked as interns in this field, I'm going to assume you know nothing about working a felony case, let alone a murder case, until I see otherwise. Fair enough?" Gerald and Dex nodded, but Parker seemed distracted and Morgan wanted her attention. "Parker, why don't you explain what an indictment is?"

"It's a charging instrument."

"In English."

"It's a document that sets forth the allegations of the case. It puts the defendant on notice as to what the State has to prove in order to get a conviction."

"How does someone get indicted?"

"The State presents evidence to the grand jury and, if the grand jury believes there is enough evidence to establish probable cause both that a crime occurred and that the defendant committed it, then they return a true bill of indictment, which is a formal charge."

"How much proof do you need to show probable cause?"

Parker broke the stream of robotic, technical answers. "Not much." Dex and Gerald laughed and Morgan realized that in her attempt to be more formal with Parker, her questioning technique had become more like an interrogation.

"Look, there's no need for this to be so formulaic. You've had a chance to look over the indictment. It will be our guide for determining whether the State has enough to get a conviction. We'll see their actual evidence tomorrow, but for now, I've got copies of the probable cause affidavit for you to review." Morgan handed out stapled packets to each of her students. Ford had delivered the document to her office earlier and she had skimmed it before meeting with them. She was anxious to hear their reaction to the uphill battle the team was about to face.

"What's this?" Gerald asked.

"Dex, want to answer that?" Morgan asked.

"It's kind of a summary of the police report. The investigating officers have to swear out an affidavit in order to get an arrest warrant." He shook the papers in his hand. "These should give us an idea of what evidence they have against Luis."

"Right. Take a moment to look it over." Morgan waited for the several minutes it took each of them to read over the document before continuing. "Okay, what can you tell me about our case?"

Gerald was the first to respond. "We're screwed."

As much as she didn't like him, Morgan had to laugh at the raw truth of Gerald's conclusion. "All right then. Let's pretend for a minute you work for the other side. Gerald, what are the strong points of your case?"

"What aren't the strong points?" he replied sarcastically. "The guy was seen standing over Camille Burke's dead body with a gun in his hand. He ran off and hid from the police. And as if that weren't enough, his fingerprints were on the gun and his boot prints are all over the scene."

Gerald's bluster got under Morgan's skin and she silently cursed Yolanda for forcing her to make Gerald part of the team. "First of all, our client has a name—Luis. He's not 'the guy,'" Morgan said. "His liberty is in our hands, so let's not forget he's a real person, not an abstract suspect." She turned to Dex and Parker. "Either of you see anything in the affidavit that's helpful to our case?"

Dex was the first to respond. His tone was more respectful than Gerald's, but his conclusion was the same. "Not really, no." He shook his head. "Things look pretty bleak for Mr. Chavez."

Parker's expression told Morgan she had her own opinion about the matter. "Parker, what do you think?"

"Frankly, it doesn't surprise me that everything in this report points to Luis as the killer. After all, the police wrote it. I think that once they heard the details about Luis at the murder scene, they didn't look for another suspect." Parker's expression turned grim. "Having said that, I have to say defending Luis is going to be tough. Especially since there doesn't appear to be evidence pointing to anyone else."

Morgan was glad to know someone besides her didn't let the daunting prospect of defending against the odds cancel out the fact the police report was naturally biased. *Smart and handsome. Makes her even harder to resist.* "You're absolutely right. Refuting the State's evidence is going to be difficult, and we're not going to get any help from the other side. So we better get started."

Morgan spent the rest of the hour leading the group through the litany of proof the State would need and that they would have to counter. She continued to be impressed with Parker's command of the law and wondered how Parker came by her extensive knowledge. She almost asked, but caution held her back. She was reluctant to engage Parker more than the other students in the group, partly because she was concerned her feelings would show through. The last thing she needed was for the rest of the class to think she had a crush on one of her students, but that was exactly how she felt.

The cases Parker had worked on the past summer in neighboring Tarrant County hadn't prepared her for the jittery feeling coursing through her as she walked through the familiar courtroom doors. Assisting the court public defender meant paying your dues by working out easy pleas, serving as gofer during trial, and, occasionally if she was lucky, getting to cross-examine a nonsubstantive witness. She hadn't minded the busywork; it gave her exposure to the way things were done on the other side and beefed up the experience on her résumé. Working on this case would be different. Though she'd spent years working as a homicide detective, she had yet to work a murder case from the other side.

Morgan and the others hadn't arrived. Parker glanced at her watch and noted she was a few minutes early. The team was gathering at the courthouse for a meeting with the prosecutor and the lead detective on the case to review the evidence in the file. They would also be meeting with Ford Rupley, the public defender who would be working with them on the case. Parker knew Ford and wondered if he would remember her. He was the most talented attorney at the PD's office and she often wondered why he didn't strike out on his own in private practice.

Parker entered the first set of double doors to Criminal District Court 10 and looked through the windows on the inner doors and noted with the exception of the bailiffs, the courtroom was empty. She glanced at the doors on either side of her. The one on the right led to the DA workroom. She had spent hours in these workrooms, one of which was located in each court. Assistant district attorneys spent their mornings in these rooms, meeting with defense attorneys, interviewing witnesses, and preparing cases for trial. In the afternoons, the die-hard prosecutors stayed in the cramped workroom, while those using the job as a stepping stone to higher-paying nongovernment jobs adjourned to tiny individual offices on the eleventh floor of the building. Parker started toward the slightly open door on the right before she caught herself and turned instead to the less familiar door on her left, the defense counsel workroom. As she turned the knob, she winced at the sound of a familiar voice behind her.

"Casey?"

Parker turned slowly and stood face-to-face with her former lover, Skye Keaton. She stifled a low moan at the raw energy crackling between them and bit out her words.

"Skye. It's been a long time."

Skye Keaton's usually stoic face was flushed, but Parker didn't truly register the impact of their reunion until she felt Skye's hand grasp her arm. The touch, though brief and light, branded her with memories. They stood in the tiny hall lined with doors as people pushed past, but to Parker it felt like they were completely alone.

Skye broke the silence and gave Parker a frank appraisal. "You look good, Parker."

Parker traded looks with equal measure. Detective Skye Keaton looked exactly the same as she had the last time Parker had seen her, tall and blond with velvet gray eyes sporting a jaunty glint. Time had been kind to her former partner in the homicide department of the DPD. "So do you. Bet you never thought you'd see me back here."

"Not again, no, I didn't." Skye stared hard into Parker's eyes. "You're not in trouble, are you?" A softness broke through her cop's tough tone and Parker was touched.

"Good afternoon, Parker." They started at the approach of Morgan Bradley. Spell broken, Parker registered how close she was standing to Skye, and the flash of Morgan's eyes told her she had noticed.

Morgan stuck out a hand in Skye's direction. "I'm Morgan Bradley. And you are?"

Skye shook Morgan's outstretched hand. "Detective Keaton."

"I see. Aren't you the lead on the Burke case?" At Skye's nod, Morgan continued. "Then you'll be joining us?"

"Us?" Skye shot a questioning look at Parker. "Uh, yes. I think we're meeting in the jury room. I'll get Gibson and meet you there." Skye looked at Parker again and shook her head before stepping into the DA workroom.

"Do you know her?" Morgan asked, her tone a blend of curiosity and suspicion.

"I used to." Parker let her answer fall flat. She hadn't had a moment alone with Morgan since seeing her at the vigil for Camille Burke. The last thing she wanted to do in these few seconds was to talk about Skye Keaton. "Morgan, I—"

Skye emerged from the workroom with a skinny blonde in tow, cutting Parker's words short. "Parker Casey, Morgan Bradley, this is Valerie Gibson. She's prosecuting the case."

Gibson asked, "Shall we get started?"

"Lead the way. Ford's trapped in a hearing, but we're expecting two others and they should be here shortly. They—" Morgan stopped short as the outer doors opened and Gerald and Dex walked through. "Here they are. Let's get started."

Gibson ran the show, but it was obvious Skye's knowledge of the case far outweighed the young prosecutor's. Skye laid out the evidence she and her partner, Detective Peterson, had gathered, which included the autopsy and ballistics reports, crime scene photos, statements from various employees of the Burke household, and the most damning evidence of all, Teddy Burke's statement placing Luis over Camille Burke's dead body. As Skye outlined the evidence against Luis, she was as cocky as Parker remembered.

"As you can see here, we have a ballistics match on the gun and Chavez's prints were all over it. As if that weren't enough, Chavez's boot prints were all over the scene, and when he was arrested he was wearing the very same boots, with traces of the vic's blood on the soles. I guess he was too busy running from his deed to think about buying new shoes." Parker winced at Skye's sarcastic tone.

"Detective, I assume you are prepared to provide us with copies of any statements you obtained from our client?" Morgan was the only one who would ask any questions during the meeting.

Skye shot Morgan a withering glance that Parker knew she reserved for all defense attorneys, but Morgan just smiled. "He admitted to being there, all right, but he just made up some crazy story about how he just found the body. Claims he didn't kill her."

Morgan pressed her. "And you have a copy for us to review?"

"Sure. You're welcome to review all the damning evidence against your client before he goes to the pen."

"Thank you." Morgan's tone was syrupy sweet. "I'll be sure to take a careful look at everything."

Parker was miserable for the entire hour they spent in the meeting. Morgan was distant, barely looking her way. Parker ached to talk to Morgan privately and resented the need to explain the interaction with Skye. While competing emotions warred within, outwardly she made a show of carefully reviewing the evidence and filed away her thoughts to be shared when the air was clear.

The session wrapped up, Skye and the prosecutor gathered up the evidence and escorted the defense team back through the courtroom. While Morgan spoke to the prosecutor about the logistics of obtaining copies of the evidence they had reviewed, Skye grabbed Parker by the arm and pulled her aside.

"Would you like to tell me what the hell you are doing here, working on this case?"

Parker struggled to ignore the fact Skye's lips were so close she could feel the intense vibration of her angry tone. "Excuse me?"

"Don't be coy. You know what I mean. Since when did you cross over to the dark side?"

Parker couldn't believe Skye could ask such an impudent question knowing all Parker had gone through and that she was the cause of much of her pain. Parker made no attempt to hide her anger, and her voice shook with intensity. "Since standing in the light burned away my soul." Shrugging off Skye's hand, she turned to leave and ran smack into Dex and Gerald talking to Ford. All three men stopped their conversation and stared at her with gaping mouths. Annoyed she would have to make up some explanation for the exchange, Parker mowed past them and made long and purposeful strides away from the courtroom.

Morgan raised her hand to knock on the door, but lowered it again. She'd walked from a nearby coffee shop having no idea the skies would open and douse her with a pounding torrent of rain. Cursing herself for not paying closer attention to the weather, she surveyed her appearance. She was drenched, her silk suit ruined.

She was only half surprised when Gerald and Dex told her Parker had already left the courthouse by the time she emerged from the prosecutor's office. They had no answer for her questions about Parker's abrupt departure. Ford, who showed up after his hearing, pulled her aside and whispered questions of his own. Morgan was determined to find answers. Something happened between Parker and the lead investigator Skye Keaton. She wasn't sure if it had happened that day or sometime in the past. The two women clearly knew each other, and the heat emanating from their interaction was clearly visible to Morgan's watchful eye. She refused to acknowledge the real reason behind her desire to know more about what she had witnessed. Instead Morgan rationalized she had a duty to check on Parker—who, according to the guys, had stormed out of the building. She navigated her way to

Parker's lower Greenville neighborhood. Something, perhaps the desire to fortify herself, made her stop at a nearby strip of businesses where she sought guidance in the form of cappuccino. Caffeinated, she left her SUV and walked the block to Parker's house.

Now, standing in front of Parker's door, she hesitated. She looked frightful, her once crisp suit now splotched and bunchy from the rain. Parker had looked amazing at the courthouse. Morgan had grown accustomed to seeing her dressed in jeans and T-shirts and was as thrown by the sight of her in a well-tailored suit as she was to see her engaged in intimate conversation with Detective Keaton. Surveying herself, Morgan decided not only did she look frightful, she wasn't confident she would be welcome. What if Parker wasn't here and one of her roommates answered? The thought wasn't fully formed when the door swung open and she was face-to-face with Kelsey James.

"Oh my God, you're soaking wet!" Kelsey grabbed Morgan's arm and pulled her into the foyer. "Let me get you a towel. I'll be right back."

Morgan stood dripping on the cool marble tiles, unable to muster a response to the display of spontaneous hospitality. For a moment, she contemplated leaving, but she knew her sudden departure back into the swirling storm would not only seem odd, it would probably result in her catching a cold, and she couldn't afford to be ill right now.

Moments later, Morgan joined Kelsey in the kitchen and watched her as she fixed a welcome cup of tea. She was as dry as a towel could get her, but she shivered in her wet clothes.

"Seriously, Morgan, I think you should change. Between your wet clothes and the air-conditioning, you're going to catch a cold. I'm going to get you a pair of scrubs. Doctor's orders."

When Kelsey returned with a well-worn set of light green scrubs, Morgan excused herself to the bathroom to change. She surveyed herself in the mirror and once again questioned her judgment in showing up on Parker's doorstep. Kelsey hadn't asked her why she was here, and at this point, Morgan was embarrassed to admit she was trailing around after Parker. She wondered what Kelsey knew about their relationship besides the fact Morgan had spent the night on at least one occasion. Was Parker even home? She tried to ignore the fact she was now barefoot and dressed in loose-fitting scrubs, and reentered the kitchen with a confidence she did not feel. Kelsey's smile was warm and the tea she handed Morgan was welcome. For the next few moments, they sat in silence.

Finally, Kelsey broke the ice. "I imagine you're looking for Parker?"

"Yes."

"She's not here. I haven't seen her since lunch. She said she was heading to the courthouse."

Morgan nodded.

"Actually, I thought she would be with you," Kelsey ventured.

"She was. But she left suddenly and I didn't get a chance to discuss an important issue with her. I was hoping to find her here." Morgan's voice trailed off and she glanced away.

Kelsey plunged in. "Morgan?"

"Yes."

"I know Parker's one of your students."

Morgan waited, knowing she wasn't finished.

"And I know there's something more personal going on between you two."

Morgan didn't know how to respond. Certainly, what she had shared with Parker in the room upstairs was personal in the same way naked want and need was personal. How could she explain to her the contrast between feeling physically intimate with Parker and feeling as if she knew nothing about her?

Kelsey saved her from her dilemma. "Look, I know you've slept together and I know your respective roles have to put some strain on the situation. I also know I haven't seen you around here since we met at breakfast a few weeks ago, and Parker's been moping around lately like she lost her best friend. Since I'm her best friend, I figure it's something else. Now you show up here in the middle of a thunderstorm, soaking wet, and I can't help but wonder if your feelings for my friend transcend your reservations about propriety."

Morgan couldn't conceal her surprise at the blunt discourse and she stared at her. "I don't know what to say."

"Say I'm right. Say you care about Parker and not merely her worth as a future lawyer. Say you'll be true to your feelings and you won't hurt her."

Morgan looked away. "I do care about Parker, but as you say, we've only shared a bed." She winced at the harsh assessment, knowing they had shared much more. "We don't know anything about each other, and the only reason we even know each other's last names is because I'm her teacher and she's my student—a situation I can't do anything about."

"Then why are you here?"

"I don't know. She was upset when she left today. I want to know why. I want to know if I can do anything about it."

"What was she upset about?"

"I don't know. She seemed to be upset after talking to a detective at the courthouse. At first, I didn't understand why, but I think I may have a little insight now."

"A detective? Who was it?"

"Skye Keaton. Why, do you know her?"

"I've only met her once."

Morgan smiled at the evasive answer. "Ms. James, you didn't answer the question."

"Touché. I don't really know her. Not personally. I know about her."

"And you're not going to tell me anything else?" At Kelsey's nod, she continued, "Even if I tell you I know Parker was on the force?"

Kelsey couldn't hide the look of surprise. "How did you find out?"

"Seriously, the courthouse is like the smallest community on earth. Parker was a homicide detective. You don't think there are more than a few attorneys who know who she is?" Morgan's words were edged with anger and she wasn't sure why. After Parker's hasty exit, Ford supplied some of the information she needed to piece together why Parker had acted so strangely around Detective Skye Keaton. Yet, in this moment, Morgan wasn't sure which part of the story surprised her more—Parker's former life as a detective or Parker's obvious feelings for Skye Keaton. *Why didn't Parker tell me?* Even as she asked herself the question, she wasn't sure which of the new revelations she had expected Parker to share. *Face it,* she told herself, *neither of you has shared anything more personal than flesh on flesh. All you've done since the day you discovered her sitting in the rows of your classroom was push her away. Did you expect her to respond by sharing her life story with you? And why do you care now?*

Morgan didn't have answers to the questions posed by her silent self. She only knew one thing with certainty. She had to see Parker and she had to see her now. Her compelling need drove her to push past Kelsey's reluctance and treat her like a hostile witness.

"Are you telling me you don't know where she is or do you know and you're not going to tell me? Which is it?" Her tone left no doubt she would not relent until she got a satisfactory answer.

"Stand down, Counselor. I don't know where she is."

Morgan read the pause and posed her next question. "But you might have an idea."

"An idea about what?"

They both turned toward the new voice in the conversation. Parker stood in the doorway of the kitchen, dripping wet. Water ran down the lines of her rumpled suit and puddled at her feet. Despite her soggy appearance, her jaw was set and her eyes were crisp with anger. She glanced from Morgan to Kelsey and back again. Though she was staring hard into Morgan's eyes, her question was clearly directed to them both.

"What the hell is going on here?"

Morgan stood, her confidence always stronger when she was on her feet. She faced Parker and was suddenly overcome. She wanted to wipe away the trails of wet the rain had left and wrap Parker in her arms, kissing away her anger.

But Morgan knew how to read people, better than most, and she read Parker's bold anger and crushing hurt. Though she didn't fully understand the source, she wanted to, and the revelation shook her to the core. Her desire for Parker wasn't limited to craving her caresses. She wanted to know everything about Parker, past, present, and future. Relying on her instincts, she knew now was not the time. Glancing at Kelsey, she said, "Parker, I was worried when you left the courthouse so suddenly. I came by to check on you."

Parker made a show of looking Morgan up and down. She reached for Morgan's sleeve and rubbed the soft cloth between her fingers. Her eyes met Morgan's and held them with fierce emotion.

"Decide to get comfortable while you waited for me, did you?"

Caught off guard, Morgan blushed, only then remembering she was dressed in Kelsey's scrubs. She barely heard Kelsey's outraged cry of protest as she delivered her own response.

"Parker, you are way out of line."

"I'm out of line? I'm out of line?" Her voice increased in volume.

"Don't you think it's a little out of line for a professor to make house calls on her students?" Parker pointed to the door, her intention clear as she spat her words. "I want you to leave, *Professor*. Now."

Morgan stood her ground. Though moments ago she had entered this house with only a vague idea of what drove her, now that she was here, she desperately wanted to stay. But as unsure as she was about her motivation for being here, she was equally sure Parker did not want her to stay. Not now, not like this. She reluctantly resolved to give Parker what she professed to want in this moment. Painfully conscious of her inability to make a dignified exit, she strode through the kitchen, grabbing her shoes and purse as she passed her drying clothes. Ignoring Kelsey's call to stay and talk, she found her way to the porch and paused just long enough to slip into her heels and ponder whether or not the Palomar had a back entrance.

❖

"What in the world was that about?"

Parker sank into the closest chair and cradled her head in her hands. "Honestly, James, I don't know."

"Well, you can't sit there and drip-dry. Don't move. I'll be right back."

Moments later Kelsey reappeared with another set of scrubs and she ordered Parker to change. In a daze, Parker stripped naked in the middle of kitchen, toweled off, and pulled on the soft, worn fabric. She knew Kelsey was waiting for her to talk about what was bothering her, but she couldn't seem to find the words. The pain of betrayal stung and she felt paralyzed.

"Casey, look at me."

Parker gazed, unseeing, at her.

"I know you saw Skye today."

Parker could only shake her head, willing away the memories spilling in. How much pain could Skye Keaton possibly inflict in this lifetime? She had buried her head in the sand. She had been foolish to think she could work in the Dallas legal community and not run into her former lover.

Kelsey gathered her close and whispered, "It's okay, sweetie. Everything will be okay."

Parker heard the soothing murmur of her voice, but couldn't agree less with Kelsey's conclusion. Everything would not be okay, and as long as she was haunted by the pain of her past, it never would be. She lashed out.

"No, it won't! You have no idea!"

The look on Kelsey's face was a combination of surprise and worry. "You're right. I don't. I don't know why you've chosen to keep what happened bottled up inside. I can only tell you whatever secret you're hiding will grind away at you until you bring it out into the light."

Parker faced her and, perhaps for the first time, realized she had never shared the whole story with anyone, though many close to her knew bits and pieces of what had happened. Even now, as she was consumed with the implications of the past roaring back into her present, she still wasn't ready to share it all.

CHAPTER NINE

I had no idea Parker Casey was going to be part of the team. Wow! What a coup!"

Ford had a busy day in court ahead, so Morgan had agreed to meet him for an early breakfast at his favorite hole in the wall. In his usual exuberant way, Ford waved his food, this time a piece of bacon, in the air. Morgan's thoughts were momentarily distracted from the painful memory of the tortured expression on Parker's face the day before, and she swore she would never work as a public defender since they seemed to eat only in greasy diners. She willed her mind away from the distractions it sought and focused on the issue at hand.

"Ford, I had no idea Parker used to be a cop. If I had, I'm not sure I would have allowed her to work on this case."

"What the hell?" Ford returned his bacon to his plate and stared her down. "Morgan, this case is a homicide. What better choice for the team than a lawyer who used to work homicide? Didn't you know what you were doing when you picked her?"

"First off, Parker's not a lawyer. Second, I didn't select the team members. Yolanda and Jim Spencer conducted the tryouts. Third, the fact she worked on the force makes me question her motivation in wanting to work on this case, on this side of the issue." Even as she spoke this last, Morgan knew it wasn't true. During the past few weeks of class, she had observed Parker's passion for defense and a thinly veiled hostility for the prosecution. True, these exercises were far from real-life courtroom experiences, but if Parker was merely acting, she was damn good.

"No need to worry about her motivation. Parker Casey has plenty of reasons to champion justice for the little guy. Her law-and-order experience certainly left a bad taste in her mouth."

Morgan's nod told him to continue even as she mentally willed him to stop. She couldn't help feeling torn between wanting to know everything there was to know about Parker, this multilayered woman, but at the same time she wanted distance: distance to do her job, distance to keep her own potentially volatile feelings in check, distance from the pain she witnessed on Parker's face and her own surging desire to soothe it away.

"Parker was a rising star. She made detective in record time and was hand-picked for homicide. She received tons of commendations and was on the fast track to become lieutenant, though I suspect she had no desire to be part of administration. She was great on the stand—a perfect prosecution witness—unflappable. Cross-examine her and you got objective facts, delivered with an engaging personality. Juries loved her, her higher-ups loved her. Detective Casey had it made." He stopped his story and waited. Morgan knew Ford well enough to know his pause was designed to make sure he had her full attention before he relayed the "and then" portion of his story.

She decided to play along. "And then?"

"And then she got set up. Skye—you remember Skye, right?" At Morgan's puzzled look, Ford urged, "Skye Keaton? Lead detective on this case?"

Morgan nodded slowly, wary of the new direction to this tale.

"She and Parker were at a suspect's house waiting around to question him. You've probably read about the case. The guy was suspected of being the Trinity River Killer. Two other detectives joined them because the guy was expected to arrive shortly and he was believed to not only be armed and dangerous, but a total whack job.

"No one knows what really happened, but apparently the guy came home and died of a gunshot wound shortly thereafter. Turns out the guy wasn't the Trinity River Killer after all."

"Why do I feel like there's more?" Morgan hesitated to ask more for fear of what might follow.

"The guy was shot in the back and even though the police administration did their best to keep that little fact out of the news, the guy's family sued the city for a host of infractions. As a result, the autopsy results became public record. The DA's office opened a public integrity investigation and the four officers involved in the case were all suspended pending investigation."

Nausea gripped Morgan and held her in its sour grasp. Every word Ford spoke seemed to lead her closer to what she professed she wanted: more information about the woman who occupied her thoughts, night and day. Yet as his story spun closer to unpleasant truths, she shied away, afraid of the effect. Ford must have sensed something was wrong because he stopped his tale to ask, "Morgan, are you okay? You look pale."

"I'm fine," she managed. "Please, finish."

"I don't know the whole story. I expect few do. Parker and the detective who fired the shot were both terminated. Keaton and the other detective were given formal reprimands, but were both reinstated. The family of the dead guy settled their lawsuit for an undisclosed amount in exchange for the city admitting no liability. Rumor is Parker sued the city herself for wrongful termination and a host of other things and won a tidy settlement, but no one's talking about the specifics."

"Why was Parker fired? What did she do wrong?" Morgan tried to hide the desperation in her voice.

Ford shrugged. "Who knows? A friend of mine in Public Integrity told me at the time in a case with this much publicity, someone had to take a fall, but I expected it would be the guy who pulled the trigger. I suppose only Parker knows for sure what happened."

Probably true, Morgan thought, wondering if she would be so bold as to ask and then wondering how in the world the topic would or could ever come up between them. After today, meaningful conversation was no longer a possibility between them. Too many unspoken thoughts and unrequited feelings filled the space between them, making the intimacy it would take to have such a dialogue unlikely.

❖

"Can I talk to you?"

Parker wasn't sure if Morgan recognized her voice. She didn't look up from her desk, but merely said, "Sure. Come on in."

Parker waited until she had her full attention before she fully entered the room, shutting the door behind her. Morgan was stunning. Last night, when Parker spent hours lying awake thinking of a graceful way to deliver her news, she had not been hampered by the distraction of her beauty. Now, with Morgan sitting in front of her, dressed in a close-cut cream silk suit, she couldn't help but falter for her opening words.

"I think it would be best if I withdrew from the team." Parker lowered her head and sighed, relieved to have the words out. She waited for the anticipated agreement from Morgan. Long, silent seconds passed. Parker raised her head and met Morgan's impenetrable gaze.

"You do?" Morgan picked up a pen and began to write in a notebook on her desk. "I would like you to tell me why."

What about what I would like, Parker asked silently. *I would like to escape this situation with as much dignity as I can. Telling you every sordid detail of my past isn't likely to leave me with much. Let it go, Morgan. Let it go.*

A long look at Morgan's face told Parker she wasn't going to get off so easy. Walls shot up and she invoked customary defenses. "I'd rather not say. It's personal. I can only say I'm sorry about the way I behaved yesterday. Kelsey's my best friend and I'm ashamed of the way I acted when I saw you two together. My reaction had nothing to do with either of you. I have other things going on and those things prevent me from being able to give my best to the team. It would be best if I withdrew."

Morgan contemplated Parker's stoic speech. The script she had delivered had probably been practiced in front of a mirror, but it was still canned and incomplete. Morgan knew there was more behind Parker's angst than a simple "I have other things going on," and she was determined to find out what those things were because she was sure these "things" held the key to figuring Parker out. Figuring out Parker vaulted to the top of her list of things to do, and she wasn't going to let anything get in the way of accomplishing her objective.

"I respectfully disagree. Parker, you're a fantastic addition to the team. I know you used to be a cop and I know something happened to take your chosen career away from you. I don't know what it was and I don't care to pry into your private life." Morgan winced inwardly at the lie. "Let's put yesterday behind us and move on. We have a lot of work to do."

Parker wasn't sure how to react. She was partly relieved to have her offer rejected, but a part of her was pissed at the way Morgan dismissed what had happened as if it was nothing. Did this woman have to take everything in stride? No wonder she could do what she did so well. She didn't let herself feel. She probably didn't care about either Luis Chavez or Camille Burke. They were nothing more than pieces in a complicated puzzle she was hell-bent on solving.

Parker, intent on her internal tirade, missed Morgan's next words. "What?"

"I said, I need you to help me with a project. Do you have a couple of hours right now?"

Put on the spot, Parker couldn't come up with a decent excuse to get away. Fact was, she didn't have anything else planned until her late afternoon Ethics class, and after the way she had acted the day before, she owed Morgan a favor. "Sure, but I have class at four."

"Great. Leave your books here and come with me." Morgan walked out the door, leaving a bewildered Parker to trail behind her.

"I thought we'd be working here."

"No, this is a field trip. I promise to have you back in time for your class. You're not scared to get in a car with me, are you?"

Parker felt the heat of a blush as she remembered her first car ride with Morgan. "Absolutely not, Professor."

❖

Morgan's Lexus whizzed through the streets of Dallas, and Parker wondered what mission she had in store. As if reading her thoughts, Morgan nodded toward the backseat and said, "Will you reach back and get that notebook?"

Parker complied and opened the notebook. Confused, she glanced through page after page of real estate descriptions, all touting the various features of East Dallas homes. She shot a questioning look at Morgan who, intent on navigating to her destination, ignored her. She was forced to ask the question. "What am I supposed to be helping you with this fine afternoon?"

"I'm house-hunting."

"You're house-hunting?" Parker repeated, vaguely aware she sounded inane.

"Yep. My realtor prepared the notebook you're holding. I'm supposed to drive by these houses and eliminate all the ones I can based on outward appearance." Morgan looked at Parker and smiled. "I thought since you lived over here, you'd be a perfect choice to help me in this little venture."

Parker was flattered and angry at the same time. Flattered Morgan wanted to spend personal time with her, and angry to be taken advantage of. Anger won out and she was about to unleash it, when Morgan spoke again.

"I know you may be angry. I did kind of take advantage of you by dragging you away under somewhat false pretenses. But, Parker, I think we need to start over if we're going to work together and we needed to get away from school to find common ground. I think you are terrific and there's no reason we can't be friendly, even if we can't be anything else. Truce?"

Morgan's words doused Parker's rising fury. Morgan was right. They needed to put to rest the brief past they had shared and start over. Fact was they would always be more than teacher and student, but if they could find a way to fashion their feelings into friendship, they would be able to move past it.

Parker smiled. "Truce." Looking at the notebook on her lap, she said, "I can tell you right now, this first house is not for you."

"You think so?"

"Absolutely. It's on my street, and the neighbors on either side are dueling Animal House contestants. Drive over to Manchester. Nice, quiet street, beautiful front yards. You'll love it."

"Because it's quiet?" Morgan asked in protest.

"Because it's beautiful," Parker replied, her words dripping with meaning.

Parker was late for her Ethics class, but for once she did not care. She slid into the seat Dex had saved and quietly opened her book to the place he indicated.

"Where have you been?" he whispered.

Feeling guilty for the white lie she was about to tell, Parker allowed her well-honed sense of self-protection to censor her account. "Running some errands. Did I miss anything?"

"No, but I'm sure Spencer noticed you were late, so expect to be called on. That's what you get for never missing class."

"Yeah, well, maybe I'm tired of always being predictable."

Dex reached over and punched her on the arm. "Hey, why do you think we get along so well? I know I can always count on you."

Wondering what Dex would think if he knew where she had spent the last few hours, Parker smiled halfheartedly and buried her face in her book. Dex was right. She could always be counted on to be on time, to get the job done, to do the right thing. She had suspended her reliability this afternoon in pursuit of a feeling, a certain comfort she felt in Morgan's presence. She'd enjoyed the afternoon of house-hunting more than she would have imagined. Maybe they could be friends after all.

CHAPTER TEN

The group of lawyers and lawyers-to-be settled in around the conference table in the faculty meeting room. Although she had received flack from both donors and other administrators about allowing her students to work on this case, Yolanda had been unwavering in her support. Ford and Morgan took up places on either side of two flip charts and Ford led the discussion.

"We have one obvious issue to resolve pretrial: Luis Chavez's 'confession.'"

Gerald Lopez interrupted. "Wait a minute. The guy confessed? Why are we going to trial, then?"

Dex and Parker rolled their eyes and Morgan looked away to hide her expression. Ford valiantly encouraged Gerald to come up with the answer on his own. "Well, Gerald. Why would a person go to trial if they had confessed to a crime? And what's your definition of a confession?"

Gerald looked around the room and noticed everyone's averted eyes. "Well, it's pretty obvious what a confession is. When you admit to doing something wrong—your admission is a confession."

Ford nodded. "Okay, fair enough. Now, let's play the video we have of the 'confession' and judge for ourselves." Ford used a remote to start the video monitor, and seconds later the screen jumped to life with the image of a weary Luis Chavez slumped in a hard-backed chair. He was in a smallish room and the black-and-white film served to accent his drab surroundings. The counter in the bottom right hand of the screen said it was moments after midnight and the counter clicked off the passing seconds.

Seconds turned into minutes and the action on the screen did not change. At one point, the audio recorded the creak of a door opening and Luis turned his head at the sound. A garbled voice asked a question and Luis merely nodded. The counter registered the passage of time.

After approximately fifteen minutes with no further activity on the tape, Luis began to fidget in his seat, an action reflected by the students watching the monitor. He glanced around and then settled back, eyes wary, as the door creaked open again. This time a person entered. The watching students could only see the individual's back leaning forward to place something on the table in front of Luis. The person left and Luis leaned forward to inspect the contents of the table. Two cans of Coke and three doughnuts didn't last long. It was obvious Luis was starving. He hastily devoured the food and the inaction of the tape resumed, marked only by the constant counter.

After another fifteen minutes, someone finally entered the room and took a seat across from Luis. Detective Skye Keaton introduced herself. Parker, the only one of the students who could have predicted the contents of the tape, screen by screen, stiffened at the appearance of her former partner as if she were actually in the room with them. The visceral reaction was not lost on Morgan, who watched from the back of the room. She wanted to move forward, place her hand on Parker's shoulder as a show of support. She stood rooted in place, knowing a display of affection could be misunderstood, but silently vowed to learn why Parker's former partner still had the power to evoke such strong emotion. As each moment ticked away on the screen, Parker's discomfort became more visible, and finally Morgan reasoned a show of support was necessary. Slowly making her way to the front of the room, she lingered beside Parker and brushed her fingers against the soft cloth covering her back. The slight touch was electric and she gave silent praise to years of practiced self-control, which kept her from crying out.

At first, Parker did not react to the touch. She too had years of training on how to keep her reactions in check. An unidentified approach from behind could mean danger, and in order to defend herself, she needed to be in control of her reflexes. True to her training, she looked for subtle clues. She could smell the familiar perfume. A glance down revealed designer heels, and the fingers resting lightly against her were long and light. She acknowledged the situation was dangerous, but relaxed into Morgan's caress anyway. The contact lasted mere seconds, but the effect lingered, producing a hazy veil of longing that clouded her awareness.

Morgan, on the other hand, noticed a sharp pair of eyes, brimming with questions, peering from across the room. She met Gerald's look without expression, shook herself, and turned her attention back to the video. She noted it had reached the portion where Detective Keaton reviewed Luis's rights. She watched Skye fish a worn card from her wallet and deliver the Miranda warning in a brisk monotone.

"Do you understand your rights as I have read them to you." Skye's words were fast and formal.

"Yes."

"Good. Let's talk about what you were doing in Ms. Burke's bedroom."

Luis fidgeted in his chair. "Can I have my phone call?"

"Who do you want to call?'

"My sister."

Skye leaned back in her chair. Seconds ticked by on the counter while she stared at Luis. When she spoke, her calm tone belied the tension in the room. "Do you have a phone?"

Morgan suppressed a snort. She caught Parker looking her way and figured they were sharing the same thought. Luis was already under arrest. His phone, if he had one, and all his other belongings would have been taken from him before he was placed in the squad car and hauled off to jail.

"No."

"Well, your rights don't say anything about getting a phone call, but I tell you what. When we're finished talking, I'll take you to a phone and you can call her." Skye sounded reasonable, almost friendly. "Now, I'd like you to tell me what you were doing in Camille Burke's bedroom the night she was murdered."

"I have a question about that paper you read to me."

Skye's didn't attempt to conceal her impatience. "What?"

"You said I can have a lawyer. When you read from the paper."

"I thought you said you understood your rights."

Luis placed his head in his hands, obviously uncomfortable about asserting even the smallest challenge to Skye's authority. "Maybe I didn't understand so well."

"Am I going to have to read them again?" Skye's expression made it clear there would be dire consequences if she was forced to repeat herself.

"No. I mean, I just thought you said something about a lawyer."

"Do you want a lawyer?"

"I think so, yes." Luis started out hesitantly, but his "yes" was emphatic.

"So, you want a lawyer now? Before we even finish talking?" Skye could not have sounded more annoyed.

Luis looked like he would rather jump off a cliff than choose between asserting his rights and pissing off Skye. Skye stared at him while he looked everywhere in the room to avoid her penetrating glare. Finally, he mustered the strength to spit out his one-word answer: "Yes."

"Fine." Skye stood up. She slowly and deliberately gathered her paper and pen, pushed in her chair, and started toward the door. "I'll see you in court."

Luis was startled out of his newfound confidence. "What?"

"We're done here. You'll get a lawyer and you can plead your case to a jury. We're done talking."

"But I didn't do anything," Luis sounded desperate. "You said I could have a lawyer present."

"You can have all the lawyers you want. I don't have to sit here and deal with them. Those are my rights." Skye's opened the door and started to walk out.

"Wait!"

Skye turned her head and waited.

"I didn't do anything. I want to tell you."

"What about the lawyer?"

"Never mind. Please, let me tell you what happened."

Skye paused as if she were giving the matter a great deal of thought. She made her way back to the table and once again pulled out the worn card from her wallet. "Do I need to read these rights to you again and make sure you understand them?"

"No, no. I understand. Let me talk to you," Luis begged, perhaps fearing any delay might result in Skye leaving before he could convince her of his innocence.

Skye beamed. "All right then. Let's hear what you have to say."

Morgan listened once again while Luis eagerly told Keaton all he knew in the anxious manner so common to those accused who hoped telling the truth would set them free. The upshot of his statement was exactly what he had already relayed to her. He admitted to having been in the house the night of Camille Burke's murder, but despite a browbeating interrogation, he supplied no other details about her gruesome death. Toward the end, Detective Keaton was losing patience, evidenced by the increasing volume and frustrated tone of her voice.

Ford turned off the tape and addressed the class. "Okay, Gerald, let's hear it. What was the essence of Luis's confession?"

Gerald shifted in his chair, glancing around the room. "Well, he did say he was in the house. So he had opportunity."

Dex broke in. "I wonder how many people work in the Burke house and have access to the residence. I would venture to say it's at least ten. So, lots of people had opportunity. His admission to being in the house doesn't equal a confession."

"Good point, Dex," Ford observed. "Gerald, what does the State have to prove in order to convict Mr. Chavez?"

Morgan idly wondered if Ford was avoiding questioning Parker since she was likely to know all the answers. How many times had Parker sat across the table from an accused person, using all the skills at her disposal to draw out a confession? Had she followed the rules to the letter, or had she developed her own set of guidelines for the right way to get to the "truth"? Morgan had a healthy respect for law enforcement. When they did their jobs properly, she truly believed the world was a better place, but over the years she had seen a fair share of everything from cut corners to outright dishonesty in the name of justice. This tape was exhibit one in the cutting corners category, and she wondered what Parker, a former cop, thought of Keaton's technique.

Gerald responded to Ford, "Motive, means, and opportunity."

Morgan bit her tongue and glared at Ford, willing him to put this doofus in his place. He did.

"Show me the part of the Code you're referring to, Gerald."

Morgan watched while he fumbled through his bright, shiny, and obviously never-cracked copy of the Penal Code searching for salvation from his own stupidity.

"Well," he equivocated, "it doesn't exactly say those words, but essentially those are the things the State has to prove."

Morgan couldn't stand it any longer. "Parker, can you help Gerald out?"

Parker shot a look at Dex, who was trying not to laugh. "I can take a stab at it. The state has to prove each element of the statute, beyond a reasonable doubt. Murder is intentionally or knowingly causing the death of another, so there are three elements: intentionally or knowingly; causing; the death of an individual. Motive and opportunity are not elements of the offense and don't have to be proved in order to sustain a conviction."

Ford chuckled. "Good stab, Parker. Now, let's talk about whether this 'confession' is admissible. Dex, you're up."

Dex didn't hesitate. "Absolutely."

Morgan wasted no time taking over from Ford. "Really, Dex?"

Dex looked puzzled that his conclusion was called into question, but he stood by the confidence of his conclusion. "Sure. She read him his rights and he waived them." He swiveled in his chair and solicited Parker's support. "Did you see anything wrong?"

Morgan hung on her answer, knowing that whatever it was it would speak volumes about what kind of cop she had been. Parker appeared uncomfortable at the prospect of dissecting Skye's methods, and her response was cagey.

"She didn't finish the warning."

Dex interjected. "She read the Miranda warning verbatim."

"I keep forgetting you worked for the Feds." Parker grinned at the reminder of their friendly rivalry. "If she's recording his statement to use at trial, she's got to ask him, on the tape, if he 'knowingly, intelligently, and voluntarily' wants to waive his rights and answer questions."

"She did," Dex insisted.

"No, she didn't. She just asked him if he understood his rights, not whether he wanted to waive them."

"Even if you're right, what's the difference? He waived his rights by answering her questions." Dex's tone suggested he thought the distinction Parker made was insignificant.

Parker's response was heated. "The difference is she's not allowed to assume he knows the difference. She has a duty to follow the law."

Morgan had been watching the exchange with interest, but she decided it was time to intervene. Parker obviously had strong feelings on the subject, though Morgan wasn't sure if the subject was Skye's methods or Skye in general. "This is perfect. Since you two have very different views on the subject, you'll be a great team to work on the research. I want a brief in support of a motion to suppress Luis's statement."

Gerald piped in. "Why do you want to suppress it if he didn't admit to anything?" His question was a challenge with a hint of sarcasm.

Morgan's answer was quick and to the point. "Because we can." Once she had everyone's attention, she continued. "I realize nothing Luis says can be construed as a confession, but look at his mannerisms. What do you see?" She rewound the tape and waited for their responses.

"He's nervous. He never looks Keaton in the eye." Dex observed.

Parker joined in. "He's sweating and look at his right leg. It looks like it's about to bounce out of its socket."

Ford joined the conversation. "And he always hesitates before he answers a question, like he's trying to figure out what to say. So, folks, what's the jury going to think about all that?"

"He looks like he's lying," Gerald volunteered.

"Or he looks like someone who was torn from his bed in the middle of the night, hauled to jail, and charged with a serious crime he didn't commit. His fear can be attributed to the fact English isn't his first language, he's been arrested before, and his citizenship may be in jeopardy." Morgan paused as she considered the pros and cons of trying to get the taped statement thrown out. Luis never wavered in his denials. He had not murdered Camille Burke. He had not struggled with her. He had not shot her. Morgan reflected, ruefully, if she was successful in suppressing the tape, the only way the jury would hear from Luis would be if he took the stand. No matter what the law said, juries wanted to hear the accused say they didn't do anything wrong. When questioned after a trial, they invariably attributed their verdict to the words, or lack thereof, from the defendant. Amazing, considering during voir dire, they all agreed they could follow the law, which requires they attribute no importance to the fact the defendant may not testify. Though it was common practice not to allow her client to testify, Morgan always kept this nugget of information in the back of her mind when planning a case. Her concerns in this particular case were focused on Luis's criminal record and how it might influence a jury. She could fight to keep the information out, but if Luis took the stand and opened the door, all bets were off. If his statement was introduced into evidence, the need for him to testify and the associated risk were diminished. She explained her concerns to the group and wrapped up their session by divvying up assignments.

"Parker and Dex, I want you two to research and prepare a motion to suppress. Ford and I will make a decision over the weekend about whether to file it in time to take it up with the judge at the pretrial hearing next week. If nothing else, it will distract the prosecutor from trial prep." She looked at Gerald, who was expectantly waiting for his assignment. She quickly came up with a do-no-harm task for him. "Gerald, I need you to catalog the rest of the evidence. Ford will show you how he wants our trial notebooks arranged and you make a checklist of anything we still need in order to be prepared." She took note of how he fumed at being assigned what was obviously busywork, but she couldn't afford to give someone so clueless a project of any consequence.

Morgan stood. "We've been at this for a while. Let's quit for the night and we'll meet again on Monday. Have a good weekend, everyone."

Dex followed Parker out of the room. "Hey, Casey, wanna a grab a bite to eat and go over this stuff?"

Parker, who had been watching Morgan make her way out of the room, struggled to wrench her attention away from Morgan's retreating form and focus on Dex's question. Funny Dex should bring up dinner. She had been thinking she would corner Morgan and tell her dinner would be a good payback for the house-hunting boondoggle earlier in the week. Surely they could break bread without breaking the boundaries of friendship. She made excuses to Dex in a hurried tone. "Sorry, pal, I already made other plans. Let's meet in the morning, my place? We'll get an early start. I'll make breakfast."

If Dex noticed Parker seemed anxious to leave, he didn't give a hint. "Sure, Casey. See you bright and early." As he strolled away,

Parker glanced around and noticed Morgan was gone. Hoping to catch her, Parker walked briskly toward the professor's office.

❖

As Morgan fumbled in her purse for her office keys, all she could think of was a hot bath and room service. *I have to buy a house soon or I will forever be spoiled by hotel living.* Leaning on the door to dig deeper for the hiding keys, she realized her door was slightly ajar as it swung open into the room. Her first assumption, that the janitorial staff was hard at work within, was dispelled by the sight of a man seated behind her desk.

"Good evening, Professor Bradley. My, you're working late hours."

Steeling herself for whatever might follow, Morgan decided to play along with this man who knew who she was and didn't seem to think introductions were necessary.

"I'm dedicated to my work."

"Clearly." His words dripped with heavy sarcasm.

"Obviously you expected to find me here this late or you wouldn't be waiting. What can I do for you?"

"What can you do for me? What can you do for me?" His repetition was mocking and his voice rose as he spoke. "You, my dear professor, can concentrate on your classes and leave your extracurricular activities to real lawyers."

Morgan resisted the urge to engage in a verbal battle. Instead, she put all her mental faculties to use in an attempt to figure out who she was dealing with. Her silence had the unintended effect of unnerving her visitor, and he spoke through the uncomfortable quiet.

"Surely you must know who I am? I find it hard to believe you haven't done your homework with regard to this case and, if you have, you must have realized I would come to call."

She was sure she had never seen him before, but there was a certain familiarity about his features. She looked hard at him. Something about the lines of his face—she had seen a similar face recently. Her memory recalled a beautiful woman, with sad eyes. The stark features of the face she recalled were reflected in this man, but there was no beauty here, only sharp features, too coarse for sadness, but hardened and shiny with hate. Finally, the pieces fell into place and she realized the identity of her after-hours visitor.

"Why, of course I know who you are, Mr. Burke. You're the late Camille Burke's brother."

"I have a name!"

The nature of his outburst was strange and Morgan wondered about his mental stability. She had been in a hurry to grab her things and leave, but she resolved to take her time sorting through this situation, sensing any sudden action on her part would stir the volatility simmering below the surface. She concentrated on making her voice sound soothing.

"Mr. Theodore Burke, everyone knows who you are."

He settled back in the chair, apparently pacified by her acknowledgment of his fame and reputation. He nodded toward a chair on the visitor's side of the desk. Morgan sat and faced him, allowing him to take the lead.

"I've come to talk to you like rational people, rational professionals."

"Certainly, I am happy to hear what you have to say."

"You cannot represent my sister's killer. I'm sure you realize it was a mistake to think you could do so. Perhaps you got yourself in too far, thinking it would be a quaint little school project." He paused as if to give her time to acknowledge his insight. She rewarded him with a slight jerk of her head, urging him to continue. "But I am here to give you a way out of your benevolence. I forbid you to work on this case."

Morgan had realized Theodore Burke was a bit off the moment she saw him seated behind her desk. She decided to cut him a little slack once she realized who he was. After all, his family gave so much money to the university, it was likely he suffered from the delusion he owned the place. And he had been through a lot with the brutal murder of his sister and having his family affairs dragged through the news day after day as the trial date of the accused murderer drew closer. However, his pronouncement forbidding her from working on the case made her wonder if more than mere emotional turmoil drove him to confront her. His eyes were red and the pupils were dilated. His appearance was unkempt despite the sleek tailoring of his designer suit. His hair looked unwashed. He seemed unbalanced, edgy, almost cracked. Again,

Morgan had to check her normal impulses, which were all telling her to waste no time ordering this man from her office. She sensed a direct confrontation would only fuel his erratic behavior. Eyeing him warily, she rose and slowly crossed the room. She offered Theodore Burke her hand.

"Mr. Burke, I am sorry for your loss. I can see the extent of your grief. I will consider, very carefully, your request." Morgan walked toward the door. "Now, I am sorry, but I must be going."

"You will not consider anything!" His eyes bulged and his shout was punctuated by the crash of Morgan's chair, which he knocked over while standing to emphasize his point. "You will withdraw immediately! I will not finance the defense of my sister's murderer!"

Morgan lost her composure and backed away from the force of his outburst, connecting hard with someone standing behind her. Turning her head slightly, she realized the impediment was Parker, glaring ferociously at Theodore Burke. Morgan felt Parker grab her around the waist and push her back, taking long strides toward the desk where Theodore seemed torn between anger and surprise at the new addition to the tableau he had created. His surprise was heightened when Parker grabbed the lapels of his fancy suit and pushed him to the floor. Standing over him, she growled, "Lower your voice." She turned back to Morgan and asked, "Is there any reason this gentleman shouldn't be leaving?" Without waiting for Morgan's response, Parker pulled Burke to his feet and propelled him toward the door, shoved him through, and shut it behind him.

Turning to Morgan, she asked, "Are you all right?"

Morgan shoved her away. "What the hell were you thinking? Do you know who he was?"

Surprise at Morgan's reaction rendered Parker incapable of response.

"Parker, talk to me."

"What do you want me to say?" Parker at once felt stupid and angry. "I thought you were in trouble and I stepped in to help. I'm sorry." She was and she wasn't. Theodore Burke was crazy. His bizarre behavior was not a very well kept secret among those on the force. Family money can cover up a lot of things, but when you have to use it as hush money, the word inevitably gets out. She was sorry Morgan was mad, but she wasn't sorry she had interfered.

"After that little display, I think we can both count on being called on the carpet tomorrow. He is Camille Burke's brother."

Parker nodded. "I know."

"Then you must know his reaction to having the law school he helps fund defend the man accused of killing his sister."

"You mean his family helps fund."

"What?"

Parker delivered her assessment confidently. "His family. Theodore Burke has never worked a day in his life. He sees any part of the Burke fortune spent to make this college a better place as an erosion of his inheritance. If Teddy Burke had anything to do with it, we'd be sitting on the floor and reading from stone tablets."

Morgan contemplated Parker from across the room. Her eyes still shone bright with anger from the confrontation and she was poised as if ready for a fight. She was sleek and sure and sexy as hell. *Great*, she thought, *Parker's going to get you kicked off the faculty and all you can think of is how her taut and ready body would feel sprawled on your desk.* Morgan grabbed her purse and briefcase and walked to the door. "He was a bit creepy, but I'm sure there's going to be hell to pay later." She pointed at the open door. "It's been a long day. Let's call it a night and we can talk about this more Monday."

Parker reached for Morgan's bags while she locked up and walked alongside her toward the faculty parking lot. When they reached her car, Morgan turned to face her.

"Whether it was warranted or not, I appreciate the rescue attempt. Have a good evening."

Parker didn't move. "I think I should follow you home."

"Oh, you do, do you?"

Parker looked confused for a moment before she realized the implication of her remark. "No, no. I only want to make sure you aren't followed."

Morgan dipped toward disappointment, but she recovered quickly. "Please, Parker, I think I can handle myself. Do you actually think Teddy Burke is lurking in the shadows ready to follow me home?"

"Maybe. Would it kill you to trust my instincts on this?" Parker wore her fighter look again, but this time it was Morgan she looked ready to take on. "My car's around the corner. Drop me off and let me follow you home. I promise once you're safely inside, I'll go quietly into the night."

Morgan examined her words and caught a wistful undercurrent to the commanding tone. She was naturally stubborn and unwilling to admit she wasn't perfectly capable of taking care of herself. Letting Parker assume the role of her protector even if it was only for a short drive across town would surely undermine her authority. *Now you're kidding yourself. As if you have any authority over this woman who has made you come more times in the past few weeks than you did in the entire time you were with Tina.* Grasping at a semblance of control, Morgan spoke.

"Fine. But you won't go quietly into the night." Morgan pointed to the open door of her Lexus. "Get in." She started the SUV and drove to Parker's Mustang, parked at the rear of the student lot. Avoiding Parker's eyes, she said, "I need a drink and I want you to join me." Catching the veiled look of surprise on Parker's face, she added, "I'm living at the Hotel Palomar. Leave your car with the valet." As Morgan sped toward the hotel, she wondered if she was speeding toward disaster.

CHAPTER ELEVEN

The Hotel Palomar was a swanky place and Parker was uncomfortably conscious of her attire. Levi's and a T-shirt were perfect for all of her usual haunts—school, bar, library, dive restaurants—but not here where the rich and pretty gathered to celebrate their wealth and beauty. When she carried a badge, she didn't much care how she looked in relation to where she was or where she wanted to go. The shine of her gold shield granted her entrance to venues denied to many. Without the shield, she sometimes felt naked. This was one of those times. *Fake it*, she told herself.

Tossing the keys to the valet, she told him to keep her car ready to go, she might need to leave in a hurry. Smothering a grin at his curious stare, she strode through the heavy draped curtains and into Morgan's boutique home.

"May I help you, ma'am?"

Parker turned to the bellman who approached. She nodded. "The bar?"

"This way, ma'am."

She followed him. At first she was annoyed at being led around, but when she saw Morgan seated alone at the glass and chrome hotel bar, she was grateful to the human shield for hiding the spark of her initial reaction. Morgan's hair was tossed back and the red highlights glinted in the shiny bar. Parker could see every inch of her long, lean legs. Her suit jacket was slung on the back of her chair and the sight of her bare arms caused Parker to catch her breath. She had seen Morgan without a speck of clothing, but hints of Morgan's skin in fine fabric seemed to turn her on even more than full exposure.

Morgan was reading from a tiny bar menu and Parker was certain she did not see her approach. She was surprised when Morgan spoke to her before she even reached the table.

"Scotch, single malt?"

"Oh, first you order me here, then you order my drink."

"Problem?"

Parker slid into the seat beside Morgan and snatched the menu from her grasp. "No, not a problem." Scanning the menu, she continued, "You pick my drink and I'll pick yours." Running her finger down the page, she read the entries. "If I'm a single malt Scotch, then what must you be?"

Morgan eyed Parker, her student, and wondered why she invited her here. They were flirting, as she must have known they would. Driving around quiet neighborhoods looking at real estate was one thing, but sitting closely in a high-toned bar was a completely different matter. She relished Parker's grin as she perused the drink menu in search of the perfect cocktail. Her dark, wavy hair fell in scattered strands across her brow. Morgan desperately wanted to reach over and brush away the strands of wayward hair. A simple gesture, but she held back because of their relative position. Did she think she would find a loss of restraint in alcohol?

"Ah, here we go. A Manhattan. A metropolitan drink for the high-powered city lawyer." Without waiting for a response, Parker flagged down the cocktail waitress and ordered a Manhattan for Morgan and a Macallan, neat, for herself.

"High-powered city lawyer? At the moment, I'm a humble college professor."

Parker laughed. "In three years of law school, I don't think I've ever met a humble professor. I suppose there's a first for everything."

Morgan feigned hurt. "So you think I'm conceited?"

Parker searched Morgan's eyes and found sincerity behind the question. The hurt on her face might be a put-on, but on some level she needed reassurance. *Interesting*, Parker thought, *I would have never guessed she ever doubted herself.* Parker placed her hand on Morgan's. "I think you're confident. And with good reason. You have an amazing track record as a trial attorney and you're an amazing teacher." She gave Morgan an earnest look before continuing. "And I think you're amazing for a variety of other reasons."

As Morgan shifted on her seat Parker withdrew her hand, wondering if she had gone too far. *She invited me here—for drinks, after all. If anyone is blurring the lines, it's not me.* She was about to deliver some equivocation when Morgan reached across the table for her hand.

"Well, Parker Casey, I think you're pretty amazing too. For a variety of reasons."

Parker pushed the point. "I feel as if we're crossing certain lines here. Lines you seemed to think were very important not so long ago."

"I see. Too many mixed messages?"

"It's only an observation. I'm not necessarily complaining." Parker had her own reservations about taking whatever it was they were doing any further. Before she could give the idea much consideration, Morgan pressed on.

"I can't explain this, but I want to get to know you better. You have many layers, Parker Casey."

Parker smiled. "More than you thought when you were having a one-night stand with the bartender, right?"

"Ouch." Morgan frowned and Parker was instantly sorry for the remark.

"Sorry. I suppose that constituted an unnecessary dig. But I am terribly curious about why you were lost in the alley." Parker hadn't realized it until that very moment, but she was indeed curious about why a successful, good-looking woman like Morgan had been standing alone in the dark by a Dumpster. When she met Morgan again, she was too stunned by the realization she was her professor to give much thought to the logistics of their one-night stand.

Morgan took a long drink from her Manhattan and stared at Parker as if trying to read her thoughts. Seconds felt like minutes before she broke her gaze, looking down at her drink. She fished a cherry from the glass and twirled it on the end of her swizzle stick. Parker waited with a cop's patience. Finally, Morgan stopped playing with her drink, ate the cherry, and downed the rest. She signaled the waitress for another round before she spoke.

"I've been staying here since I moved to Dallas."

Parker waited, certain the story was longer than those few words.

"I moved to Dallas because my partner, and I don't mean law partner, of ten years was offered a great opportunity to turn around a tech company."

Parker waited still, calling all her powers of concentration to bear in order to keep Morgan from seeing her stiffen at the mention of a partner. *Where is she going with this?*

"Tina moved here a couple of months before me. She came early to buy us a new house while I dealt with all the details of getting our home back East sold, packed, and shipped. I finished with time to spare and decided to show up a week early as a surprise. I got to the house late in the evening, but Tina wasn't in. There were a few messages on the answering machine, and from what I could tell, a group of her new Dallas friends were heading out to the bar and wanted her to come along. I had it partly right.

"I decided my early arrival would be an even better surprise if I showed up at the bar. Tina was always bitching that I never cut loose, so I decided to sex up my look. You remember the low-riding jeans, halter top, the fuck-me shoes?" Parker nodded. "Well, that outfit is not my normal fare. In fact, I rarely go to bars at all. I just thought…" Morgan's voice trailed off. Parker waited while Morgan took a drink of her Manhattan and fiddled with the ice in her glass. "I don't know what I was thinking. Tina and I spent the last ten years going our separate ways. I suppose I thought the move to Dallas would be a step back toward each other. I was wrong.

"I took a cab to the bar, sure I would have a ride home at the end of the night. I went in, got a drink, and waited for my eyes to adjust to the dark. I was sitting at the bar, sipping on one of these," Morgan held up her new drink, "when I saw them. Tina and what had to be a model melded together on the dance floor. The music was fast, but they didn't seem to notice the beat, or anything else for that matter. They were practically wearing each other's clothes, they were so close. In ten years of living together, Tina never kissed me like that, never looked at me with that much longing in her eyes. To tell the truth, she could probably say the same for me. Later, I realized seeing her direct that much passion toward someone else was exactly what I needed to finally make the break I knew was best. But when I saw her wrapped around that woman, all I could think of in that moment was getting out of there with some of my dignity intact. They had danced their way into the path of the front door, so I headed for the only other exit I could find."

"And wound up in the alley."

Morgan smiled ruefully. "I've had better exit strategies."

"What were you going to do if I hadn't come along?"

"Scale a fence, call a cab, find a place to sleep for the night. Wake up, dust myself off, and start over."

"Regrets?"

Morgan felt the weight within the question, and carefully considered her answer. "None that mattered at the time. You were everything I needed. White knight, passionate lover, gorgeous woman. I decided right then I could feel sorry for myself or I could make the best of a bad situation. I sought solace with you and you didn't even know you were salve for my wounded ego." Morgan reached across the table. "I'm sorry. I suppose I used you, and on some level I feel bad about it."

As Parker listened to Morgan's story of her first day living back in the city where she grew up, her stiffness melted. Morgan's telling was straightforward and even self-deprecating, but it invited comfort and affection, which Parker desperately wanted to give. As she listened, she realized in a way she already had, even if it wasn't the kind she felt she should offer now. Their first meeting had been about physical need, satisfaction. What she felt now was different. Now she wanted to hold Morgan in her arms and tell her she was beautiful, tell her she was amazing, tell her she was cared for.

It was Parker's turn to finish her drink. As the amber liquid burned a gentle path down her throat, she contemplated whether she felt used for the events of their first encounter. Would it even matter if they had never met again? If Morgan had been one of her usual one-night stands, she would have been resigned to never seeing her again. But fate had dealt them a curious hand, throwing them into this situation of juxtaposed power and intimate connection. She pushed the empty glass aside and reached for the new one, taking another swallow. The mellow haze of the alcohol allowed her to admit to herself she did feel used, but she was strangely proud she had been available when Morgan needed her.

A comfortable silence enveloped them as Parker negotiated her own feelings about their chance encounter and where it had taken them. They were one of only a few occupied tables in the bar and the waitress was exercising excellent diligence in her ability to anticipate their needs without interrupting either their words or silence. Parker's nod ordered their next round. She sensed her heart-to-heart with Morgan was in its infancy.

Morgan proved her correct. No sooner had she licked the sugar rim of her new glass than she posed a question for Parker.

"What is a star homicide detective doing working in a bar and going back to school?" Morgan almost winced as she delivered the words. She felt duplicitous. She did know part of the story from Ford, and Parker had to know Morgan would have ready access to courthouse gossip. But she didn't know the whole story, and she sensed the complete tale held the key to unlock the mystery. Parker was an enigma in so many ways. She was earnest and hardworking, yet she had chucked an entire career and was building a new life for herself from the beginning. It had to be hard to go back to school with students much younger and compete again for accolades she should have already earned from life. Top it off with the fact Parker worked in a bar and lived in a house with roommates. There were indeed many layers to Parker, and Morgan wanted to see more than what was visible on the surface.

Why? she asked herself. *Is it because we slept together? Has it been so long since you had a one-night stand you feel as if you have to get to know the person you were with so you can justify the relationship, however fleeting?* Despite the nagging questions, Morgan knew the reason for her need to know came from a deep place. Once again she was struck by the force of the connection she felt with Parker, whose body she had thoroughly known but whose heart she had barely glimpsed. She hung on Parker's answer.

"Star homicide detective, huh? You might want to review the evidence, Counselor. This here detective was fired from the force." Parker's expression was cold, but sadness clouded her eyes.

"Can you tell me about it?"

Interesting phrasing, Parker observed. Sure, she was capable of recounting the story of how her stellar career had crashed and burned. She knew Morgan's question was more probing than a simple inquiry about whether she could tell a tale. She wanted to know if Parker had the fortitude to survive the telling. Had time and distance severed the emotion surrounding the collapse of her aspirations? She wasn't sure, but she wanted to share her story with Morgan and she wasn't sure why. Maybe it was simply because she had asked.

Parker met Morgan's patient gaze and answered, "Yes."

Morgan waited.

"I don't want to do it here." The flat words were tinged with a plea. Parker had not told her story in its entirety to anyone. Some knew the details, but only because they had lived it with her. She had no idea how sharing her experience would affect her and she did not want to wind up blubbering in a hotel bar.

Morgan slid from her chair and motioned for Parker to wait. She sought out the waitress, ordered another round, and asked that the drinks and the bill be sent to her room. Returning to the table, she lifted her jacket from the back of her chair, shrugged into it, and walked away from the table, signaling Parker to follow.

She squelched her desire to hold Parker's hand, to put her arm around her waist and pull her close. Once in the elevator, she pushed the button for her floor, resisting the urge to jam the car between floors and exercise the physical yearning stirring in her core. She sensed Parker needed some distance for what she was about to relay, and the feelings she had for Parker outweighed the needs of her body. Idly she wondered at her shift from lust to yearning. She pushed the thought away, but the feeling lingered. What she felt in this moment for Parker was vastly different from anything she had ever felt before, with Tina, with anyone. Protective, empathetic, caring combined with infatuation, affection, and craving to form a new emotion for which she had no words.

You are falling in love.

The inner voice was strong and sure and Morgan felt certain it was not her own. Love was a structured framework reached by agreement, not this heady, lust-filled passion over which she had little, if any, control. Love was sharing the mortgage, saving for retirement, swapping household duties by turn. The emotion enveloping her now held no room for such practicalities. Lust perhaps, but love? Not a chance. She shrugged away the voice's declaration and unlocked the door to her room.

Parker followed Morgan all the way to the room without taking in a single detail of their route. She was numb. When room service arrived with a new glass of Scotch, accompanied by the rest of the bottle, the sight allowed her a small measure of relaxation. She was prepped to remain numb for the storytelling portion of the evening.

Seated on the couch, she sipped her drink and watched Morgan settle in. Slender feet slipped from designer sandals. Parker distracted herself by conjuring up a name for the pearlized copper color of Morgan's toenails. Bronze seemed too plain. She remembered rifling through a victim's medicine cabinet one night while the scene tech catalogued the contents. The nail polish names were endlessly creative: Cheer Me Up Cherry, Over the Top Orange. Maybe Morgan's could be called Penny for Your Thoughts.

After an undeterminable length of time, Morgan settled in the overstuffed chair across from her, poured herself a Scotch, and waited. Parker knew this was her cue. She leaned back and closed her eyes, picturing the events in her mind as she told the entire story for the first time ever.

"We'd worked on the case for weeks without a break, and the killings were coming faster. Each body was found wrapped in plastic and dumped in the Trinity River. Days old, still buoyant, surrounded by cast-off debris. Young women, beautiful women, their bright futures and dreams violated, suffocated and abandoned. Skye and I had delivered the news to four families and we were drained. Listening to their wails, their tears, their dashed hopes, I vowed we would bring this killer to justice, and I didn't much care what form justice took. I had no idea my resolution would spell disaster."

Parker paused. Already she could tell dredging up these memories was going to be harder than she imagined. She met Morgan's patient glance, took a drink, and pushed through.

"Vice had been investigating this guy, a sleazy little man who got his rocks off looking at blondes in torture scenes on the 'net. Not your average S&M, but full-on brutal torture—fire, baseball bats, racks. They were convinced he was a key player in a child porn ring in North Texas. Turns out they were right, though we didn't confirm it until it didn't matter anymore. They had him dead to rights on obscenity, but they decided to hold out for more. Child porn is a sure trip to the pen. One image saved on the computer is all it takes to fuck up someone's life for good.

"Turns out one of the women we found showed up in a picture

streaming from this guy's computer. Vice brought us the info, desperate to have us bring him in. Skye was all for it, but I didn't want to spook him and made the call we should wait until we had more. We were working hard to connect this guy with the killings when next thing we know Vice tips us off. The guy's booking a one-way to Rio and putting his house on the market. We didn't have time to wait for the forensics, and we decided to take a chance on talking to him to see if we could turn up any leads on the killings. The investigation was ramping up and we had nothing except the lead on this guy. We were determined to follow it and nail the bastard. He had to know something, right?"

Morgan nodded, but Parker wondered if she truly agreed. Morgan had never worked the other side, hadn't had a chance to learn frontline respect for a cop's instinct. Parker pressed, desperate to earn Morgan's respect even as she feared she would never have it. "Skye and I showed up at his house. We didn't have a warrant, but sometimes these guys—sociopaths—enjoy talking to the cops, playing with us. As we rolled up to his place, Vice showed up as well, Detectives Morales and Ranell. I'm sure they were either watching his house or following us to see where our investigation was leading. Probably both.

"Sure enough, the guy, Edward Tucker, invites us in, dripping hospitality. He offers to serve us afternoon tea, complete with finger sandwiches and tiny cakes. Morales and Ranell left the questioning to us and Tucker was more than accommodating. He went on and on about how horrified he was to know the Trinity River Killer was still on the loose and gushed about the fear all young women in the city must be feeling to know this evil force had yet to be apprehended. He was very convincing and he knew it. I wanted to punch him until the sneaky gleam in his eyes died away.

"I didn't hit him, but I didn't live up to my gold shield either. I guess I'll never be entirely sure of what happened next.

"Tucker excused himself to the kitchen. While he was gone, I talked to Skye about ways to break him, make him tell us something we could use to wedge open a lead. I was more concerned about cracking the case than following procedure—otherwise I wouldn't have let him wander off. Next thing I knew, Ranell was whispering in Skye's ear and I noticed his partner was MIA. I started to ask where he went, but before the words hit the air, they were blasted by the sound of gunfire. We drew our guns and ran toward the back of the house. I knew in my gut this was going to end badly." Parker looked down at her hands, only mildly surprised to find they were shaking. She released the iron grip on the half-full glass in her hand and eased it onto the table, fighting the drive to drink it down. She had battled similar urges back then and she willed herself to do so again. At least until she could finish telling her story.

"Tucker wasn't so cocky anymore. He was lying face down in a pool of blood, the back of his shirt ripped through from the bullet that snuffed his life. Morales was standing a few feet away, his gun still trained on Tucker's body.

"I checked his pulse, but I knew it was pointless. I asked what the hell happened, but nobody had anything to say. Morales completely ignored me. He finally put his gun away and started frantically opening doors and drawers in the room. Ranell joins in and the two of them start tearing apart the room. Skye just stood there. She wouldn't look me in the eye. My first instinct was to call in the shooting, but I ignored it. I wanted to know what the hell they were up to. Since Morales was ignoring me, I grabbed his arm and got in his face and yelled at him to tell me what had happened.

"Nothing could have prepared me for what he said. During my conversation with Tucker, he had decided to do a little warrantless searching, hoping to find some evidence in plain sight so he could justify an arrest. While he talked I lost track of the number of ways I had disgraced my badge during the afternoon. I was so intent on engaging Tucker, I hadn't even noticed Morales leave the room.

"He had found Tucker's study, the room where we were standing. As I looked around, I could tell Morales thought he'd hit the mother lode. The room was full of computer equipment, complete with sophisticated webcams and high-speed disc-writing drives. Morales said he'd barely scratched the surface when Tucker snuck up behind him.

"Tucker started taunting Morales, telling him he knew what he was looking for and asking if Morales thought he was stupid enough, careless enough, to leave evidence lying around. He turned his back on Morales and reached in a drawer, all the while needling Morales about his inferior investigative skills. Tucker pulled something out of the drawer and raised it over his head, saying, 'I know how to protect myself.'

"Morales heard his words and saw something shiny. He didn't

hestitate. He drew his weapon and fired point blank. The bullet hit Tucker in the back and kept on going, blasting out of his chest. Morales raced across the room and grabbed the shiny object out of Tucker's hand. It was a CD. Wiping software. A hard-core program not sold in stores. Standard weapon for all serious child pornographers. There was no gun."

"But he didn't know that when he fired." Morgan's voice was gentle, her words couched in compassion.

Parker shook her head. "Maybe so. I would have found it a lot easier to believe him except for what happened next. Morales finished telling his story and went right back to searching the room. I finally managed to recover enough to make him tell me what he was doing. He acted like I was an idiot. 'What do you think I'm doing? I just shot a guy in the back. A worthless piece of scum who deserved to die and I'm not going down for it. I'm sure he owns a gun and before we call this in, the gun is going to be in his hand, freshly fired. Now, you can help me or stay out of my way. Your choice, but shut up with the questions.' He and Ranell went back to their search as if I wasn't there.

"It was becoming clear these guys were on a mission and they weren't going to tolerate anyone getting in their way. I looked at Skye, but she woudn't look back. Her face was set and stern. I'd known her for years, and while I never questioned her ethics, I was well acquainted with her aversion to rocking the boat. Over the years, she had gone to great pains to keep her private life secret for fear an out lesbian would garner less respect on the force. She thought her sexual orientation was a closely guarded secret, but I'm sure all the guys she wouldn't give the time of day to had no doubt about her preferences. She made up for her inability to emulate a straight woman by fitting in as one of the guys in a brotherhood that demanded unfettered loyalty.

"Now, our loyalty to our brothers was being put on the line, and while we both thought our choices were clear, we ended up on completely different sides. This was never clearer to me than when Skye pulled a throw-down from an ankle holster and handed it to Morales. As I watched her hand him the gun, the key to their cover-up, I decided I was on my own. I radioed in and reported the shooting. I clicked off when the questions from dispatch started coming fast and furious.

"Skye pulled me aside and impressed upon me the importance of sticking together. I had no idea her insecurities were so strong. Once they realized I had no intention of joining forces, they huddled together and talked as if I wasn't in the room and couldn't hear their every word. Next thing we knew the place was flooded with cops to take over the investigation and union reps, one for each of us. Then the suits from IAD arrived and our helpful union representatives gave us the only advice they had to offer: give a statement or lose the job. We were separated at that point. For all I know Skye and other two stuck to the story they'd concocted. I turned over my gun and badge and left in the department vehicle, accompanied by a uniformed rookie who was clueless about why he was charged with the task of dropping me off at home and then driving my vehicle back to the station."

"What a horrible betrayal." Morgan's voice was full of anger now. "Your partner should have had your back."

"You can't even imagine the many layers of Skye's disloyalty." Parker winced at the memory of the pain inflicted by her former lover. "The next few months were a blur. We were all suspended pending investigation. I told the investigators the truth about the shooting, though not the whole of it. I couldn't bring myself to go so far as to nail Skye with the truth of her role in the cover-up and I couldn't figure out a way to pin it on the other detectives without bringing her down as well. It didn't take me long to realize no one wanted to hear anything I had to say. The normally brutal IAD detectives lobbed me chance after chance to bring my story in line with the others. I was tempted, but the truth was I had no idea if Skye and the others were sticking to the story they cooked up at Tucker's house. I told them everything I heard and saw, but I pretended to have no idea where the gun in Tucker's hand had come from. And I didn't. I had no idea Skye carried a throw-down weapon. I learned I knew very little about her. I got more and more disgruntled every time I was called back down to the station. The lawyer the union hired was a spineless bastard who exerted more effort trying to get me to conform than he did trying to defend me.

"I was number one in my class at the academy. I earned my gold shield faster than any cop in the department. I had been decorated for valor and had a list of commendations longer than my arm. My accomplishments were meaningless in the wake of the train of deception shooting down the tracks, and my 'brothers' were the ones who had tied me down. I was fired for cause, stripped of rank, pay, and retirement. I was so devastated I got no comfort from the fact Morales was fired as well. The outcome of the administrative hearing was Morales had acted badly in snooping around the house and shooting a guy in the back and I, as the lead detective, knew or should have known he was a loose cannon. Never mind the fact he was a detective in his own right and belonged to a different department. I got the message behind my firing. I hadn't gone along. I had betrayed the loyalty of the brotherhood and I was no longer trusted to do the right thing, however loosely defined the right thing was."

Parker stared at the half-empty bottle of Scotch sitting on the table. She had no recollection of drinking while she talked and shook her head to assess the buzz she felt. It was strong, but not strong enough. She leaned forward and filled her glass, drinking deeply through the silence. Seconds stretched into minutes and, hearing no response, she turned to meet Morgan's face, fortifying herself for whatever expression she might find there.

She saw pain and she wondered vaguely at the source. Finally, Morgan spoke.

"Did it end there?"

"Not quite. Tucker's family crawled out of the woodwork to sue the department for wrongful death. Actually, they seemed like nice people and I'm sure they saw the lawsuit as a way to compensate for the pain of raising a child who, despite their efforts, turned out to be a monster. I was subpoenaed as a witness and wound up hiring a lawyer on my own to discuss the pros and cons of taking the Fifth. Out of a job, I had precious little money, but I didn't trust the union hack who had 'represented my interests' to the department. My lawyer convinced me to fight my termination and I wound up suing the department and taking advantage of their desire to keep all their wrongful acts out of the public forum. My settlement is paying for law school. You could say I was inspired by my experience to use my powers to fight for the underdog.

"The irony of it all is Tucker wasn't the Trinity River Killer. Everyone thought for sure he was the one since the killings stopped right after he died, but the family gave permission for a DNA test and there was no match. I think they wanted to know for themselves whether his life had any redeeming value. The killer's still out there. Maybe he'll call on me to represent him someday."

Parker's final words on the subject were delivered with thick sarcasm, but Morgan could read the pain behind them. She ached to draw Parker close, hold her and comfort her, but Parker was distant and she feared pulling her close would break rather than forge any connection they had.

Morgan contemplated the rush of feeling she had experienced in the elevator. Was she indeed falling in love? To the outside observer, her feelings were well placed. Not only was Parker smart and beautiful, she was brave and honorable as well. Morgan pondered whether what she felt for Parker was real or whether it was the by-product of Parker having saved the day the night she came to town. As she reflected on that night, she had no doubt the physical attraction was real, but what about this intense desire that had developed that was entirely separate from their sexual attraction? Love and lust started to wind their way around each other and Morgan wasn't sure she could trust her ability to tell them apart. She decided that until she did, she wouldn't act on either. To do so was to risk hurting Parker, and she had suffered enough betrayal from others who lacked the courage of their convictions. Morgan resolved she would keep her feelings to herself until she was sure.

CHAPTER TWELVE

Parker walked in from the garage and headed straight to the kitchen. She wanted coffee, but she needed water more. She had woken up about forty-five minutes before, sprawled on the couch in Morgan's hotel room. They were both fully dressed and Parker felt the dull throb of a hangover begin to take hold. She eased her way out of the room, casting a wistful glance at Morgan sound asleep on the couch. It had been a strange night. The only one they had shared without sleeping together, yet it was the most intimate by far. Now, as she chugged a bottle of cold water, Parker regretted not stealing a kiss before she left.

Parker was so wrapped up in the memory, she didn't notice the presence of anyone else in the kitchen. The scraping sound of a throat clearing caused her to turn abruptly and smack her head on the refrigerator door.

"What the hell?" She rubbed her head and stared at Kelsey and Dex, who were standing in the middle of the kitchen staring right back at her. Slowly, her memory started to return. Dex. Research. Saturday morning. Shit. She wondered if they had seen her come in from the garage, dressed in yesterday's clothes. Feeling like a kid caught with her hand in the cookie jar, she scrambled. "Oh, hi, Dex. Sorry, I had to run out this morning and get some stuff. Give me five minutes and I'll be raring to go." She grabbed the bottle of water and jogged out of the room without waiting for a response.

❖

They had been working for almost two hours when Dex abruptly pushed the button on the computer monitor. As the screen faded to black, Parker exclaimed, "Hey, I was reading a case!"

Dex settled into the chair next to her. "We need to talk."

Parker squirmed in her seat. "Dex dear, we've been talking. We've talked all morning. I think we're getting close to having this motion briefed. Can we finish please?"

"In a minute." Dex took a deep breath. "Gerald Lopez came by to see me last night."

"Is he feeling a little left out? I'll never figure out how he made the team in the first place."

"Yeah, me neither. But apparently he's got a pretty big chip on his shoulder and it has to do with you."

Gerald had never hidden his jealousy for her success in school. He believed he was entitled to accomplishment because his daddy was a hotshot lawyer, alum, and major contributor to the law school. He viewed Parker as a lowly cop, which figured into his calculation that he was more deserving of success than she. Parker had no idea what Dex was about to say, but whatever it was, she wasn't surprised about the fact Gerald didn't like her. She was surprised, though, that Gerald had bothered to talk to Dex about his feelings, since he had to know Dex and Parker were tight.

"Gerald has it in his head you and Professor Bradley have a thing."

Not in a million years did she expect this revelation. Her feelings furiously treaded water while her thoughts swam in search of an acceptable response. "A thing? What's that supposed to mean?"

Dex gave Parker a knowing look. "Don't make me spell it out. You know what I mean. He says he saw you two, quote, 'cuddling up in class' and riding off somewhere together last night."

"What did you say to him?"

"I threatened to beat the shit out of him." Dex gave her a pointed look. "Was my bluster unfounded?"

Parker managed to return Dex's look, but couldn't find words to convey a simple answer to his question complete with an explanation of the complexity of her relationship with Morgan. She had trouble understanding the situation herself. How could she expect Dex to comprehend? As she watched his expectant expression, she realized their friendship demanded she at least try to explain. Knowing Dex, Gerald had suffered for even bringing up the issue, and she owed Dex for his loyalty.

Parker told Dex everything, from the first moment in the alley to her soul-baring episode of the evening before. She omitted no detail, not even her involved past with Skye, and was surprised at the sense of relief she felt at the telling. Years of training allowed Dex to listen without reacting, giving Parker no idea how he felt about her revelations. When she finished she waited expectantly.

"Wow." The one word revealed the surprise his flat tone was meant to hide.

"Wow? You don't have anything to say but wow?" Parker waited for his thoughts to catch up to his feelings.

Dex shook his head. "So you've slept with both the lead detective on the Chavez case and the lead defense attorney. Gee, Parker, any other major players on this case you haven't bagged?"

Parker stood abruptly, knocking over the reams of research they had compiled. "You're an ass."

"Come on, Parker. What the hell did you expect me to say? 'Way to go'?"

Parker was furious at Dex for his callous reaction and furious with herself for sharing with him. "I don't expect anything from you. We're done here, aren't we?"

Realizing he was being dismissed, Dex stomped across the room and gathered his things. "Sure, Parker. We're done. Since you seem to have the inside track, why don't you finish briefing the motion? I'm sure your work will be more than satisfactory."

Parker glared through his departure. She waited until she heard the front door slam shut before grabbing the nearest text and hurling it across the room. Where did he get off? Their friendly competition to graduate first in their class seemed to have morphed into a brawl at her revelation. Surely he didn't think she slept with Morgan to come out on top? She glanced up at the sound of approaching footsteps and saw Kelsey standing in the doorway.

"Are you done throwing things?"

Parker met Kelsey's questioning look. "I don't know. The first throw barely scratched the surface of my anger." She grimaced. "Enter with caution."

To her surprise, Kelsey marched across the room and gathered her up in a fierce hug. "Parker Casey, you're not angry. You're confused. You've gotten yourself wrapped up in a complicated situation and you can't seem to find a way out of it."

"What are you talking about?"

"Come on, Parker. You've got a crush on your teacher."

Parker felt the blood drain from her face. She was intrigued by Morgan. She admired her. She was irresistibly attracted to her. But a crush? Not a chance. Before she could eke out the words to challenge Kelsey's assumption, Kelsey put a finger over her lips.

"Not a word out of you. You're about to vehemently deny my conclusion. Forget it, Parker. I'm a doctor, which makes me a practiced observer of physical and emotional signs. I know you didn't come home last night and I'm quite sure I know who you were with. When it comes to Morgan Bradley, you exhibit all the classic symptoms of a woman who is infatuated. Whatever you have to say isn't going to change my diagnosis. Think about it and get used to the idea. Because you're going to have to do something about it before you trample all your friends beating a trail away from your feelings." Kelsey released Parker from her grasp and held her at arm's length. "I'm going downstairs to make dinner. Beat your pillows with a tennis racket, take a warm bath, count to a hundred. Do whatever you need to do to regain your composure and then join me in the kitchen. I expect you to eat."

Parker stood transfixed as Kelsey left the room. *Infatuated, my ass*, she thought. Surely Kelsey was reading more into recent events than she should. After all, last night had been nothing more than a drink-induced truthfest with nothing loverlike about it. All she remembered was baring her soul, drinking most of a bottle of good Scotch, and waking up with Morgan at her side. She had for a moment wondered if more had happened, but seeing Morgan fully dressed next to her on the sofa put to rest any questions she might have had.

She turned Kelsey's words over and over in her mind, searching for truth. After a few minutes' consideration, she opted to ignore the bulk of Kelsey's advice. She spent the next hour furiously banging on her laptop keyboard, then she printed her work, proofed it, and made her way downstairs to feign an appetite.

Chapter Thirteen

Morgan, Dex, and Luis were seated at the defense counsel's table, waiting for the judge to take the bench. Morgan leaned over to her client and gave him an idea of what to expect from the hearing they were about to have. She told him they would be discussing various procedural issues, including the expected length of the trial and any issues that needed a ruling in advance from the court. Morgan told him the judge might decide to hear testimony about the motion to suppress she had filed the day before.

Luis was dressed in a jail-issue black and white striped jumpsuit and faux Crocs. Morgan noticed his sister was in the gallery and she leaned over to ask Dex to remind her that Luis would need street clothes for the actual trial. Satisfied that detail was addressed, Morgan focused on the brief Dex and Parker had prepared on the suppression issue. They had done a fantastic job, but the decision could go either way. The judge was likely to focus on whether Luis had constructively waived his rights by continuing to answer questions after his rights were read to him. A lot would hinge on the testimony of Skye Keaton, who was waiting with the prosecutor. If the judge decided to take up the motion, Skye would be the State's star witness.

Morgan wanted to claw the woman's eyes out. Everything about her, from the cocky comfort of her reclining pose to the smirk playing along the edge of her lips, fueled the fire of Morgan's rage. *Channel it*, she told herself. *Use her cockiness. Let her hang herself with pride.* Morgan took a deep breath and forced the strength of calm to take over. This wasn't the time or place to bring up Skye Keaton's internal affairs record. With no jury in the box, the shock value would be minimal, and it was likely the judge already knew about her record. After all, she had probably testified in this court on numerous other occasions since her reprimand and the damage to her credibility was old news to the man on the bench. Morgan forced herself to wait, knowing she would get much more play from the shock value of Keaton's disciplinary record in front of a jury. Resisting protective, personal feelings urging her to tear this witness apart here and now, Morgan focused on the legal grounds of her argument.

She was still torn about whether or not to fight this battle. She had watched the tape at least a dozen times and its contents never changed. Truth be told, she was fighting this battle because it was expected and she didn't want to show her hand to the prosecutor, who was trained to expect the expected. Morgan reflected if she were prosecuting this case, she would be tempted to forego admitting the defendant's statement into evidence—a move designed to force him to take the stand and give his side of the story. As she turned the thought over in her mind, she shot a look across the room, sizing up her competition.

Valerie Gibson was young, trim, and blond. She looked like so many of her fellow female prosecutors, Morgan had given up trying to identify her in the hallways of the courthouse. Probably a graduate of a local school with good, but not great grades, she was either zealously committed to the idea of putting away bad guys or viewed this job as a stepping stone to private practice. In any event, her age meant she had little real-life experience and though she had probably prosecuted dozens of DWIs and petty thefts, it was unlikely she had tried many violent crimes, especially not murder. Remembering her first big case, Morgan speculated Valerie was either excited beyond belief or scared out of her mind at the prospect of trying this high-profile case.

Morgan found it interesting that after all Lester and Teddy Burke's comments to the media about the death of their dear Camille, the district attorney had not found it necessary to assign this important trial to one of their more seasoned prosecutors. Though the elected DA rarely tried cases himself, he would normally assign a sensitive case like this to one of the several super chiefs who oversaw the prosecutors in the trenches. Morgan scratched a note on a Post-it to remind her to ask Ford some pointed questions. He was in tune with courthouse gossip and if he didn't know the answer, he could usually be counted on to have a source.

Moments later Judge Thompson doddered through the door behind the bench and arranged himself in his seat.

"Counsel, are you ready to proceed?"

Gibson half stood. "The State is ready, your honor."

Morgan, Dex, and Luis rose as one and Morgan announced, "Morgan Bradley and Dex Gallagher for Mr. Chavez. We're ready as well."

Judge Thompson leaned across the bench and pulled his glasses down. "Why, Morgan Bradley, I haven't seen you in years. I'm told you're teaching at the university."

Morgan nodded. She was used to be recognized and remembered. "Yes, Your Honor, I am. Mr. Gallagher is one of my students. He, along with a few others, will be working with Mr. Rupley and myself on this case."

"What a nice surprise. Well, you be sure and tell your father hello for me. I haven't seen him in a while. I suppose he's making the most of his retirement." Morgan smiled as she realized it was her father, the retired judge, who was being remembered, not her.

Judge Thompson's tone became more formal as he discussed the preliminary issues to be resolved. Both sides agreed the trial would likely take a week and the judge set the trial date for two weeks out. Then he addressed the prosecutor. "Ms. Gibson, do you have your witnesses ready for the motion to suppress?" When she responded in the affirmative, he instructed her to proceed. Even though Morgan had filed the motion, the burden of proof was on the prosecution to show that Luis's constitutional rights had not been violated by the way his statement was obtained. The remedy, if his rights were violated, was to throw out that piece of evidence.

Gibson called Skye to the stand and asked her a rote series of questions about how Luis came to be in custody and the procedural steps she took before she started questioning him. As she watched her adversary questioning Detective Keaton, Morgan realized how excited she was to be back in the courtroom. The hum of anticipation vibrated to a steady pitch as she waited impatiently for Gibson to finish laying a foundation for the video. Yes, teaching was gratifying, but the well of the courtroom was where she belonged, using the skills she merely simulated in the classroom.

"Judge, I have the video cued up if you'd like to watch it now."

Judge Thompson inclined his head toward the defense table, offering Morgan the opportunity to object. She stood.

"Judge, we have no objection to you watching the tape at this time. In chambers." She didn't want the gawking public to see a tape she was trying to suppress.

The prosecutor started to voice her own objection, but her trial partner grabbed her by the arm and whispered a word of advice. Half standing, she called out to the bench. "The state has no objection to a recess to allow the court time to view the tape."

Morgan stood again. "I'm sure Ms. Gibson would like the court to have the benefit of all the information at its disposal, so I want to make sure the tape is cued to the very beginning—from the moment Mr. Chavez is placed in the interrogation room." Instinctually, she knew the prosecutor would have started the tape, for the judge's viewing, where the actual questioning began, ignoring the full thirty minutes where Luis sat gulping down food and otherwise looking furtive.

"Ms. Gibson, how long is this tape?" The judge's tone conveyed his feelings about how long he thought it should be.

The young prosecutor equivocated. "Judge, I'm not entirely sure of the length. I imagine it's under an hour."

Morgan interjected in a helpful tone. "Actually, Judge, the tape is ninety-eight minutes." She knew the information would be like a burr under a saddle. Ford had told her Judge Thompson was not a patient man. He preferred counsel resolve issues among themselves so he would not have to engage in any pesky legal analysis. Rarely did cases come back on appeal when the lawyers had worked out all the issues by themselves. No way was he going to be happy about having to watch a movie-length tape laced with legal pitfalls and then have to render a judgment about its admissibility. Hell, at his age he might not even be able to stay awake that long. She could hear the whirring sound of the prosecutor unraveling in the silence. Glancing over, she could see Valerie Gibson engaged in a barely whispered exchange with her trial partner. Morgan waited.

"Your honor, may we approach?"

The judge looked around, his tiny allotment of patience tapped out. "Ms. Gibson, there's no jury present. What is it you want?"

"Sorry, Judge. I was hoping we might have a short moment to confer with opposing counsel."

"If it will save the Court valuable time," he delivered a pointed look, "you may have ten minutes. Detective, you may step down."

Skye stood and started to walk through the well of the courtroom. She stood before the rail, ostensibly to wait for further instruction from Gibson, but her eyes searched the gallery. Morgan knew without looking in the direction of Skye's gaze she was searching for Parker. Preparation for this hearing meant Morgan hadn't had an opportunity to share more than meaningful glances with Parker since their night of mutual disclosure. Though Parker hadn't included personal details about Skye in the tale of her separation from the force, Morgan was certain Skye's betrayal extended beyond a dispute between fellow officers. She had no doubt these women had been lovers. The sparks their encounters ignited were searing and deeply personal. And Parker's expression when she spoke of Skye contained more hurt than would be left by a professional betrayal alone. Masking her own mixed feelings of jealousy and anger, she forced her features into a relaxed expression and leaned back in her chair, waiting for the prosecutor to approach.

"Can we talk?"

Morgan smiled widely at the young woman. "Of course. Have a seat."

"In my office."

Morgan pointed at Mr. Chavez sitting next to her. "I'm pretty sure whatever you have to say is going to impact my client. Don't you think he should hear it for himself?" She was deliberately goading the prosecutor. Strategy discussions were rarely held in the presence of the person to whom they mattered most. Morgan did a better job than most making her clients feel they were part of the process. After all, it was their freedom at stake. But once formal proceedings began, she was like most lawyers, needing space from the raw emotion of the accused in order to make the razor-sharp tactical decisions required to defend them. She waited a beat and then shrugged. "Fine, I'll hear what you have to say. Mr. Chavez, I'll be right back." She stood, motioning to the bailiff, who came over to take Mr. Chavez back into the holdover.

Seated in the DA workroom, Morgan crossed her legs and waited.

"You realize you don't have good grounds to suppress this tape, don't you?"

"Oh, I don't know. Judge Thompson might not be too happy when he sees how long your detective kept my client caged without explaining his rights, waiting for an opportunity to explain himself. How she conveniently left off the waiver portion of the the Miranda warning and clearly ignored his invocation of his right to counsel. Then there's the matter of how many times your detective feels the need to mention his prior record on the tape."

"If we redact those portions, will you withdraw your motion to suppress the tape?"

Morgan forced herself to sound reluctant. "I'll agree to hold off on my motion. But I reserve the right to submit any issues about its admissibility to the jury, and I want them to see the tape from the beginning. You know, the part you didn't think was important enough for this judge. Furthermore, I want you to agree to instruct your witnesses not to mention Mr. Chavez's record in open court and to approach the bench for a ruling before you ask any questions about his record. Do we have a deal?" Morgan stuck out her hand.

The prosecutor shook her hand and told her trial partner to let the judge know they wouldn't need to finish the hearing. Morgan was certain she felt like she had won this round. *You keep thinking that way, sweetie. You just got snookered.* Morgan focused on maintaining a neutral expression, hiding her relief that Luis would not need to take the stand to tell his side of the story. The tape would do the trick, and now that the prosecutor thought Morgan didn't really want the tape in evidence, there was no doubt she would play it for the jury.

Parker was itching to know what Morgan and the prosecutor were talking about, almost as much as she was itching to talk to Morgan about their conversation at Morgan's hotel. Scotch hadn't dimmed her memory and she had a clear remembrance of the level of personal detail she had shared. She had cursed herself repeatedly for taking off that morning while Morgan was still asleep. Her hasty exit, and the fact they had been too occupied with work on the case to talk about it since, left her feeling frazzled. Dex's revelation about Gerald's crazy suspicions and Kelsey's diagnosis of her feelings were also weighing on her mind. Parker wanted to tie up the loose ends and she needed to find a few moments alone with Morgan to make that happen.

For now, she had to wait in the gallery. The judge allowed only two attorneys at a time to sit at the counsel table. Today Dex occupied the second spot. Parker wondered how they would handle the issue of who got to sit where at trial. Her experience at the public defender's office told her juries had mixed feelings about seeing a gaggle of attorneys surrounding the defendant. On one hand the presence of so many legal minds gave the appearance of power, but power doesn't always equal right. Sometimes the best approach when your client was dressed in mismatched clothes gathered from the public defender's suit closet was to take advantage of the David and Goliath scenario and play it for all it was worth. No crowd of expensive suit–wearing lawyers sporting fancy watches and taking notes with Montblanc pens. Only one attorney and one client facing the might of the State of Texas. She imagined Morgan and Ford would sit at the table with Luis while she and the other students would position themselves in the first row of seats behind the railing—within spitting distance.

Parker watched Morgan and the DA make their way to the back of the courtroom. With Morgan gone from the room, Parker felt the slow burn of eyes focused her way. She knew, without looking up, the eyes were gray, beautiful, and flame-throwing. She had once admired Skye's ferociousness. There was a time when their intensity was evenly matched. Parker realized her own fervor was now tempered by perspective. She feared Skye hadn't learned a thing from witnessing Parker's ride on the rail out of the department. Instead, Skye clung to the safety of believing if Parker had stood up for justice, she would still be standing strong with her law enforcement brethren on the right side of good versus evil. It was so easy to believe your cause was the right one when you never had to see things from the opposite point of view. *I was no different. I thought the people we arrested were scum, and defense attorneys no better, especially the ones like Morgan who gave blow-by-blow accounts of decimating the prosecution on Court TV. Yet here I am. Ready to defend this man accused of breaking the law with the same zeal I used to enforce it.* Skye's first words summed up every ounce of what Parker was feeling.

"You've changed."

Parker shook her head, then stopped abruptly to acknowledge the truth her former lover spoke. "Well, Skye, you've finally caught on." When Skye didn't reply, Parker turned to go find Morgan, but she felt a tug on her arm.

"Have dinner with me." Skye's tone was not questioning.

"You've got to be kidding." Parker was sure she must be.

"You still eat, don't you? We'll go to Campasis, have some wine."

Parker couldn't find enough words to express how much she didn't want to break bread with Skye. The search left her speechless.

"I'll pick you up at seven." Skye's confidence was still alive and well.

Parker finally found the words she was looking for. "No. No way. Not in a million years."

"Why not?" Skye asked as if she could not imagine a single reason Parker might turn her down.

Parker looked deep into Skye's eyes, but she could not see beneath the veneer of bravado Skye had in place. Ignoring Skye's question, she shrugged and turned away again. Within a second she felt the warm whisper of Skye's voice in her ear.

"Another time then. See you at trial." Skye slipped away.

Parker looked around, but Morgan had yet to emerge from her meeting with the prosecutor. Moments later, Parker nearly jumped out of her skin at the sound of another voice over her shoulder.

"So, what do you think they're talking about back there?"

Dex. Parker wondered if he overheard any part of her encounter with Skye and prayed he had not. Things had been strained enough between them since the scene at her house when he found out about her fling with the professor. Because they'd been thrown into working together, their relationship survived out of necessity. Parker missed their camaraderie but feared she had lost the thing she wanted most from Dex—his respect. *Maybe he'll come around*, Parker hoped.

"Maybe they're working out a plea. And then we can go back to the way things were." Parker intended every layer of meaning and she silently willed Dex to hear her plea.

"Maybe they are. Frankly, I'd prefer we go to trial. I'm beginning to appreciate seeing things from another perspective." Dex feigned nonchalance, but Parker knew him well enough to peel away the indifference. Knowing he relied on her to maintain a stoic front, she rewarded his overture of friendship with a simple nod.

"Good point. Let's go make sure we get to trial."

He pointed to the door. "Are you ready to go?"

Parker glanced at the closed door of the DA workroom, then at her watch. Even if she waited for Morgan, it was doubtful she would have a chance to talk to her alone. The entire group was meeting for lunch in twenty minutes. She decided to leave with Dex and catch Morgan alone later. As they left the courtroom, Parker locked arms with Dex, grateful they had reconnected.

CHAPTER FOURTEEN

The trial team gathered for lunch at Market Diner. Ford saved them one of the only large tables in the back. Morgan resigned herself to having to eat greasy diner food for the duration of the case and gave a recap of the morning's action against the noisy backdrop of the lunch crowd. Gerald, who had not attended the hearing, had a ton of questions, and his tone insinuated he didn't think she knew what she was doing.

"I don't understand why you didn't try harder to suppress Luis's statement. Especially after all the time and research that went into preparing the motion."

Morgan started to respond with an observation that Gerald couldn't take any credit for the hard work on the motion, but Parker and Dex both started talking at once. Dex punched Parker in the shoulder and won the right to deliver his response first. His tone was engaging, as if he was trying to win the grumbling student over. "She made the prosecutor think she didn't want the tape in evidence, which means it's definitely coming in. And she reserved the right to challenge it again at trial."

Gerald wasn't buying it. "My father says you should never concede a point to the other side."

This time it was Ford who responded first, and he shut Gerald down. Ford said, "I know your father well and I can assure you if he knew the situation, he would have made the same decisions Morgan did." Ford's tone made it clear he would not tolerate any more grousing from Gerald.

Morgan smiled a look of appreciation. Ford had not been able to attend the pretrial hearing because of a conflict in another court, but he embraced Morgan's strategy as if they had planned it in advance.

With the issue of Luis's statement resolved for the time being, Morgan decided it was time to talk about the defense investigation. Trial was two weeks away and the investigator assigned to work with the public defenders was clearly pulled in too many different directions. Ford was able to name three cases set for trial in the coming weeks the investigator was working on, all of them "top priority." Ford hadn't been able to get a solid answer on the status of the work on this particular case and he expressed his concern to the group.

"I think we should file a motion asking Judge Thompson for money to hire a private investigator," Ford suggested. "We'll just explain the situation about the PD's in-house investigator."

Morgan agreed. "We don't have any time to waste. We need to start interviewing people we think are going to be on the State's witness list. We should draft the motion and take it to the judge today. Any volunteers to write the motion?"

Dex, who had been exchanging whispered conversation with Parker, was quick to answer. "I'll do it." Morgan caught him exchange a conspiratorial look with Parker and wondered what was up. "Okay, I'll need it by three. Gerald, talk to Ford about some additional items he wants to include in the trial notebooks, and, Parker, I'd like you to prepare a list of proposed jury instructions." Morgan let her gaze linger on Parker. "I'll be in touch soon to go over your first draft." She wondered if Parker realized she didn't want to talk about jury instructions, or evidence, or anything else related to this trial. She only wanted to see Parker alone so they could reconcile the blazing passion of their first encounters with the tender intimacy of their last night together. She wanted to explore her feelings, figure out if the connection between them was forged from stronger stuff than a physical craving. Even as she had the thought, she decided it would be a mistake to delve any deeper. It was obvious Parker was still smarting from the betrayal she had suffered from her fellow officers, Skye in particular. She didn't need to be the subject of Morgan's self-discovery, didn't need to have her feelings put at risk. Better they stick to the clearly defined roles of teacher and student than to wade into murkier waters.

❖

Parker drove Dex back to the courthouse to retrieve his car. Once they got in the car, Dex couldn't wait to unveil his plan.

"I think you and I should do the investigation ourselves."

Parker gave him a look that indicated she thought he had lost his mind. "Morgan—" Seeing Dex's raised eyebrows, she hastily said, "I mean, Professor Bradley, will never go for it." While Ford had insisted the students call him by his first name, Morgan had not made a similar offer.

"Why not?" Dex asked.

"I think she has a healthy dose of cynicism about law enforcement types."

"Most PIs are former cops. She has to know that."

"I'm sure she does. We just might not be 'former' enough. Besides, we're technically the lawyers on the case. We can't testify." Parker voiced what they both knew. A non-lawyer investigator was necessary, especially for witness interviews. If a witness took the stand and said something different than they stated in a previous interview, the person who conducted the interview would be called to the stand to impeach the witness's credibility, which meant they were done in their role as the attorney. A lawyer testifying in his or her own client's case was too confusing for juries and raised too many questions about bias and motivation.

"I know, I know. But if we help with the investigation, then we'll be able to get it done more quickly. We can type up the witness summaries and we'll have firsthand accounts to pass along to Ford and Professor Bradley." Dex was excited about the prospect of doing something other than research and writing. "Come on, this is right up our alley. Especially yours."

Parker had to admit the prospect was exciting. The one thing she missed about her former career was the challenge of sifting through pieces of information to solve the whodunit puzzle. Though the State believed Luis was the only possible answer to the question of who, why he had killed Camille Burke was still a missing piece. Parker couldn't help but think if they could find out why someone had wanted Camille dead, the resulting picture might not be what everyone expected.

"All right. I'm in. But you have to do the asking. By yourself. Do it this afternoon when you take the motion to Morgan." Parker gave up trying to remember to call her Professor Bradley with Dex, but she didn't want to admit she didn't want to risk seeing Morgan outside the formal bounds of their teacher-student relationship. The fast pace of trial preparation meant she hadn't spent any time alone with Morgan since she had poured out her soul in Morgan's hotel room the week before. In the context of preparing, she had seen her plenty and on every occasion she heard Kelsey's words, whispering truth. She struggled to ignore her feelings, knowing there was no hope they would be returned. Morgan was her teacher and had expressed clear regret every time she had crossed the line of propriety. Parker figured if Morgan felt something more than physical attraction, she would find a way to disregard the boundaries, but obviously that was not the case. Parker pondered whether she should let Morgan know about Gerald's accusation. If he decided to, he could try to make trouble for them both. But it wasn't as if Gerald had said anything directly to her. If she told Morgan, she'd have to admit Dex knew something was going on between them. She decided telling Morgan would merely heighten her anxiety about the impropriety of their relationship, and that was the last thing she wanted to do. Besides, it was pretty clear there wasn't going to be a relationship anyway, so Gerald's supposed bombshell would turn out to be a dud.

❖

Hours later, Parker sat in her room pretending to study. Dex was supposed to come by this evening and let Parker know where things stood. Parker was finding it hard to be little more than an observer in the case and hoped Ford and Morgan would allow them the more active investigative role. Waiting to hear from Dex contributed to her inability to focus, and when she heard the doorbell, she jumped at the sound. Before she could make it to the hall, she heard Erin call out, "I'll get it." She waited upstairs, knowing Erin would tell Dex to go on up. Moments later, she looked up to see Erin in her doorway with a furrowed brow.

"Hey, Parker, there's someone here to see you. Not Dex."

"Any idea who it is?" Parker asked.

"Not a clue and she wouldn't tell me. She said she wanted to surprise you."

Parker smothered a grin. Of course, Erin hadn't met Morgan so she wouldn't have a clue who she was. Well, except for the fact Dex was supposed to show up any moment, Morgan's visit was a very pleasant surprise. Though they had agreed on friendship, it seemed their chance encounters were laced with something more. Each had stolen glances at the other during class and trial preparation, and more than once their surreptitious outreach happened simultaneously. When it did, the effect was smoldering. Parker refused to let herself reflect on the meaning of the physical force she felt every time she caught Morgan's eyes locked on her. For once in her life, she chose to revel in the feeling and ignore the consequences. If they were nothing more than friends, then surely these feelings would subside at some point. In the meantime, she felt good, right, and warm. She wasn't in the mood to let meaning steal those feelings away.

Parker told Erin she would be right down, then glanced in the mirror and ran her hands through her unruly hair. Straightening her shirt and smoothing out the wrinkles in her pants, she smiled at herself before she turned to head downstairs. She took the steps two at a time, not caring if she looked like she was skipping with excitement. As she reached the bottom of the staircase, she saw Skye Keaton waiting for her in the foyer, balancing a pizza box on the fingers of her right hand. Parker lurched to a stop.

"Skye! What the hell are you doing here?" Parker stayed on the last step.

"Helluva greeting for someone with dinner on board." Skye smiled as if Parker's visceral reaction had no effect. Shoving the pizza box toward Parker, she said, "I brought your favorite."

Parker was furious, but fought down her emotions. She had no desire to let Skye see she could still have such a strong impact on her. Coupled with her anger was piercing disappointment at seeing Skye instead of Morgan. Imagining Morgan and then seeing Skye instead left her reeling with feelings she put aside to examine later. She struggled for an even tone. "Skye, you don't know me well enough to know what my favorite anything is. Now, take yourself and your pizza and leave."

"I see you're going to need a little more time to come around." Skye spoke as if Parker had merely said, "I'm in the middle of something, can you come back later?" Setting the pizza box on a table in the entryway, Skye leaned toward Parker and hugged her. "I'll check in with you later. After all, we'll have lots of opportunities to see each other now since you've managed to get a gig working on my biggest case." Turning toward the door, she called over her shoulder, "Enjoy the pizza!"

Parker watched her leave, unable to move from where she was rooted on the stairs. Erin poked her head in the foyer and, seeing the pizza box and Parker standing alone, asked, "Is everything okay?"

Parker started to answer, when the doorbell rang.

"Don't answer."

Erin stared at her, trying to decipher her strange behavior. "Parker, what's wrong?"

The doorbell rang again.

"Nothing. Don't answer. She'll go away."

A fist pounded on the heavy wooden door and Erin looked back and forth between the door and Parker, trying to decide what to do. A voice yelling from the other side made the decision clear.

"Parker, open the door!" The voice was loud, male, and Dex's. Parker moved past Erin and opened the door herself.

"What took you so long? I know it's a big house, but I swear I was standing out here forever." Spying the pizza box, he asked, "Was the chick who just left the pizza delivery person? She was hot. What kind did you get?"

Parker almost closed the door right in his face but instead resigned herself to having to explain. "You dope. She wasn't a pizza delivery person. She was Skye Keaton. Great powers of observation you have." Ignoring the shocked look on his face, she said, "And I wager the pizza is from Campasis, all the way, well done." It was still her favorite and of course Skye would remember. For all their differences, Parker had to concede Skye was a stellar detective with amazing powers of observation and ability to memorize detail, though Parker wasn't particularly impressed Skye remembered her favorite kind of pizza.

"Well, we may as well eat while you tell me what's going on." He picked up the pizza box and waited for Parker to follow him to the kitchen. Erin followed along and joined them at the table. Dex grabbed a slice of pizza and nodded toward Parker, urging her to start talking.

"I don't know what to say. I don't know why she showed up here tonight." Parker didn't feel like getting into the fact Skye had asked her out this morning. "Asked" wasn't the word for it anyway. She had more like ordered Parker to go out with her. Her authoritarian ways had always been a source of contention in both their personal and professional lives. Parker often told Skye she needed someone much more pliant, someone who actually liked being bossed around. Skye's consistent reply had been that it wouldn't be as much fun if the other person gave in without a fight. Funny, Parker thought, for someone who professed to like a good fight, Skye sure had caved when Parker asked her to fight for what was right. *It may be she just likes to fight.* Parker rolled the revelation around in her mind and decided the assessment fit. Skye liked conflict, and she and Parker had been consumed with it when they were together. The heat of their conflict inflamed both passion and anger by turns, but at the end of the day, Parker decided she craved the consistency of compromise.

She gave Erin an abbreviated explanation. "Skye used to be my partner on the force. She's the lead detective on the case we're working on now. I saw her this morning at the courthouse and she expressed an interest in meeting. I said it wouldn't be appropriate, but Skye has her own ideas about what's appropriate and what's not. I sent her packing."

Dex interjected, "But not without getting her to leave the pizza— smooth move, Parker."

Erin sighed. "As usual, your life is way more exciting than mine. I'm on my way over to Bob's. Mind if I grab a few slices to take with?"

After Erin left Dex casually finished off the pizza. Parker begged off, her stomach shut down after the events of the day.

"So," Dex asked, "are you going to tell me the real reason Skye was here?"

"Pretty much what I told Erin. If Skye had some other reason for coming here than getting under my skin, I don't have a clue what it was. I didn't exactly invite her in for tea and conversation."

"Weird."

"Not if you know her. She probably wanted to pump me for information on the defense. Skye's scruples allow her lots of leeway when she's working on a case. Speaking of cases, what's the word on our little side project?"

Dex's face lit up. "It's a go. Professor Bradley's hired an investigator who works with Ray Ramirez's firm. If the judge denies our motion, Morgan will foot the bill herself. You and I will team up with him to interview witnesses and go through the rest of the evidence. We have our first meeting tomorrow."

"Piece of cake. Way to go!"

Dex shook his head. "It wasn't as easy. Professor Bradley required a lot of convincing. You were right. She has a bit of a hang-up about having us former law enforcement types doing the investigating. Has she never worked the other side?"

"No, she hasn't. But remember, my friend, up until this semester, I never would've pictured you working for the defense. Did it ever occur to you her reservations might be because we're students and this is a high-profile murder case? She might be a little worried about trusting us because of our lack of legal experience."

Dex threw a pizza crust at her. "There you go. Sticking up for your girlfriend. I knew this is how things would shake out."

Parker's mouth fell open and Dex quickly added, "Parker, I was kidding."

His expression was earnest and Parker rolled his words around in her head. At first she wanted to beat him over the head with the pizza box, but one word in particular gave her pause. *Girlfriend.* She repeated it silently to herself. Despite her growing pessimism about any sort of future with Morgan, she had to admit "girlfriend" had a nice ring.

CHAPTER FIFTEEN

W hy, if it isn't Parker Casey. How're ya doing, girl?"
Jake Simons hadn't changed one bit since the last time
Parker saw him. He was still the same grandfatherly man, dressed in a
tan poplin suit, smelling of tobacco and peppermint. Parker speculated
he must own at least half a dozen of the same suits, since she had never
seen him sporting any other outfit. His close-cropped hair was whiter
than she remembered. Parker had known Jake since she graduated from
the academy. A former cop himself, he had been a regular fixture at the
department, always scouting out leads and keeping up acquaintances
with those who had the power and resources to funnel information his
way. Parker had had only a few interactions with him and, frankly, she
was surprised he remembered her.

"I'm good, Jake, real good. You've met Dex?"

Jake nodded toward Dex. "Sure have. He filled me in on the
basic details. Ms. Bradley just called to say she was on her way. In the
meantime, why don't we sort through all these papers and let's see what
we have?"

The three settled around the oak table in the small conference
room at the Ramirez Law Firm. Ray Ramirez had generously donated
the space to the Chavez defense team for a war room. Already the room
was covered with flip charts and flow charts detailing strategy for the
upcoming trial. Empty food and drink containers filled the trash cans to
overflowing. Although the police detectives spent weeks investigating
Camille Burke's death, the fruits of their labor had only recently been
released to the defense. The students on the team were appalled to
learn how late in the game they might receive this information. Morgan

and Ford had explained they'd received some of the information even sooner than the law required. The moment the case was set for trial, the defense team filed discovery motions requesting copies of the evidence against their client as well as any evidence in the possession of the State favorable to Luis's case. This latter type of evidence was called *Brady* evidence in honor of the Supreme Court case requiring prosecutors to hand exonerating information over to the defense. However, with a few narrow exceptions, the State was not required to hand over most of the evidence requested in a defendant's discovery motion until moments before they intended to use it. It was not uncommon in the courtroom for crime scene photos to be tossed on the desk of opposing counsel seconds before the prosecutor questioned the witness who had taken the photos.

Some prosecutors believed the primary reason for sharing evidence before trial was to advance plea negotiations while others held a genuine belief the system worked better when the playing field was leveled, at least to some extent, by sharing the evidence before the start of trial. Gibson rode the fence. She provided more than she had to, but later than many would have. Certainly, it had been clear once Morgan entered the case, that plea deals were out of the question. Morgan had a reputation as a trial lawyer for a reason. She wasn't afraid to try the tough cases and her appearance in a case usually meant a jury would decide her client's fate.

The group was reviewing the catalog of evidence in the trial notebooks Gerald had prepared, when Morgan entered the room. She caught Parker's glance and winced at the well of hurt in her eyes. Morgan willed herself not to respond with anything more than a pleasant smile. She had made peace with her decision that no personal contact was the only way for both of them to emerge unscarred through the gauntlet of emotions laid down by their shared intimacy. Morgan's plan would sting now but, like ripping off a bandage, the pain would be over quickly. Resigned to her plan, Morgan focused on the purpose of the meeting.

"I'm going to get you started, but then I have to meet with Ford to go over our plan for jury selection." Morgan flipped through the notebook in front of her. "I'd like you to focus on witnesses. We don't have the State's witness list yet, but we can construct a likely list from the individuals identified on the police report. I know we've talked about motive and how the State doesn't have to prove Luis had a motive to kill Camille, but juries want to know the 'why.' Chaos isn't comfortable, and for someone to kill a person for no reason at all, especially when he hasn't exhibited any violent tendencies in the past, can provide exactly the kind of doubt we can argue is reasonable enough to merit an acquittal."

Dex chimed in. "So, you want us to find out if someone else had a motive?"

"Precisely," Morgan answered. "Start with the rest of the staff at the Burke household. Most of them have already been interviewed by the police. Luis says he was working on the plumbing when he heard gunshots. Someone in the house must have seen him working. Then find out who Camille's friends are and interview them. We know virtually nothing about her other than she was the only daughter in a fabulously wealthy family. Contact as many people as you can and have summaries of your interviews ready by the end of the week."

"What about character witnesses?" Jake asked. "Would you like us to hold off on that?"

"Go ahead and identify some, but you can wait on those interviews till next week. We'll use most of the character witnesses for the punishment phase of the trial." Morgan grinned. "I like to be prepared, but I'm a little superstitious about preparing for a loss.

"I have to run. Any questions?" Seeing there were no questions, Morgan made a hasty exit, avoiding any eye contact with Parker.

❖

Parker watched Morgan's retreat and pondered the coolness of their recent interactions. She couldn't put her finger on the problem. She didn't feel any animosity between them, but there was a distinct formality that didn't usually exist between people who had seen each other naked. Parker realized she had her answer about what Morgan wanted from her. The answer was sex, and she had gotten all she wanted and was ready to move on. *Fine, I can move on too.* Saying it was the easy part.

"Hey, Parker, wake up." Dex snapped his fingers in her direction. "Any ideas how to find out who Camille's friends are?"

Parker shook off her malaise and brought her mind back to the task at hand. "Maybe we can get her transcript, talk to her teachers, find out who else was enrolled in her classes." She paused as a nugget of information struggled its way into her consciousness. "Seems like I talked to someone recently who knew her." She drummed her fingers on the table. "Oh yeah! My roommate, Erin. She was in her undergraduate class. She might have some ideas."

Dex grinned. "She's cute. I'll talk to her."

"Settle down, playboy. She has a boyfriend."

"For now."

"Enough, you two." Jake interrupted their friendly banter. "I'll get a subpoena for Camille's transcript, but go ahead and talk to Erin. She might have some leads on folks we can talk to who Camille knew outside of school."

Parker nodded agreement with his plan. As Jake and Dex started a list of the known witnesses, she flipped through the pages of the autopsy report. "Hey, Jake, is Doc Hudson still practicing? He must be a hundred years old by now."

Jake shook his head at the mention of the doddering pathologist. "A hundred and ten, and yes, he's still posing as a doctor. The only redeeming fact is he's only allowed to work on dead bodies."

"I don't see the toxicology report. Any idea where it might be?"

"Why would they have done a tox screen?" Dex asked. "Wasn't she found shot to death in her own bedroom at home?"

"Toxicology screens are usually standard requests on suspected homicides." Parker was puzzled but then she realized he probably didn't work many homicides as a DEA agent. "The object of the autopsy is to rule out causes of death, not to merely accept the obvious. It's a simple test and it doesn't require any extra effort beyond filling out the request and sending off the samples. There's no reason not to do one. Let's put it in our list of follow-up items."

While Dex made a note, Jake placed the papers in front of him to the side and said, "I'm going over to the jail later this afternoon to see Luis. Do either of you have any insight about his version of what happened?"

"He's not much help. Like Professor Bradley said, Luis says he was working on the plumbing in one of the downstairs hall bathrooms when he heard what sounded like a gunshot. He went inside to investigate, heard sounds upstairs, and found Camille Burke lying in a pool of blood with her face missing."

"His prints are on the gun and his boot prints are all over the room," Jake observed.

"He picked up the gun and he must have gotten blood on his boots when he was checking to see if she was still alive."

Parker chimed in. "Does he have an explanation for why he ran from the house?"

"Not a good one. He said Teddy Burke saw him holding the gun, so he dropped it and took off. He ran because he was scared he would be blamed."

Jake shook his head. "Full of holes. How the hell are we going to explain the fact he didn't call the cops, that he hid out?"

"Well, he has his reasons, but we can't use them. About eight years ago, Luis was arrested with his nephew, Raul, who was driving a car he had 'borrowed.' While investigating whether the car was stolen, the cops found drugs in the car. Luis says he didn't know the drugs were in the car, but he took the fall for his nephew. Raul was enrolled in school and would've lost his scholarship. Luis figured he didn't have as much to lose as Raul, so he took the heat. The public defender who handled his case got him probation, but the prior can be used against him if he were to testify. Luis says the cops treated him like shit before and he was in no hurry to call them in on this occasion. He figured there was no way they would believe he wasn't involved."

"So your fella has a bad habit of being in the wrong place at the wrong time."

Parker's first reaction to Jake's words was to vehemently defend her client and ask Jake how the hell he could work for their side when he was obviously already convinced of Luis's guilt. She forced herself to hear beyond the actual words and realized Jake's cynicism represented a major obstacle they would need to overcome with the jury. It was absolutely necessary that they keep Luis's record out of the evidence, and the only way to ensure it would stay out was for him not to testify. The pressure was on. They needed something to present in Luis's defense besides Luis himself, and she was committed to finding that something.

"Jake, while you go see Luis, Dex and I will find out what we can about Camille's friends. How about we meet up in the morning and start interviewing whoever we've identified?"

Jake and Dex nodded their agreement.

While she helped Dex construct a list of the people they would need to interview, Parker shuffled through the crime scene photos again. The image of Camille's body sprawled in the throes of a violent death clawed at a memory of another lurid crime scene she would never forget. When Dex wasn't looking, she stuffed a copy of the autopsy report and a few of the photos in her notebook. She told Dex she had an errand to run before she could get started on their project. Her actual plan was to do a little research about the missing toxicology screen. She cringed inside at the semi-lie, but she wasn't ready to explain why she was so focused on the autopsy report since her instincts were probably off.

Chapter Sixteen

Parker paced the room. She hated this place. Necessity had called her to this section of SWIFS, the Southwestern Institute of Forensic Sciences, on too many occasions to count, and her insides twisted up without fail whenever she walked through the door. No amount of cold air and sterile solution could block out the heavy stink of death. Every room in the building reeked and she knew when she left she would carry the scent.

"Detective Casey?"

Parker was startled at the use of her former title. The woman standing before her was wearing a white lab coat and sporting a clipboard. She was younger than Parker expected her to be. And way better looking. *Ah*, she thought, *now I understand why Kelsey developed this "professional" relationship.*

"I'm Parker Casey. I assume you're Dr. Williams."

The woman extended her hand. "Lauren Williams. Dr. James said you had some toxicology questions. If you'll follow me to my office, we can talk there." She started off down the hall without waiting for a reply. "This way, Detective."

The use of the title jarred her still. Kelsey must have used it to secure this meeting, banking on the pretense of authority to get Parker in the door. Parker vowed to correct the misimpression the moment they reached the privacy of Dr. Williams's office. She wanted information, but not at the expense of lying to get it. Parker considered contacting one of the many doctors she knew in the pathology department from her time on the force. When she'd run through the list of potential contacts, she realized she had no idea how any one of them would react to hearing from her. She had cut herself off completely from the department and, as a result, severed her connection to anyone she knew in her professional capacity as a cop. If she had it to do over, she might have figured out a way to preserve her valuable contacts, but she spent all her energy in the weeks and months after she was fired trying to find the energy to get out of bed. Networking for a future career seemed a waste of time when she didn't foresee a future at all.

The crime scene photos and the autopsy report raised more questions than they answered. Parker had turned to Kelsey for assistance filling in the blanks, and Kelsey had set up this appointment with Dr. Williams. Parker pulled up a chair and settled in across from Dr. Williams's desk.

"Before we get started, I need you to know I'm not a detective. I used to be, but I'm now a law student working on a case. A homicide. Your office did the autopsy and I have some questions about it."

Dr. Williams looked at the papers in Parker's hand. "Did I do the report?"

"No, you didn't."

"You should be talking to the doctor who did the report. Even if I were to tell you something different, I would have a conflict if you asked me to testify against one of my colleagues."

"Who said anything about testifying?" Parker hedged. She was here to get answers about procedure. She wasn't asking her to reach a different conclusion than Dr. Hudson, but she did want someone to say a tox screen should have been done and list the reasons why. It would be best if the testimony came from someone who knew the protocol for this office and, if this doctor was willing to commit, Parker would have Jake here with a subpoena in no time flat. Then the judge could decide if the doctor's conflict was more important than the truth. "I'm not here to get you to give a different conclusion. I would like to ask some questions about protocol. For my own edification."

"Fair enough. Dr. James is a friend and I told her I would help. What are your questions?"

Parker felt like she was cheating. She'd already gone over her questions with Kelsey, who had done a rotation in pathology, and knew what the answers should be. With Kelsey's help and her own experience watching dozens of autopsies performed, she was ready to poke holes of reasonable doubt into the report prepared by Dr. Hudson. She laid the report and the crime scene photos in front of Dr. Williams and gave her a moment to flip through the pages before posing her first question. "When is it appropriate not to request a toxicology screen?"

"I'm not sure what you're asking. A tox screen is part of the protocol on all autopsies. If we do an autopsy, we do a tox screen."

"Are there any circumstances where you wouldn't wait on the results before assigning a cause of death?"

"Sure. If the cause of death was readily apparently from the physical exam, there would be no need to wait on the results of the tox screen."

"Okay, so conversely, what, if anything, would cause you to wait?"

Dr. Williams picked up the crime scene photos and studied them before answering. "Why do I think you already know the answer to the question?" Dr. Williams smiled.

Parker returned the smile. "Because a good lawyer never asks a question when she doesn't already know the answer?" Leaning in, she assumed her very best earnest expression. "Seriously, Doctor, I know what I think the answer should be, but I want to know your opinion. I think the cause of death determination should have been suspended until the toxicology results were in. I think the findings in this report were based on the obvious, but not the actual cause of death. Maybe I'm wrong, but there's only one way to find out."

"As much as I'd love to play Nancy Drew with you, if a tox screen wasn't done, I can't order one."

"Can't or won't?" Parker challenged.

"If you were indeed a detective, you know this office has procedures we are required to follow. First, this isn't my case—you should be talking to Dr. Hudson. Second, even if it were my case, I don't act at the direction of defense counsel. I work for the county." She examined the photos again. "Now, if the detective or prosecutor assigned to the case asked for additional information, I'd be happy to oblige." Dr. Williams's expression shouted what her words did not say and Parker got the message loud and clear. The good doctor harbored some measure of interest in learning if there was more to Camille Burke's death than the conclusory results contained in the "final" version of the autopsy report. Yet she was making it clear Parker would have to show her hand if she wanted to find the answers to her questions about Camille Burke's cause of death.

Parker gathered her papers, thanked the doctor, and left the palace of death stoked with purpose. She needed to talk to Morgan about their options. She had enough experience to know the defense couldn't order the medical examiner to run tests. That would amount to asking them to create evidence. The defense could certainly ask for their own expert to run tests on the evidence in possession of the medical examiner, but they would have to file a motion with the judge to obtain access. In addition, because Luis was indigent, they would have to ask the judge for money to hire their own expert to conduct the tests. If the defense wanted tests, they would have to give the judge a damn good reason why. Parker had a hunch, but she wasn't confident her hunch would meet the judge's definition of good cause.

❖

Aimee's unexpected visit was a pleasant surprise, though Morgan suspected it was hardly a coincidence. Yolanda escorted Aimee to Morgan's office offering some lame story about how she and Aimee just had lunch. As it happened Aimee had an updated list of homes to give Morgan, and Yolanda suggested she might be in her office.

Morgan had to admit she was relieved to be sifting through sheets of home details rather than the gory evidence of Camille Burke's demise, even if the whole ruse of Aimee's appearance was Yolanda trying to play matchmaker. Fact was, she could do worse than Aimee. They had spent a fair amount of time together over the past month looking at houses. Morgan liked the way Aimee adjusted the search based on her expressed likes and dislikes. She reasoned away the fact she didn't feel anything for her beyond surface-level attraction. There was no burning, no yearning, to be in her presence, but Aimee did provide a pleasant personal distraction from the stress of the murder case. And, Morgan reflected, spending time with Aimee was completely appropriate. Although they had a professional relationship, they were both adults capable of distinguishing their roles based on circumstance. A nagging inner voice queried whether she thought of Parker as an adult. *Well, of course she's an adult, but our roles are different. I'm in the position of deciding a part of her future and that places us in decidedly different places.* Even as Morgan had the thought, she questioned the rationale.

Her feelings for Parker were vastly different than the shade of attraction she felt for Aimee. She burned and yearned to feel a glance from Parker, to run her hands through her wild hair, and to fall back into the strong and gentle arms of the tough yet sensitive woman who sat in the third row of her trial practice class.

Morgan shook off the sensory memory and focused on Aimee. Aimee Howard was smart, beautiful, and interested. Those factors, combined with the fact she didn't make her feel feverish, probably meant Aimee was the perfect choice for a distraction. Morgan was rocking around several ideas for letting Aimee know she might be up for more than a little house-hunting, when her office door swung open.

❖

Parker didn't have a clue what she would say to Morgan, but she wanted to share her theory with the person she was sure would appreciate it most. Parker toyed with the idea of calling Dex or Jake first, but she ultimately decided in favor of impressing the teacher. *Who am I kidding*, she thought, *I want an excuse to see her. Alone.*

Parker pushed open the door to Morgan's office. "Morgan, you are not going to believe—"

The blonde's bright smile smashed Parker's thoughts into little bits and Parker was too thrown to pick up the pieces. All she could digest was that a curvaceous beauty was comfortably sprawled along the edge of Morgan's desk and leaning too close to the object of Parker's desire. It was the blonde from the Lakeside. The one Morgan had been sharing wine and laughs with weeks ago. Parker's mind slowly opened to the flood of facts pouring in. The beautiful woman who was breaking bread with Morgan was here now, in her office, looking for all the world like she owned the place. Giggles, whispers. Could this have been Morgan's ex? Maybe. There was no doubt there was something going on between them. *Must. Leave.*

"Sorry, I should've knocked." Parker left faster than the apology fell from her lips, and the last words trailed behind her as she stalked down the hallway.

❖

"Sensitive student?" Aimee asked after Parker's abrupt departure.

"We're working on a special project and my students are used to ready access." Morgan knew her response sounded lame the moment it left her lips. She wanted to run after Parker but knew she couldn't, at least not without looking foolish. As she wondered what was behind Parker's strange reaction, she missed Aimee's next words. It wasn't until Aimee's parting words, "I'm looking forward to Friday night," that she realized she had made a date with Aimee.

Parker paced the tiny entryway to Skye's duplex while she debated if coming to this place was a smart decision. She acknowledged smart choices weren't her forte lately, and her silent admission was loud and clear. She couldn't help but think of Morgan. Every day, she listened to her sharp and sure voice, witnessed her poise, and delighted in the fire dancing in her eyes. Morgan Bradley was everything she could ever want and nothing she could ever have. Seeing her every day was painful. Seeing her today in the presence of a woman who so obviously desired her was unbearable. Every time she saw Morgan she was hungry for more. She had had countless encounters with women and rarely repeated the exercise. Though Dallas was a big city, she hadn't been able to completely avoid seeing some of these one-night stands again, but none had ever left her empty, wanting. Not like this.

Poor judgment be damned, she thought, and raised her hand to ring the bell. Skye Keaton had been more than a one-night stand and look how their relationship had ended. Skye, her partner, her lover, had killed Parker's ability to feel. Until now.

"Casey, I knew you'd come around. I don't have any pizza to offer, but you're welcome to come in." Skye was dressed in a wrinkled T-shirt and cut-offs, her hair mussed, her eyes sleepy. She looked great.

"Hey, Skye, I'm not hungry, but I want to talk to you about something important." Parker looked around. Not a change in sight. Like its resident, the apartment was exactly the same as she remembered. Parker made her way to the living room and settled on the couch. Skye watched her as if assessing the "something important" Parker was there to discuss. Her eyes strayed to the folder Parker had placed on the coffee table.

"What's in the folder?"

Parker decided she wasn't ready to get into the reason for her visit. Her past consisted of a host of memories, many of them shared with Skye. Looking into her eyes, Parker felt long-dead feelings stir in anguish. She needed to numb those feelings before she could talk business.

"Do you have any beer?"

Skye didn't blink at the non sequitur. She left the room, returning moments later with two cold bottles. She pushed aside a random array of junk mail, indicating an old magazine to serve as a coaster. Parker downed half her beer and leaned back.

"Casey, I'm trying not to take personally your need to preface whatever you have to talk to me about with alcohol. But if you wait much longer to spit it out, I'm going to get the wrong idea."

Parker tilted the bottle and fortified herself with another healthy draft. She could sense that whatever her original reason for being here, she was about to start down a path she hadn't expected and the alcohol was a necessary provision. "Skye, did you ever love me?"

Skye's sharp intake of breath was the only sound in the room. Parker watched her face but couldn't read anything from Skye's expression. Gone was the cocky jeer of the Teflon-coated detective. Parker saw fear replace shock and then settle into pain. Skye's pain cried out and Parker answered with her own. "Then why?"

The one-word question packed a punch and Skye looked worn from the blow. "You know why. You made me choose. I only picked what I thought you would've picked. No one was more surprised than me when you decided to be all honorable and throw yourself on your sword. I thought we had an understanding. We meant something to each other, but the job meant more. I didn't have any idea it wasn't the same for you. Not until you decided to walk the plank, all to protect the reputation of a crazy pervert."

"Don't you think you're simplifying things a bit? You lied. You should've known me well enough to know I would never lie for anything, not even the job, and I certainly would never ask you to lie for me."

"We're different. I loved you in my way." Skye contemplated her beer bottle for a very long time and then met Parker's eyes. "I still love you, you know."

Parker shook her head. The revelation fizzled and her reply referenced a past long gone. "I loved you too, Skye, but it was different. It is different."

"We don't have to 'love' each other to have a good time. I seem to remember some great times." The edge softened into want and Skye drew closer, clearly angling for a kiss. Parker stiffened at first, then questioned her own hesitancy. *What the hell? I'm here and she wants me. Maybe this is all there is. Longing and gratification. Love is too fancy a concept when all you need is to satisfy a craving.* Her lips touched Skye's and her mind stopped whirring. She melted against her waiting mouth and gave in to the embrace. Skye's fingers sliding under her soft cotton shirt left a trail of want in their path to her breasts. Breaths, deep and quick, registered the passion. Passion she did not want to feel and did not seek. The beer was not working. She was anything but numb. Ignoring the sour taste of love's memory, she met Skye's kiss with equal fervor, seeking new flavor to replace the taint of the past.

Locked in passion, they exchanged hungry grasps with lips and hands. Parker's head was spinning as she whipped through feelings she didn't recognize—torrid, hungry feelings. Skye was toxic and as she drank her in, her mind spun in heady clouds that hid rational judgment. No one else ever made her feel this way. Wait—a thought fought its way forward. The way she felt with Morgan was like this. No, she insisted, it was different. Her fuzzy head acknowledged she was right. It was different. What she felt with Morgan was as consuming, but it was not toxic. If she slept with Skye, she would feel empty afterward. Yet after passion with Morgan, she was full. It was the desire to maintain the satisfaction that kept her wanting more.

Parker placed a hand on Skye's chest and eased her back. "Skye, look at me." Skye eased open hazy lids and cast a dreamy look at her. "This isn't why I came here tonight."

"Plans change, Casey."

"Not for me, they don't." Parker pulled back farther. "I'm sorry I let things get out of hand."

Skye adjusted herself into a more powerful seated position and shrugged. "Things are nowhere near out of hand. I was having a good time. I guess you don't know how anymore." She was petulant. This Skye was as familiar to Parker as the cocky cop who showed no fear in the streets or the courtroom. Parker knew she better act fast before

Skye's mood turned stormy, which was likely when she hadn't gotten her way. She reached for the folder on the coffee table. "Here, I want you to look at something."

As Skye flipped through the pages, she shook her head. "Casey, we can't talk about this."

"Why not? The evidence is what the evidence is. Are you scared I'm going to read your mind about the prosecution's theory? Seriously, Skye, like I don't already know what Gibson thinks. Luis Chavez was an ungrateful employee of the Burke family who lusted after their prize daughter until he couldn't stand it anymore. One fateful evening he decided to take what wasn't offered and when he was spurned, he delivered a fateful blow. Am I close?"

"Okay, so you've got it all figured out. What do you want from me?"

Parker shoved a couple of the crime scene photos under Skye's nose. "Take a good look at these and tell me you don't see something wrong."

Skye barely glanced at the photos before replying. "You're not kidding. Camille Burke's deader than a doornail."

"You always were the sensitive type."

"Don't get all self-righteous on me, Casey. You sure picked the wrong side of the law to show you care about innocent victims."

Parker shook the photos. "Skye, don't get off track here. Take a close look and tell me what you see."

Skye focused on the photos. Camille Burke was in the grip of death, a pool of blood fanned out from her head. The medical examiner estimated the time of death to have occurred within a couple of hours of the police's arrival, not surprising since Teddy Burke made the 911 call from the house moments after he heard shots fired. Camille Burke had been shot in the face at close range. The result was a pulped-up wreckage of brains and blood. No eyes, no nose, no mouth. Camille wouldn't need the senses those parts provided anymore. The shooter made sure. No matter how many times Parker looked at photos of the mangled, lifeless victims of murder, she would never stop feeling pain. She took small pleasure from the grimace that crossed Skye's face. It was nice to know she hadn't become completely desensitized.

"Give me a clue, Parker. What am I supposed to be looking for beyond the obvious?"

"Look at her arms, legs, her hands." Parker gestured at the lifeless form of Camille Burke. Her limbs were contorted, her hands frozen into fists, clutching only air. "The ME noted rigor at the scene. When was the last time you saw a two-hour-old corpse in full rigor?"

"Maybe he made a typo."

"Give me a break, Skye. I know you well enough to know you've reviewed the autopsy report already and you probably observed the exam. If you thought there was a mistake, you would have made sure it was corrected. The photos leave no doubt. She was in rigor probably before you even got to the scene."

"So what?"

"So, maybe she didn't die from the gunshot wound."

Skye snorted. "You've lost your mind." She shoved one of the photos at Parker. "Look at her face!"

"Skye, look at the rest of her! She's balled up like someone shocked her with a cattle prod. Have you ever seen a gunshot victim twisted up that way?"

Skye didn't reply, but she appeared unable to look away from the gruesome corpse in the photo. Parker read her silence as a tacit invitation to continue. "I have an idea about what would have caused what you're seeing there."

"You do, huh?"

"Poison. Strychnine. It has that effect on the body, causes severe convulsions, quick onset of rigor. Dr. Hudson should have caught the signs and ordered a tox screen. Hell, he should have ordered a tox screen no matter what."

"Gimme a break. Why waste the taxpayer's money? Her fucking head was blown off. Even if you're right, it doesn't matter."

Parker looked hard at her. Though it had been several years since they worked side by side, she could tell the difference between confident conclusions and plain old bluster. This was bluster and Parker was determined to get beneath it. "Humor me, Skye. You don't want the defense to try to drum up reasonable doubt. Order a tox screen, then decide for yourself if the results make a difference in how you see the case." When Skye didn't immediately respond, Parker pushed a hair more. "If you don't want to piss off Hudson, get Dr. Williams to do it. I think she's actually interested in finding out what happened.

Frankly, I thought you'd be concerned about anything that casts a shade of reasonable doubt all over your case."

It took less than a second for Parker to realize she had said too much. Skye went ballistic. "Dr. Williams, huh? What the hell does she know about this case?" Skye pressed on. "Did you talk to her behind my back?"

Years apart hadn't changed a thing. Skye knew how to press her buttons. "Behind your back? Since when are all county employees subject to your bidding? I have every right to talk to whoever I want. In fact, I have a duty to do whatever it takes to zealously represent my client."

"Your client? Your client is a murderer. He deserves nothing less than to rot in prison for the rest of his hopefully very long life. Don't act all self-righteous about your duty. I have a duty too—to protect the citizens of Dallas County, and before you dis it, you might want to remember it wasn't so long ago you took an oath to do the same."

Parker bit back the sharp retort hovering on her lips. Would there ever be a time she and Skye could talk about things that mattered without battling? *You didn't fight when you were talking about love.* Parker shook away the thought and focused on the topic of the moment. She knew Skye well enough to know once she was this worked up, she would only get more agitated if Parker persisted. Holding up a hand, Parker gave in. "I hear you. Let's forget I asked." Noting Skye's surprised look, she realized Skye fully expected her to put up more of a fight. "I have a lot to do, so I'm going to head out. Thanks for talking to me." Parker left, smug with the knowledge Skye wasn't getting the battle she was armed to fight.

CHAPTER SEVENTEEN

Is this a date or did you feel obligated to go out with me because I'm the best realtor in town and you're desperate to find a house?"

Morgan stopped fiddling with her salad and looked solidly into Aimee's questioning eyes. "Honestly?" She waited for Aimee's nod. "I don't know."

"I get the impression you're distracted."

Morgan reached for words to express how she was feeling, a task made difficult by the fact she didn't know what she was feeling. "It's this case we're working on," Morgan lied. "It's complicated and all-consuming." She struggled to deliver the statement without betraying its untruth.

"Uh-huh." Aimee's tone conveyed clear disbelief.

"And I have some personal things going on right now." Morgan's voice trailed off.

"At the risk of prying, Yolanda told me the reason you're in the market for a house is because you recently broke it off with a longtime partner."

Had she broken it off, or had things between her and Tina merely broken? Once she might have been annoyed with Yolanda for sharing such personal information, but tonight she was actually relieved since it gave her the perfect out. Try as she might, she wasn't up for dating, and as appealing as Aimee might be, she wasn't... Morgan quit the thought with full knowledge she planned to insert Parker's name.

"It's true I recently went through a civil, but nonetheless nasty breakup." Morgan declined to add more, thinking it was safer to let Aimee fill in the blanks.

"Too bad. You're stunning, and smart too. I was hoping you were available."

Morgan laughed at her frank assessment of the situation. She liked Aimee Howard. She was a competent professional and cute and funny to boot. But even pushing aside the allure of the handsome Parker Casey, she could envision only friendship with Aimee. "Sorry to disappoint. I could use a friend, though."

Aimee sighed dramatically and grabbed the bread basket. "Friend it is. Pass the butter. Now that I'm no longer trying to impress you, I may as well eat what I please."

❖

"She's a great catch."

Morgan hid her surprise at seeing Yolanda standing in the hall outside her office. She had returned to the law school after her date with Aimee and didn't think anyone else was in the building "She is. If you're fishing."

Continuing the metaphor, Yolanda tossed back a line. "Or depending on what you're fishing for. You don't have to marry her, for crying out loud, but you could at least have a good time. You're back too early to have had a good time."

"Spoken like a true old married lady."

"I am not a lady. Please, allow me to live vicariously through you. Now that you're single, you're bound to have a ton of great adventures and I want to hear about every one. Don't shoot me for speeding things along."

Morgan sighed and resigned herself to Yolanda's good intentions. "Tell me your own life isn't so boring you waited here to find out about my dinner."

Yolanda's features rearranged into a more serious expression. "Actually, no. I need to talk to you about something and I wanted to get it out of the way. Can we talk now?"

Morgan gestured Yolanda into her office. "Okay if we talk in here?"

As Yolanda took a seat across from her desk, Morgan wondered if the Burke family had gone over the dean's head to try to keep Morgan and her students from working on the case. She had told Yolanda about the incident with Teddy the day after it happened. The day after she and Parker downed a bottle of Scotch, she remembered. Yolanda told Morgan not to worry about Teddy's outburst. She had made it clear to his father the university had to be free from monetary influences when it came to student projects. She had told him she regretted this particular project would have an impact on his daughter's case, but their grief did not give his son, Teddy, free rein to threaten one of her valuable and popular professors. Morgan hadn't heard from Teddy Burke since, but she wondered if perhaps he found a sympathetic ear on the board of regents. She was completely unprepared for the real reason behind Yolanda's late night visit.

"Are you romantically involved with Parker Casey?"

Morgan looked at the earnest expression on her face. Frantic thoughts raced while she fought to hide a telling reaction. She made a snap decision to deflect. "What in the world would give you that idea?" She struggled not to wince at the insincerity of her response. Yolanda was her friend. She had shared years of life's ups and downs with her, yet she couldn't bring herself to answer the question directly. Should she share her feelings or the reality of the situation? She had decided nothing was going to develop between her and Parker, but she couldn't deny the steady pull of attraction whenever she thought about her. The allure extended beyond the desire to touch. Her glimpse of Parker's vulnerable side tempted her to seek out the bigger picture of her heart and soul, but she was firmly set against giving in to temptation. *Aren't I?*

Yolanda waited through the silence as if giving Morgan time to reconsider her initial response. Morgan took the cue. "No. And yes." Noting Yolanda's raised eyebrow, she pressed on. "Remember at the beginning of the semester, you and I had brunch at La Duni?"

"Yes," Yolanda replied, hesitantly.

"We talked about the first night I arrived back in Dallas? I went out to surprise Tina and I was the one who got surprised?"

Yolanda nodded as she recalled their beginning of the semester brunch. "Of course. Yes. I remember—Tina was all over some other woman right there in front of you." She stopped as if waiting for Morgan to say more, but Morgan merely widened her eyes, urging Yolanda to remember more details. Realization dawned in shades. "Wait, I remember! You met some hot woman, had mind-blowing sex, and went home the next morning with nothing but a smile to commemorate your night of wild abandon." She smiled when Morgan confirmed her recollection, then frowned. "What does your night of passion have to do with my question?"

Morgan dove in. "The hot woman with whom I had mind-blowing sex? Well, that would be Parker Casey."

"Fuck."

"Well said."

"Seriously, Morgan. This isn't good."

"What was I supposed to do? It wasn't like I knew who she was."

"Tell me this—have you had sex with Parker since you found out she was one of your students?"

Silence. Morgan knew her lack of response spoke volumes and she waited for Yolanda's judgment.

"Shit."

"Language. I don't think I've ever heard you cuss so much."

"I'm upset. This is a grave situation and you don't seem to be taking it seriously."

Morgan considered her assessment and decided Yolanda was wrong. She did take the situation seriously. After all, wasn't she the one who had been so adamant with Parker about their inability to see each other anymore, once they discovered their respective roles? Why was she so resistant to let Yolanda see how seriously she considered these circumstances? Well, for one thing, she wasn't used to having a boss. For years, Morgan ran her own show and was used to operating by her own set of rules. Plus she and Parker were both adults. She knew her assessment was shallow and Yolanda considered this a serious situation. She held a position of authority over Parker and even though her strong ethics enabled her to separate personal feelings from her professional ones, the mere appearance of impropriety would be enough for someone to question any grade she gave Parker, high or low.

"Morgan?"

"I heard you. I don't know what to say without making you mad. Maybe I'm not cut out for this teacher gig after all. All my life, my every move has been calculated toward a specific end. I have one spontaneous tryst and next thing you know, I've thrown off the balance of the universe. If I were back in practice, this never would have happened." Even as she spoke the words, she cringed at her lapse of logic.

"What, you never would have slept with her?"

"I don't know. All I know is things wouldn't be so complicated if I hadn't."

Yolanda looked long and hard at her, then said, "You haven't acted like things were complicated. I never would have known if someone hadn't said something."

"Who?"

"Who what?"

Glaring, Morgan asked, "Who said something?"

"I can't tell you who." As Morgan's face become heated with anger, she held up a hand. "I can't tell you, because I'm required to keep anonymous the identity of anyone who reports a violation of the honor code." She continued deliberately as if willing Morgan to hear beyond her words, "Because, if you knew the individual's identity, you might be inclined to retaliate against him," she paused for a few beats, "or her by taking some action like," long pause again, "giving whoever it is a bad grade." Yolanda's long, hard stare punctuated the obvious meaning of her words.

Morgan turned through each phrase carefully and considered. *So, a male student in one of my classes ratted on me. He must be in the Advanced Evidence class because it was the only place he would have seen us together. He chose to report me, not Parker, so he must be mad at me for some reason.* The answer was crystal clear. She could see him now, fuming over his assignment to make trial notebooks for the team, while the others handled more substantive work. What in the hell could he have witnessed and why was he so sure his story would be believed? Like a flash, Morgan recalled the day she offered subtle comfort to Parker in class. Gerald's eyes had watched her, full of rancor.

Morgan stored away the knowledge that Gerald Lopez had it in for her and directed her attention to dealing with Yolanda. "So, what are you going to do about this?"

"I guess it depends on what you're going to do."

"What kind of answer is that?"

"A reasoned one." Yolanda sighed. "I don't know what to do, but I have to figure out something. I have no doubt if I don't deal with this, I'll have another formal complaint to deal with"

"And I've been the cause of all of them." As Yolanda started to protest, Morgan waved her off. "Seriously, Yo, it's true. I don't mean to cause so many problems. I'm not cut out for the politics of academia and, frankly, I don't want to be. You better start looking for my replacement."

"Whoa, there. I'm not replacing you, but we do need to figure out how to handle this. Go, do your trial, and when it's over, we'll figure this out."

"What about Parker? Are you going to talk to her about this?" Morgan silently willed Yolanda to wait until after the trial. She didn't want her action to rob Parker of the ability to work on the case, and she knew whatever Yolanda decided, she would be better equipped to deal with the fallout if this case were behind her.

"I do need to talk to her and I intend to. This situation affects her most of all." Yolanda looked hard at Morgan, reading her plea. "It can keep another week. Go get ready for trial."

❖

Morgan stewed in her office for another hour after Yolanda left. She didn't accomplish any real work, but did manage to work up quite a storm of anger over the complications caused by Yolanda's late-night visit. She had half a mind to pack up her office and leave university life behind. Then she could see whoever she wanted and everyone else could be damned.

Did she want a relationship with Parker so badly she would pull up roots here so soon after having found a place to settle? The question sent her spinning. She could name a few things she knew she wanted, but none of them answered the larger question about a relationship. She wanted to crawl up next to Parker and trade whispered versions of their most intimate secrets. She wanted to run her fingers through her thick, unruly hair while listening to her share her favorite color, her favorite food, her favorite music. She wanted to gently slide her hands along the buttons of Parker's jeans and feel her passion on her fingers while they shared their dreams and fears.

Strong knocks jerked Morgan from her thoughts. She scrambled to compose her heated thoughts and croaked "Come in" toward her office door.

"Burning the midnight oil?"

She was surprised to see Jim Spencer. Though their offices were next door to each other, she'd been too busy over the last few weeks to do more than give him a quick wave as they passed in the hall. Ever since their outing at Rangers Ballpark, he made a point of stopping by her office each week to renew his offer to help her with anything, anything at all. While she appreciated his earnest desire to make her feel at home, she had actually settled in on her own. Other than asking him to judge the competition to determine who would work on the Chavez trial team, she brushed off his regular offers of assistance. Seeing him here, late at night, she felt a twinge of guilt at not having reciprocated with some goodwill of her own.

"Actually, I might be merely burning out." She waved him in. "What in the world are you doing here so late on a Friday night?"

"Ruining my reputation as a Casanova, apparently." He grinned. "I had no idea anyone else was here. I could lie to you and say I ran by here after a hot date, but frankly I was on a geeky exam-writing roll and didn't want to risk losing the evil genius mindset. Then I saw Yolanda leaving your office and was overcome with curiosity as to what she would be doing here so late on a Friday night. So I came over to see if you have any juicy gossip you'd care to share. It is your turn, you know."

Morgan stared at his eager expression and pondered an appropriate lie. She decided her efforts to dissemble weren't worth the energy and she plunged in before she could change her mind. "I have a hypothetical question for you."

"Go ahead."

"Suppose a professor had an affair with one of her, or his, students." She stopped to gauge his initial reaction. He nodded, encouraging her to continue. "Is there any way to resolve the situation without sending the world crashing down around them?"

"Pretty broad question, Professor," Jim said, pointedly. "I assume both parties are legally adults?" He waited for her nod. "And the student is currently enrolled in the professor's class?"

Morgan nodded again and added, "The affair started before they ever even knew they would have a teacher-student relationship."

Jim rubbed his chin. "Interesting. So they started seeing each other when there was no professional benefit to be gained by either party."

"Right."

"And they kept seeing each other after they entered into the professional relationship?"

Morgan squirmed a little at the word "seeing," certain Jim assigned more to its meaning than the casual sex she'd experienced so far with Parker. She almost corrected him, but held back. Though she kept referring to her encounters with Parker as casual, they were anything but. Casual sex by definition wouldn't have left her filled with such raw and open need for more.

"And I assume part of the problem stems from the fact neither wants to end the personal part of the relationship."

She had no idea how Parker felt about their relationship or even if Parker thought what they had constituted a relationship. As for herself, she was no closer to an answer about what she wanted. She decided since the question was supposed to be hypothetical, she may as well go out on a limb. "Yes, they want a chance to see where the relationship goes."

"Pass/Fail."

"Excuse me?"

"Pass/Fail. If both parties agree, then she, the student, can get a pass/fail grade, thereby eliminating any suspicion her loving professor gave her a good grade in class because she gets good grades outside the classroom, if you know what I mean. It's more of a big deal for the student, since if she was on track for an excellent grade, her transcript will suffer, but it's better than having to take the whole class over or have no credit for the class at all."

Morgan rolled the thought over in her head. "Interesting solution."

"Sure it is. Of course, my advice is worth what it cost you."

"Then I better pay you something to make it golden. I went to dinner already, but I didn't feel like eating. Are you hungry?"

"Always."

"Lead the way." As she turned off the light to her office, Morgan wondered how Parker would feel about Jim's solution. Even as she had the thought she felt silly. Parker had a lot at stake. She was on track to graduate at the top of her class with an impeccable transcript full of high marks. What in the world was she thinking to consider asking Parker to take a simple "Pass" for six hours of grueling coursework in her chosen field, all because Morgan wanted to see if they had a chance at a relationship? Hell, she didn't have a clue if Parker wanted anything more than what they had already shared. Considering she wasn't sure herself, she had no business asking Parker to join her in disclosing a relationship, especially in light of Parker's past. Parker had already suffered enormous loss as a result of telling the truth. Morgan wasn't going to ask her to risk a similar sacrifice. Doubt crawled in and chilled her warm thoughts of happily ever after. *No, better to finish the trial and bow quietly out of this politically charged teaching gig.* There would still be enough time left in the semester for someone else to take over and assign a real grade to the star student.

CHAPTER EIGHTEEN

W e've talked to most of her friends and we keep hearing the same thing. 'Camille was a wonderful person, a kind and gentle friend. We can't imagine anyone who would want to hurt her.'" Dex pushed aside his notes and rubbed his red eyes. None of them had gotten much sleep in the last week and Parker and Dex, still carrying a full class schedule, were both feeling the pain. They were gathered in a conference room at the law school on Friday afternoon to begin a weekend's worth of last-ditch trial preparation.

"We have one more name: Leslie Hammond. She's out of the country, but she gets back Tuesday. I'll hang out near her apartment and try and catch her when she gets in from the airport," Jake volunteered, seemingly undaunted by the schedule they had all been keeping the last week.

"Okay, but I don't think she'll have anything to add. Even Camille's acquaintances can't imagine she would have any enemies." Parker looked toward the door of their makeshift war room, wondering when Morgan and Ford would join them. The team had worked on separate assignments during the past week, so she hadn't seen much of Morgan and when she had they had been in the company of others, which meant they hadn't spoken about the "incident." Parker was ambivalent. She wanted to square things with Morgan, but she wasn't sure what "square" meant in these circumstances. She was horribly embarrassed that she had run like a chicken at the sight of Morgan with another woman. Hell, they'd only been talking. For all she knew there was nothing going on between them. Even as she finished the thought, she knew she was deluding herself. The blonde had been drooling. And who wouldn't? Morgan was a supreme catch. She was brilliant, tough, sharp, and witty. As if those attributes weren't enough to attract hordes of admirers, she was beautiful as well. Parker resigned herself to the fact she was only one of many admirers and even though she felt like there was more of a connection, Morgan's actions since the other night put a chill on any such thoughts. Morgan had been polite but cool. No more subtle touches and grabbed chances to be close. No more glances held beyond the bounds of professional courtesy. All weekend long, Morgan had directed more questions at Dex and Gerald and rarely met Parker's eyes. She seemed to be making a point to keep both a physical and emotional boundary erected between them. It was as if she had decided to adhere to her original resolution, shared on the park bench the first day of classes, to keep their relationship completely compartmentalized. *Fine,* Parker thought, *I can compartmentalize too. The only chinks in the boundary are a few rounds of sex and me spilling my guts after too much alcohol. Consider it forgotten.* But it wasn't, and she knew in a place deep inside that she had been more intimate with Morgan than with any other person in her life.

❖

"Sorry we're late." Morgan and Ford entered the room, and the group launched into a discussion of what was left to do to prepare for trial. Stealing a glance at Parker, Morgan fought to put her discussion with Yolanda out of her head and concentrate on trial prep.

The one thing Morgan knew she couldn't teach was the most important thing of all. Flexibility. She remembered her first trial. Though she was the lead attorney, a partner at the firm had sat second chair. She wasn't sure at the time if his presence was to provide assistance or to take over when she got so nervous she threw up. She didn't throw up, but she did learn the limited value of the many nights she spent carefully planning the clever cross-examination questions she would ask and the insightful objections she would raise.

Months later, during her fifth trial, she reflected there was only so much preparation you could do for the real thing. Though good defense attorneys hired investigators and researched every angle before the big day, there was no way to prepare for the stories witnesses concocted, often for the first time, while they were on the stand—this after having taken an oath, hand raised high, to tell the truth, nothing but the truth, so help me God. She was often tempted to ask the judge to make the witness show his other hand so she could make sure fingers weren't crossed. After years of trying cases, she had come to the conclusion most witnesses made shit up, and the shit they made up was so necessary to preserving their view of the ways things should have happened or must have happened that they would have gambled their lives on the truth of their testimony.

She'd once tried a murder case where six witnesses testified, consistently, the dead man was really and truly dead when they had come upon him. But the victim's father was the seventh witness and, not privy to what the other witnesses revealed about the condition of his son during their testimony, no sooner did he take his oath than he blurted out a revelation: his son had made a dying declaration. With his last breath, the poor boy confided to his father that Morgan's client shot him, point blank. Hell, even the prosecutor almost fell out of his chair at the revelation. But he recovered nicely and asked the necessary follow-up questions to ensure the grieving father's revelation would be admissible into evidence. Morgan would never know for certain whether the prosecutor's surprise at this astounding piece of evidence was feigned. There was no doubt, however, of the effect it had on the jury. They hung on the grieving father's every word and attributed not a whit of importance to the fact he had been interviewed by the police four times and hadn't mentioned the fact his son named his killer with his last breath to either them or a single other soul before he offered it up in open court. No amount of preparation could have equipped Morgan to deal with his lies, and only years of experience enabled her to continue the trial without letting anyone see she wanted to throw up in the middle of the courtroom. Remembering the nauseated feeling as if it were yesterday, Morgan knew her students would have to suffer plenty of nausea on their own if they were going to develop into good litigators.

As she glanced around the room, her gaze settled on Parker and she realized she was spending more time thinking about her than she was the facts of this case. Of all of her students, Parker was the one in whose abilities she was most confident. She had already perfected the art of questioning witnesses, although her experiences had taken place in less sterile environments than the courtroom. Equally impressive was the fact she had testified in dozens of complicated cases over the years. Though she had a lot to learn about lawyering, Parker came equipped with the skills to learn fast and well. Once she graduated, she would make a fantastic addition to whatever practice she chose to join. Morgan vowed not to do anything to jeopardize Parker's chances at success.

They went around the room and offered their reports. Morgan would pick the jury with Dex and Gerald taking notes. She added Gerald to this task only after her talk with Yolanda and because she felt she needed to throw her a bone. Ford and Morgan would split the witnesses. Morgan reserved Detective Keaton for herself, ignoring Parker's raised eyebrows at this pronouncement. Dex and Parker would be responsible for working with Jake to run down any new issues likely to crop up during trial, as well as handling witnesses for the defense. This last was a lean task since Luis had only one sister who lived in the States and no one else had been convinced to step forward to speak on his behalf. Jake was still working to convince at least some of the other Burke family employees to vouch for the good character of the handyman or tell what they might know about what he was actually doing in the house that night, but the Burke influence easily extended its reach to curb the willingness of their staff to speak in favor of the man who allegedly brutalized their only daughter.

After they settled on their respective assignments, Morgan asked if anyone had anything to report. Jake reported he had one more friend of Camille's to talk to and he was going to get in contact with her when she returned to the United States, but he didn't hold out much hope the interview would yield any helpful evidence. Morgan was about to adjourn the meeting when Parker cleared her throat. She had avoided direct eye contact with her up until this point and barely broke the barrier now. Waving a hand in Parker's direction, she indicated she should speak.

"I've been looking over the autopsy report and the crime scene photos with a doctor friend of mine." Parker hesitated. She had a theory but nothing concrete to support it. And even if her theory was spot on, she didn't have a clue what it meant. Here they were, the weekend before trial. Was this the time to be throwing a wrench in the works?

Ignoring the internal questions, she spat out her conclusion before she could censor it to death. "I think Camille Burke was poisoned."

Gerald smirked and Ford coughed away a snort of laughter. Dex, steadfastly loyal, maintained a neutral expression. But the reaction Parker focused on was Morgan's raised eyebrows and she met her eyes straight on.

"You do, do you?" Morgan's tone conveyed her disbelief.

Parker resisted the urge to bristle. Logic told her even the members of her team would think her crazy poison theory didn't have legs to stand on. There wasn't much to it anyway. She surmised Camille Burke had been poisoned before she was shot in the face, but her theory stopped there. She had no idea how or why and had not a clue as to how this piece of the puzzle fit into their mission of defending Luis Chavez. If Luis shot Camille, did it even matter whether or not she had been poisoned? Was she already dead when she was shot? Parker realized her theory raised more questions than answers, but there was value in the uncertainty. The jury would be instructed to acquit Luis if they had a reasonable doubt about his guilt. Any reasonable doubt. Parker knew her theory that Camille Burke was poisoned did little to answer the question of who killed her, but it certainly raised some reasonable doubt. Why would a handyman with a gun take the time to poison Camille before shooting her?

Parker channeled her thoughts into a simple answer. "Yes. And if she was poisoned before she was shot, it raises some doubt as to the identity of her killer or even as to whether she was already dead when she was shot." Her words were directed at Morgan and for the next few moments it felt as if they were the only ones in the room.

"What support do you have for the proposition she was poisoned?" Morgan's question was direct and Parker felt like she was on the witness stand.

"I was looking at the crime scene photos and realized something seemed off. Teddy Burke told the cops he heard a gunshot and within moments called nine-one-one. The first police unit arrived on the scene within fifteen minutes. The autopsy report puts the time of death right around the time of the nine-one-one call."

Parker paused and Ford prompted her along. "Nothing out of the ordinary there."

"Look at the photos," Parker responded. "These were taken by the crime scene investigator, about an hour after the first unit arrived on the scene. Camille Burke is in full rigor." Parker pointed at one of the photographs. "No gunshot victim goes into rigor that fast."

"How do you make the jump she was poisoned?" Ford asked.

"It's a hunch. I worked a case once where an angry wife put a heaping dose of strychnine in her husband's morning coffee. She waited till he finished convulsing and called for an ambulance. She told the paramedics who found him dead under the kitchen table that he had a history of heart disease and that he had probably suffered a heart attack. The hospital doctor was suspicious about the condition of his body and ordered a toxicology report. The guy, like Camille, was in full rigor mortis, just an hour after he had died. The toxicology report showed the presence of large amounts of strychnine, which causes the body to experience such strong convulsions that the victim's body contorts into weird positions and rigor mortis sets in almost immediately after death. That just doesn't happen from a gunshot wound."

Ford pressed. "What were the toxicology results?"

"No report was done." Parker took a deep breath. Even as she spoke, she sensed Morgan and the others doubted she had the expertise necessary to draw the conclusion she had. She ended with a statement designed to bolster her supposition. "When I discussed this information with Dr. Williams, I detected a reaction from her. If this were her case, she would've ordered a tox screen to see if she could confirm the poison angle." She instantly regretted her words.

Morgan came up out of her chair. "You discussed this with who?"

"Dr. Williams. A medical examiner. Not the one who did the autopsy. She said we would need to get the prosecutor or detective to instruct her to run additional tests or obtain a court order."

"Parker, what the hell were you thinking? She's a county employee. Anything you tell her, she's going to run off and share with the prosecutor. If you had a valid theory—big if—then we would bring in an independent expert to determine if it was something worth following up on. Now, even if you are onto something, the other side knows it and can do whatever they think necessary to subvert our efforts. Typical cop—not thinking things through." Morgan was so angry, she didn't realize she had spoken the last thought out loud, but she could tell her words cut Parker to the core. She could see the pain in Parker's eyes and she fought dueling desires to comfort and to push away. She decided the latter was the best path for both of them and she resisted the urge to soften her blows. "I'm tempted to ask you to leave the team."

Parker hid her hurt, but let her anger show full force. Staring directly at Morgan, she pronounced, "No need. Consider me gone."

Morgan felt foolish as she watched Parker stalk out of the room. She hadn't expected her to actually leave. She'd imagined they would exchange more angry words but would then put their differences aside. The last thing she wanted was for Parker to quit the team, especially now that she had decided to forgo a chance at a relationship. If Parker quit now, she wouldn't get any credit for the long semester's work. Addressing the group, she suggested they take a break. The words were no sooner out of her mouth than Jake and Dex shot out of the room. Ford pulled up a chair to sit beside her and asked, "Do you want to talk about what's going on?"

"You mean my lack of temperament for this teaching job?" Morgan knew what he meant and she wondered how many of the others caught the undercurrent of the conflict between her and Parker. She loved Ford like a brother, but she couldn't get into the details now. She needed every ounce of her composure for the battles of the week ahead. Avoiding his eyes, she said, "I'm sorry for the outburst. I'm not used to being ambushed by someone on my side. I know she was trying to help, but her methods took me by surprise."

Ford looked at her for an extended time as if divining her true thoughts. Finally, he spoke and his words were layered with meaning. "She's not your average law student."

Parker's strides were long and carried her quickly down the hall. She heard light footfalls behind her but ignored them in her haste to get away.

"Parker, wait. I want to talk to you."

Parker glanced back and saw Gerald trying to catch up to her. What the hell was he doing? *Of all the people I thought might try to get me to come back, he's the last candidate. Besides Morgan*, she added.

After all, she's the one who wanted me to leave so badly she would shame me in front of the rest of the group. Curiosity overtook her desire to flee and she stopped.

"What is it, Gerald?" she snapped.

"Don't be mad at me. I'm not the one who threw you off the team."

Parker tempered her tone. "Sorry. Look, I'm in a hurry to get out of here. Is there something you want?"

"I was checking to see if you were all right."

The gleam in his eyes told Parker right away he was lying. *Checking to see if I'm all right. Fat chance.* More like he was gloating at her distress. *This guy isn't even human.* Parker wasn't up for another confrontation, though, and she decided it would be easier to play along.

"I'm fine. I just need to get out of here. Did you need something else?" The question was dismissive. Parker wasn't remotely prepared for Gerald's next words.

"I mean, it must hurt to have your lover betray you, especially in front of so many others."

Parker felt a slow sour curl in her belly and the taste of bile rendered her speechless. Gerald took her silence as tacit permission to continue his ramblings.

"She's not all that. You could do so much better. I know it must have been nice to be her favorite, considering you're so focused on beating everyone else out to graduate first in our class. I know you would do anything to achieve your goals, but her? She's washed up. If she isn't, then why is she here teaching? How lucky for you she's a man-hating dyke. Too bad she's also a user. She used you for a good time and gave you nothing in return. Bet you were counting on a much bigger return on your investment. Well, you'll be happy to know she won't be teaching here much longer, so I guess all your efforts were for nothing."

Roaring rage blacked out all other emotion. Parker grabbed Gerald's shirt and slammed him against the wall. She twisted the cloth of his shirt and watched with satisfaction as red rose from his constricted neck to his scared and darting eyes. She twisted harder, ignoring the pull of strong hands on her shoulders.

"Parker, for crying out loud, let him go." It took both Dex and Jake to pull her off the whimpering Gerald. She was in kill mode and continued to fight against their grasp even as Gerald ran down the hall, far away from her fury.

With Gerald gone, Parker directed her anger at the others. "Leave me alone."

Dex grabbed her shoulders and shook her. "Why? So you can beat the hell out of Gerald? What did he say to you?"

Parker struggled to regain her composure. She had no desire to rehash what had transpired. More than anything she wanted to get away from this place since it no longer held familiarity and comfort. Getting involved with Morgan was the stupidest move she had ever made. She had broken her rule of mixing work and pleasure, and the price she paid was safety. Years of education, her stellar GPA, her class standing—all were no longer safe because she traded a few grabs at lust for the prize of scholarship and success. Apparently, the lessons she learned from her lost career had been for nothing. All she wanted right now was to be alone—her only sanctuary.

She faced him. "Dex, let me go. I swear I won't go after him."

He held her for several seconds longer as if unsure whether to believe her assurances. Finally, he released his grasp. "Wanna talk about what just happened?"

"No." She started to say more but saw Jake standing patiently behind Dex. "Not right now."

"Forget about him. Come work out with me."

"I don't have the energy." Parker knew Dex was trying to distract her from the swirl of thoughts and maybe he was right. A brutal hour of weightlifting might be exactly what she needed. Trade one kind of pain for another. She was torn, but her desire to be alone and safe won out. "All I want to do right now is leave here." Seeing the hurt look in Dex's eyes, she tossed out a compromise. "Let's talk later. Call me."

He nodded and she almost felt bad. She knew she wouldn't answer when he called. She was already erecting walls and couldn't risk her safety by allowing anyone in. She would say whatever was necessary to leave in peace and begin her task.

❖

Parker heard the doorbell and ignored it. She didn't want to see or talk to anyone. The doorbell kept up its insistent ringing and she willed her mind to another place. Finally, she heard the front door open and the ringing stopped. The sound of a woman's insistent voice roused her from her stupor.

"I need to talk to Parker. Now."

Kelsey's reply was forceful. "Look, Detective. Unless you have a warrant, you don't have any right to push your way in here. Tell me what you want and then I'll decide if it's worth bothering her."

"Kelsey, I know you're trying to protect her, but I'm only here to help. I have some information Parker asked me to get. I think she's going to want to see it."

"Go away, Skye. Don't you think you've caused her enough pain in one lifetime?"

Skye entreated again. "Please, Kelsey. I know Parker doesn't want to have anything to do with me, but I wouldn't be here if it weren't important."

Kelsey relented. "Come in, but wait down here. I'll ask if she wants to see you. If she doesn't, I'll need you to leave. Understood?"

As Parker listened to Kelsey climb the stairs, she wondered what Skye was doing on her doorstep on a Sunday afternoon. Maybe it wasn't Sunday. Parker couldn't really be sure. Kelsey didn't knock before she entered. The room was dimly lit, but Kelsey's gasp told Parker she'd been spotted. Parker looked over at the mirror and saw she was dressed in the same clothes she'd worn home Friday night. Dark circles surrounded her red-rimmed eyes. Her usually wavy hair hung limp and lifeless. Kelsey sat on the arm of her chair and drew her close. Stroking her head, she murmured endearing comforts. "Honey, whatever it is you're going to be okay. We've gotten through worse before, I'm sure of it. Let it go, sweetheart, let it go."

Parker leaned into Kelsey's arms and tried to let go of the hurt, the pain. She'd spent the last two days thinking, and her thoughts were driving her further inward. She knew it wasn't healthy. She knew action had the greater power to heal, but she wasn't ready to heal. She had only enough energy to wallow in her pain, soak it in, and make sure the memory of it was so ingrained in her being she could never allow it to catch her by surprise again.

Kelsey held Parker for a long time before broaching the subject of Parker's visitor. "Parker, Skye's downstairs. She insists she needs to see you."

When the doorbell rang, Parker had half expected it to be Morgan. She had refused to take any of Morgan's many calls. Kelsey had finally unplugged the phone. Parker told herself seeing Morgan was the last thing she wanted, but she had to admit it wasn't completely true. Even so, Parker experienced relief that the woman who showed up on her doorstep was Skye. *Things have certainly changed.*

"What does she want?"

"I don't know. If you don't want to see her, I'll gladly send her packing. She has a folder and said she has some information you want."

Parker had no doubt Kelsey could send Skye firmly on her way, and normally, she would enjoy watching her loyal friend drive Skye from the house. But her inner voice told her it would have taken a complete submersion of pride for Skye to show up here again so soon after being rejected. Parker's curiosity won out.

"As much as I'd like to see you kick her ass, I want to know what's she's got to show me more." Parker glanced down at herself. "I'm pretty ripe. Let me grab a quick shower and I'll be right down."

Kelsey smiled. "I'll tell her you'll be down when you're damn well ready."

❖

"Skye?"

"You look pretty ragged."

Parker managed a grin. "You always know the perfect thing to say." Waving off a retort, she added, "Should've seen me thirty minutes ago." Pointing at the folder in Skye's hand, she asked, "Kelsey said you had something for me."

"I do." Skye shoved the folder toward Parker, but held tightly to one end. "I haven't shown this to anyone else."

Parker read her entreaty and nodded solemnly. She opened the folder and her eyes darted across the top of the first page inside. Toxicology report for Camille Burke. She shot a glance at Skye, then carried the folder into the living room, sank into a chair, and devoured the report. Strychnine, extremely high levels present in the blood.

Addendum to the full autopsy report concluding Camille Burke had been poisoned prior to being shot. Probable cause of death—poison. The new report was signed by Dr. Lauren Williams.

When Parker finished reading, she met Skye's impatient eyes. "Well, don't you have anything to say?" Skye asked.

"How did you get her to do this?"

Skye grinned. "I can be very persuasive when I want to be."

"Give me a break. I met Williams. She was impervious to my charms."

"Maybe you don't have the right charms. I was on my best 'gee, I'm a hardworking cop who is seeking justice' behavior. Women find it hard to resist."

"Not this woman. Don't let Kelsey know you put the moves on the good Dr. Williams. I'm pretty sure she has the hots for her."

"Well, you know me. I got what I want, I'm on to the next." Skye cast her eyes down even as she delivered the flippant remark. Parker knew her flip was all bluster. She knew how hard it must have been for Skye to not only ask for, but to hand over the new report. Skye's Sunday delivery was a peace offering of sorts and she took it in the spirit in which it was intended.

Parker asked, "Have you shown this to the prosecutor?"

"Not yet. I'm on my way to see her now."

Proof positive Skye was intent on making up for the past. While delivery of the toxicology report didn't heal all wounds, it was definitely a salve. Parker reached out a hand. "Peace?"

Skye grasped her firmly. "Peace."

Parker held up the folder. "I wish I knew what this means."

"You have until tomorrow to figure it out. And since I need to grab something to eat before I have the energy to face the know-it-all Ms. Gibson, you have a couple of hours' head start."

Parker shook her head as she watched her leave.

CHAPTER NINETEEN

Morgan stood with the rest of the attorneys and spectators as sixty potential jurors filed into the room. The process was slow as each juror handed a clipboard containing a completed questionnaire to one of the bailiffs and another bailiff pointed out where they should be seated. While Dex and Gerald scribbled notes as they entered the room, Morgan concentrated on making eye contact with each person who would be a judge of the facts of the case.

Though the process was called jury selection, it was actually jury deselection. At the end of a couple of hours of questioning, each side would strike six of these individuals from the pool of potential jurors for reasons ranging from their answers to questions, to simple assessment of their body language. In addition, each side could suggest potential jurors be dismissed for cause—such as they couldn't follow the law or they couldn't understand English. The key to figuring out who to strike was to get them to talk, hence the name *voir dire*: "to speak the truth."

As Morgan contemplated the individuals lining up in the aisles of the courtroom, she thought, not for the first time, there would be little truth telling during the next couple of hours. Some would consciously lie to get out of jury service and some would lie, all the while believing their words to be the rock-solid truth. This latter group would say they respected the presumption of innocence and no, they wouldn't hold it against the defendant if he didn't testify. Morgan was sure they believed they could be impartial, but the truth was the defendant in any case, having been arrested and indicted by a grand jury, faced an uphill battle fighting a strong presumption of "why are we here if he didn't do something wrong?"

The panel was seated and the judge began with simple questions: who has a vacation planned this week, who doesn't understand English—asked in English, of course. Morgan projected a relaxed appearance, but under the surface she was struggling to focus on the task at hand: listening. Normally, Morgan's attention was laser sharp, but today she fought distraction and the primary source was the folder tucked in her briefcase and the woman, standing in the back of the room, who brought it to her early this morning.

❖

Parker had dressed for court even though she had no intention of participating in the proceedings. Her singular goal was to hand off the folder to Jake and Dex and head out. She'd made a late-afternoon appointment with Dean Ramirez and she intended to keep it. But from the moment she reached the courthouse, her plans spun out of her control. She had called Jake the night before and told him the gist of the report, but now that she was here, Ford and Morgan wanted to hear all the details for themselves. Parker felt the heat of Morgan's attempts to meet her eyes, but she avoided the temptation of reconnecting. Facing the others, she recounted Skye's eve-of-trial delivery. The guys on the team expressed excitement at the various ways the information could be used while Morgan quietly read the report for herself. Parker watched her bowed head and wished they were alone. She wanted to apologize for storming out of the prep session on Friday. She wanted to know what Gerald had done and if Morgan was hurt because of it. Come to think of it, where was the little bastard? She glanced around, but he was nowhere to be found. As she turned back, she was struck by the powerful impact of Morgan's eyes boring into her own. They spoke over each other.

"I'm sorry."

"Me too." Parker felt Morgan's hand on her arm and she registered Dex and Jake had slipped away. She opened her mouth to say more, but the sear of Morgan's touch blocked out any professional comment she could have made and the personal was, well, too personal. Flushed, she broke eye contact and stepped back. "You should get in there." She nodded toward the courtroom doors. "And I should go." She didn't wait for a response, instead she walked down the wide hall of the courthouse. She knew without looking back that Morgan was rooted in place.

Parker was riding the escalator to the first floor when she felt a hand on her shoulder. Jake's gravelly voice was unmistakable. "Where you think you're off to?"

"Air, Jake. I need some air."

"I don't blame you for not wanting to settle back in around here."

Parker was startled by his frank assessment, but she realized she shouldn't be. Certainly, Jake had been privy to the gossip over her departure from the force. Try as she might to put it behind her, fact was the shade of the past would dance its shadows into her professional life for the foreseeable future. "If only it were so simple, Jake."

Jake's hard yet gentle stare dared her to a different conclusion.

"Jake, I have some things I need to do."

He didn't relent. "But here I was counting on you to help me out. We have a witness to go see. Leslie Hammond."

"I thought she wasn't back in town until later this week."

"I got wind she blew back in town last night. Accounting for jet lag, I figure she should be awake and moving around by now. Come on, let's make a trip to her house and see what she has to say."

Parker looked at her watch. She had plenty of time before her afternoon meeting. She could do this small task and feel like she hadn't abandoned the team altogether. "Fine. You'll hate riding in my noisy car, though, so you're driving."

"Fair enough."

❖

Camille's friend Leslie had means, though you'd have to know the neighborhood well to realize it. The small Tudor house was situated on a postage stamp lot. Parker figured the house had no more than two bedrooms, one bath, and a small detached garage, but the house's location, smack in the middle of the M Streets, meant it was valued at close to a half million dollars. Pretty swank for a college student.

Jake eased his sedan into Hammond's driveway, pulling up close to the Porsche 911 nestled against the house. Parker followed him to the door, intent on merely observing this interview. A tousled twentysomething male answered the door, steaming mug of coffee in hand.

"Can I help you?"

"Maybe. We're looking for Leslie Hammond?"

The affable young man nodded and replied, "I'm Leslie."

Jake glanced at Parker and both attempted to mask their surprise. The man in the doorway grinned. "Let me guess. You expected a nice young lady to answer the door? No worries, it happens all the time. I think my parents are the last holdouts on using old family names long after they've gone out of style."

Jake smiled. "Can we come in for a moment?"

"You're not selling anything, are you?"

"No, we're here about Camille Burke."

Leslie's face paled and he waved them in. Heading to a table in the kitchen, he motioned for them to be seated. "I heard what happened. Weeks after the fact. I've been in a remote area of Africa working on a research project." As he talked he ran his hand through his unruly blond waves.

Parker was struck with a thought. Did Leslie return early so he could be a witness for the prosecution? What would he have to say that would help the case against Luis Chavez? "If you don't mind my asking, why did you come back early?"

If Leslie was puzzled at the fact Parker knew his schedule, he didn't show it. "I finished up ahead of schedule and frankly, I missed having hot running water."

Relieved, Parker said, "We'd like to ask you some questions about Camille. But before we begin, I want to let you know we are working with the team representing the person on trial for her death."

"The handyman, right?" At their nod, he continued, "I don't get it. Camille was the sweetest person I had ever known. I have no idea why he, or anyone, would want to kill her." Leslie choked as he spoke the last words and Parker watched him carefully, suddenly clear about something.

"Leslie, were you in love with her?"

His expression was tinged with sadness, but he smiled nevertheless. "Pretty obvious, huh? Yes, I loved her. I wanted to marry her and thought she wanted me too. I was wrong."

Parker leaned forward. "What happened?"

"I don't know. She broke it off with me the day before I left. She was vague."

Parker pushed. "Vague how?"

"She said the usual amorphous break-up lines. 'It's not you, it's me,' 'I need some space.' You know."

Parker nodded. Even though she carefully avoided relationships, she had delivered similar phrases to keep from hurting another woman's feelings. But the lines she had spoken in the past had always been true—it was her and she did need space. Her thoughts strayed unbidden to Morgan and she couldn't help but think space was the last thing she wanted. How unlike her to crave closeness. Shaking herself, she focused on the young man seated in front of her.

"Leslie, did you have any contact with Camille while you were out of the country?"

"I didn't speak with her at all. I didn't speak to anyone at home. Our location was so remote, I didn't even receive mail. I did write to her, but I have no way of knowing if she received my letters." Leslie kept up a strong front, but the crack in his voice betrayed his attempts to hide his hurt. Camille Burke had broken his heart and he was still in love. Now she was dead and he would never have an opportunity to win her back. Parker felt tendrils of his pain wrap around her and squeeze. As his heartache held her in its grasp, it became her own. What if she was in love with Morgan? What if she lost the opportunity to explore her feelings? A cynical voice inside told her it didn't matter. Morgan clearly needed nothing more than the physical encounters they had shared. The curvaceous blonde salivating in her office was now fulfilling Morgan's needs. Parker's questions battled her cynical conclusions. She needed answers, but right now she needed to leave before she suffocated in the reflection of her own anguish. Turning to Jake, she realized she had monopolized the interview and gladly turned it back over to him.

"Jake, can you think of anything else?"

While Jake asked Leslie a few additional questions to round out background information, Parker walked around the room. Mementos of Leslie's love were scattered around like wildflowers, coloring his otherwise stark bachelor pad. Smiling for the camera, he and Camille had embraced in a host of exotic locales, and their love was framed and displayed for all to see. Parker tried to imagine a photo of her and Morgan sporting leis and cuddling on the beach. *Focus, Parker. She's not interested in anything more than what we've already had. Especially since what we already had has almost cost her job.* Parker looked at her watch. If they hurried, she still had time to make her meeting with Dean Ramirez. Glancing once more at Leslie's photographs, she mentally noted if he was this upset about the breakup weeks later, he must have been livid at the time.

Jake indicated he was finished and handed Leslie his card. Parker begged off riding back to the courthouse, instead asking Jake to drop her off on campus. All she wanted to do was see Morgan, but she had to see to something else first.

❖

"Ms. Bradley, I have some additional discovery for you." Valerie Gibson thrust an envelope forward. "These lab tests were delivered today. Nothing of any consequence, but I wanted to make sure I provided you with them prior to the start of evidence."

Morgan looked at the envelope but didn't reach for it. "I suppose you missed the section of my discovery motion asking for *Brady* material." Morgan's voice dripped sarcasm. The prosecutor knew she had an obligation to turn over any exculpatory evidence, and ethics should have compelled her to do so even if Morgan hadn't specifically asked.

"Who said there's anything exculpatory here?" Gibson shook the envelope.

"Not you, though you should have. Don't you think the fact Camille Burke was poisoned sheds some doubt on your theory my client shot her dead?" Morgan watched for Gibson to register the fact Morgan already knew the contents of the envelope. It didn't take long for the prosecutor's face to redden, but she pushed away embarrassment at being caught in a breach of ethics.

In a blatant display of denial, Gibson responded, "Obviously you already knew about the poison, so you can't claim your case has been prejudiced by not having this report sooner. Frankly, I don't think this report makes a lick of difference to my case."

Morgan faced her squarely. "You're bluffing, and if you think any of the twelve fine people we selected to serve won't see through it, you have severely underestimated both them and me." With a pointed look at the envelope still in Gibson's hand, she shook her head, turned, and walked out of the courtroom. She would study the copy of the report she already had. Skye Keaton was likely to be the prosecution's first witness and it would be much more fun to use the copy of the report Skye herself had provided when she ripped into the credibility of the State's key witness.

Her intense concentration on the lineup of the next day distracted her and she ran directly into Skye as she made her way out of the courtroom.

"Ms. Bradley."

"Detective." Morgan snarled her response to Skye's acknowledgment.

"Did I do something to piss you off?"

Skye's question caught Morgan off guard and she realized Skye probably expected a different reception from her, especially since she had provided the report casting doubt on the prosecution's case. But for once Morgan couldn't compartmentalize her feelings. Skye had pierced the heart of the woman whose heart Morgan wanted for her own. Anger rose through her core and struggled to lash out. Skye had been privileged to receive Parker's most treasured feelings, yet she'd crushed them as if they had no value. Morgan tallied the value of Parker's intimacy and trust and wished she could afford the price. Knowing neither she nor Parker had the means to take the feelings they had any further, she resented Skye all the more for throwing away her own opportunities. Her resentment wrestled with the strong façade of self-control for which she was famous, but the resentment battled forward.

"Yes, matter of fact, you did."

"Mind telling what it was?" Skye's expression was genuinely puzzled.

"You hurt someone I care about." Skye's puzzled expression remained and Morgan was sorry she had said anything. "Never mind." She pushed past the detective and started out of the room.

Skye grabbed her arm, but her touch was gentle. As Morgan faced her, she saw the questioning lines on Skye's face settle into a knowing look. After all, there was only one person it could be. Skye's response was a whisper. "I'm sorry for what I did, but it was a long time ago. She's forgiven me."

"She may have forgiven you, but she still bears the scars." Morgan shook off Skye's hand. She didn't want to be having this conversation with Skye for a multitude of reasons, including the fact she would be skewering this witness on the stand first thing in the morning. If there was anyone she should be talking to it was Parker. Parker, with her sparkling charm in public, but guarded pain in private. Morgan wanted to erase the hurt that haunted Parker and see the affection she felt reflected in her eyes.

"I'm sorry."

Morgan looked into Skye's face, and noted her cocky demeanor had been replaced with genuine angst. She nodded and walked out.

❖

Parker answered the phone because she knew no one else was home. If Kelsey or Erin had been there, she would have enlisted them to screen her calls. Parker imagined Dex was calling to give her a blow-by-blow of the first day of the trial and she knew him well enough to know if he wasn't able to reach her by phone, he would show up at her door. She was torn about wanting to hear the details of the trial. Dex would be gushing about Morgan's prowess and justifiably so, but she didn't want to talk about Morgan. She had done enough talking about her professor during her afternoon appointment with the dean, and it had worn her out. She focused on making her voice sound sleepy, hoping he would take the hint and keep the conversation short.

"Parker? You sound like you've been sleeping. Well, get up, girl. We have things to do."

It was Jake. Parker's first reaction was to tell him she was off the case and explain her work earlier in the day had been a freebie but she was officially retired from the Chavez defense team. She started to form the words, but curiosity forced a different response. "Gimme five minutes. I'll be out front."

Parker waited on the porch, watching for the lights of Jake's car. She wondered at her eagerness to jump back into the case when she'd spent the afternoon explaining to Dean Ramirez why she was dropping the Advanced Evidence class. Her decision to drop the class was calculated to protect Morgan, but she couldn't deny the small part of her that hoped removing their professional relationship might open the door to something more. If nothing else, now that she was no longer one of Morgan's students, she could work on the case without jeopardizing Morgan's career.

Jake's car pulled into the driveway and Parker shrugged off the lingering questions about her motivation and climbed into Jake's sedan. "Okay, Sherlock, where are we going?"

"Leslie Hammond got a letter in the mail and he wants to show it to us."

"A letter?"

"Yep. From Camille Burke."

"Here it is." Leslie's hand shook as he passed the envelope to Parker. Clearly he deemed her to be in charge of the investigation. Parker took the envelope and carefully pulled a sheaf of pages from it. Casting a gentle look at the tearful young man, she asked, "May I?" He nodded and Parker began to read. Camille Burke's last letter was both gripping and horrific. Parker was caught between the desire to race to the end and the urge to cram the gruesome story back into the envelope. When she finished, she handed the pages to Jake and focused her attention on Leslie. "When did you receive this?"

"It's postmarked the day she died. It was in a pile of mail being held at the post office until I returned."

"Before you got this, did you have any idea?"

"No. I knew she was troubled, haunted even." His voice choked. "She was breaking up with me, for God's sake. I thought her distress was all about me, wanting to end things with me, wanting to be rid of me. I had no idea, none, she was in her own personal hell. I never would have left if I had known." He wiped away tears. "I loved her."

She was sure he did and equally sure it would be a long time before he recovered from the knowledge the woman he had loved had been systematically victimized for years by her own brother. She knew Teddy Burke was a talented sociopath, but the juxtaposition of his public persona with the tale of horrific abuse he heaped on the sibling he purported to love would repulse even the most jaded. Parker, who had felt the raw pain of too many sickening revelations during her career as a cop, was no less sensitive from her experience, but necessity demanded she stuff her feelings. They had work to do.

"We need to let the police know. I'll tell them." Indicating the letter, she asked, "May I take this?" Leslie nodded.

❖

The rest of the night was a blur. She directed Jake to the Palomar and led him to the door of Morgan's room. She ignored Morgan's surprised look to find them in the hall of her hotel at the late hour. Parker watched intently while Morgan sat on the end of her bed and burned through the pages Camille Burke had penned. She wanted nothing more than to go to Morgan. She needed the close warmth of Morgan to melt away the pain inside her soul. Instead, she waited quietly for Morgan to finish reading.

"She killed herself." Morgan looked at Parker as she spoke the words and her look conveyed sorrow for Camille as well as apology to Parker for not having lent credence to Parker's theories.

"Yes, and who could blame her? Teddy Burke has spent his life skating around the edge of trouble but never coming close enough to be caught. No one would have ever believed he had been raping his sister for years. I'd be willing to bet he paid off Dr. Hudson to make sure there was no tox screen done. If there was a suicide note at the scene, it's probably long gone. Camille had nowhere to go, no one to tell. I'm sure she was so ashamed, she thought Leslie Hammond would drop her once he found out. Clearly, she loved him. She wrote this letter to him to make sure he knew he wasn't the reason she broke things off."

Morgan grasped Parker's hand. She sensed Parker was internalizing Camille's pain and she wanted to ground her in the here and now. "Parker, there's nothing anyone could have done. Camille kept the secret and by doing so, she shut out anyone who could have helped her break free." Placing her hand under Parker's chin, she tilted her face until she was staring into her eyes. The connection was electric.

The rough sound of a throat clearing broke the wordless bond. Morgan looked across the room where Jake waited patiently.

"Ladies, I think we need to make some decisions."

Morgan nodded. "I have Gibson's cell phone number. She's probably practicing a stinging opening argument. I'll take great pleasure in interrupting her. Jake, will you give Ford a call and let him know what's going on?"

"Yep." He fished a cell phone from his jacket pocket. "I think I'll call from downstairs so we don't talk over each other. Parker, meet me downstairs when you're done helping Ms. Bradley explain the situation to Ms. Gibson." Nodding, he left the room.

Parker looked down at Morgan's hand still clasping her own. "Subtle."

"Has he always been so perceptive?"

"He's a regular Sherlock Holmes." Parker fastened her gaze on Morgan. "I have so much I want to say to you." All she wanted to do at this very moment was lean in and take. Take Morgan's hair and sweep it back from her face. Take Morgan's full lips with her own and kiss away the distance between them. Take Morgan's clothes and tear away all barriers to her soft and lovely skin. But before she could take, she had to know Morgan wanted to be taken, and now was not the time to solve the case of the unrequited love. Love? Was she feeling love? Surely she desired Morgan; she craved her, even. But love? She turned the question over in her mind and examined it from all angles. The answer was clear, but this was not the time to take the chance. "We'll talk later. Right now, you need to make a call."

Morgan's steady stare almost dissolved Parker. Her brain sent signals telling her to ignore her doubts and take what she wanted, but before the synapse fired her into action, Morgan picked up the phone and started dialing. Parker barely caught herself and settled in to listen. Later, she thought. Later.

Chapter Twenty

I would like a brief continuance to investigate this matter."
Judge Thompson looked down his nose at Valerie Gibson before glancing at Morgan and Ford. "I assume you two have something to say about this." Morgan had been up half the night strategizing, but she was poised to respond to the prosecutor's request. They were scheduled to present opening statements in thirty minutes and Ford was prepared to deliver one for the defense. Immediately following, Teddy Burke was scheduled to take the stand. Morgan had been up late revising her cross-examination, including damning questions about his role in his sister's death, whether it was suicide or murder. Despite her hours of preparation, she was willing to bet they wouldn't be presenting anything to the jury today.

"Certainly, we do, Judge. We think the prosecutor already has enough information to dismiss the charges against our client. A county medical examiner will testify Ms. Burke was poisoned and now the prosecutor has a suicide note. I'm not sure what she intends to investigate, but certainly her case is already riddled with enough reasonable doubt for an acquittal." Despite her attempts to persuade, Morgan knew the judge would most likely grant a short continuance to the prosecutor, who had been as surprised by last evening's revelations as she was, but she didn't have to agree to it. The delay was likely to be very short considering the fact they had a jury sworn and in the box ready to go. Judges weren't in favor of inconveniencing those citizens who actually showed up for jury duty, especially since those same citizens were likely to vote in the next election.

"Judge, this new evidence hasn't been entirely verified. Plus, it's not as if any of this information negates the fact Mr. Chavez's fingerprints were on the gun that shot Camille Burke in the face and he was found standing over her dead body. I'm asking for a day to sort through this. One day is all I ask."

"Granted. We'll reconvene tomorrow morning at eight thirty. Ms. Bradley, do you have any motions to make at this time?"

She was ready. "Yes, judge. Mr. Chavez has been in jail for several months pending the trial of this matter. In light of the new evidence and the additional delay, we respectfully ask he be released on a personal bond."

Valerie Gibson flew out of her seat shouting "Your honor, defense counsel's request is premature. We're only asking for a day delay."

Judge Thompson studiously avoided looking at Gibson as he made his ruling. "Defense motion for personal bond is granted. Bring me an order and I'll sign it." He stood to indicate their meeting was over and everyone should leave his chambers. Morgan and Ford filed past the stunned Gibson on their way to let Luis know the good news. Luis was to be released on his own recognizance pending the outcome of the case. The judge had made known his opinion about the state of the evidence by his ruling. If he thought the trial was going to proceed in a day, it was unlikely he would have agreed to the bond. Morgan knew she should waste no time in case the tide turned, and she planned to spend the rest of the day reviewing her notes even though she knew the adrenaline pumping through her veins would likely rob her of the ability to concentrate. She pondered ways of channeling her energy, but practicality settled in. A resolution about her feelings for Parker would have to wait the outcome of this case. Even as she had the thought, she knew that where Parker was concerned, her feelings were already resolved.

❖

Bag of bagels in hand, Parker approached the door to Skye's duplex. It was a beautiful fall morning and she felt good. She had talked to Dex and gotten a full report on the morning's activities at the courthouse. He added in that the prosecutor was ranting about the fact both her key witness and lead detective were missing in action. Parker figured Teddy Burke had gotten wind of Camille's letter. His family's influence had always saved his ass in the past, and no doubt someone at the courthouse had tipped him off. As for Skye, she was probably taking cover till the chaos at the courthouse blew over. Gibson couldn't be happy with her for getting the tox screen, and now that her case was falling apart, Skye would be the most convenient scapegoat. Parker didn't wish that on anyone.

By the looks of things, the Chavez case would be over soon and then she and Morgan could have the talk they had both alluded to. She was so immersed in her own perspective she had only a vague idea of how Morgan felt, but she at least wanted to let Morgan know her job was no longer in jeopardy even if nothing were to come from the feelings she harbored. No matter what, she had to face her past before she could find a future with Morgan, or anyone else. So, bagels in hand, she raised her hand to ring the bell and make one last visit back in time.

Parker stopped with her hand in midair. Skye's front door was slightly ajar, a small but clear signal something was wrong. Cops weren't careless. Parker bent down and carefully placed the bag of bagels to the side of the porch. Instinctively, she reached around her waist for the gun she no longer wore. After years of carrying a weapon, she still felt naked without it. Parker leaned forward, almost touching the door frame, and listened through the crack. Tense, whispered voices drifted through Skye's small home, and though she couldn't make out the words, Parker felt urgent action was required. She gently pushed Skye's front door open until she could slip through the opening.

Parker stepped quietly through the small hallway and glanced into each room she passed. Skye's place was modest—one bedroom, one bath, living area, and kitchen. The whispered voices stopped and Parker had only her instincts to guide her. Each room appeared to be empty until she reached the kitchen where she saw the shadow of a figure seated at the small dinette. Parker could only see the figure's back, but she knew it wasn't Skye—it was a man. She watched as the stranger raised a mug and drank, slowly, as if enjoying a leisurely cup of morning coffee. There was no turning back now. She knew Skye was in trouble and she had to face this man in order to save her. She had faced him before, but something about the cool, confident way he made himself at home here shook her steady resolve, but only for a moment.

She knew she had to display more control than he if she was to wrest away his confidence. She channeled all the hurt and anger from Camille Burke's last words and drew strength from Camille's pain.

"Why, Teddy Burke, don't you know everyone in town is looking for you?"

He swiveled in his chair and faced her. She caught a glimpse of fear in his eyes before his expression settled back into calm. When he spoke he displayed no affect.

"Well, hello, former Detective Casey. If you, a discharged and disgraced detective, found me, I can't be so very hard to locate, now can I?"

Parker stifled natural responses and merely stared at him. She'd known for years Teddy Burke was a sociopath, but she'd had no idea he was capable of the torment he'd inflicted on his own sister. She was consumed with worry about Skye. Her car was parked outside. She had to be here somewhere. Parker concentrated her full attention on him. She knew her every word, her every action, could mean the difference in whether both she and Skye escaped unharmed. She played along.

"I suppose you're right. I imagine others will be here soon to look for you."

His lack of affect was unsettling. "Certainly. We have time to share a cup of coffee. Sit. Drink with me." He pointed to an empty chair at the table.

The last thing Parker wanted to do was sit. She knew it was imperative to remain in a position of readiness. In addition, she had no desire to drink anything Teddy Burke might offer. But she also knew she needed to buy time, time to learn Skye's location and time to figure out a way to take control of the situation. She sat and took the mug he offered. Parker drew on years of practice coaxing criminals into telling their stories and offered Teddy the chance to tell his tale.

"I assume you know Camille left a suicide note."

"I heard something to that effect."

"She said a number of things about you in the note. Despicable things. I'm sure you'd like a chance to refute her accusations, substitute truth for her lies."

His eyes flashed anger. "Are you calling my sister, my flesh and blood, a liar?"

Parker realized she was pushing too hard, too fast. "No, no. Not at all. I don't know why she wrote the things she did." She took a different tack. "Perhaps someone forced her to write those awful accusations. Someone who was jealous of your relationship with her."

Teddy Burke stroked his chin and leaned back in his chair, eyes half closed. "There were many who were."

Ah, I've hit on something here. Parker tamped down on her excitement and continued in an easy tone. "I have no doubt you loved her. It must have been hard to know she was desired by many others."

He looked through her as he answered, his eyes and thoughts focused on a past scene. "If I tell you everything, you will understand."

It was part declaration, part question. Parker answered simply, "Yes."

❖

"I went to be with her as I had many nights before. Camille was my true love and she always welcomed me. Our bond was special, everlasting.

"I looked for her in the bed. It was late and she should have been waiting for me. Her bed was empty. I looked around and found her lying near her desk, curled into a hideous display of the grotesque. Her arms and legs were sprawled into spasm and her face was frozen into a mask of horror. The sight of her was revolting. I could barely stand to look at her.

"On her desk, I found a letter full of lies and hurt, obviously conjured by a jealous lover who made her write painful words designed to pierce me to the core. My darling would never speak such lies.

"I knew she wouldn't want to be found like this. Wouldn't want people to think she was weak. Taking your own life is weak, even if you're pressured by forces stronger than your own. I burned the note. She would have wanted me to. I would fix her death scene so no one would ever know she had succumbed to frailty.

"When I was done, I stared at the gun in my hand, willing it to draw back the bullet with the same force it had expended to send the metal hurtling into my beloved's face. Seconds seemed like hours as I stood still, contemplating the consequences of this final act. I raised the gun to my own temple and sorted through the reasons death would bring me peace. Like a rush of cold, my composure returned and I chose to survive. She would've wanted me to go on. I found a handkerchief in my pocket, and slowly and deliberately, I wiped the black casing of the weapon to a mighty shine.

"I was just finishing when I heard rough boots running up the stairs. I shoved the cloth in my pocket, tossed the gun on the floor, and ducked into the adjoining study. Peering through the slightly cracked door, I watched the dirty handyman burst into my beloved's sanctuary, leaving spots of grass and dirt to mark his path. He stopped short at the sight of her lying in a massive pool of her own blood, but not short enough. His boots trailed the essence of her being everywhere he stepped. I watched him look at her face, perhaps searching for signs of breath. He even leaned close, barely touching. Seeing no indication of life, he backed away, his heavy boots catching on the gun lying behind him, sending it skittering across the wood plank floors. As if entranced, he followed its path and, joy of joys, picked up the shiny weapon and held it in his rough and grimy hands. I was barely able to conceal my glee. Tiptoeing to the hall, I charged into the room and surprised him, standing over her body.

"The handyman…what kind of name is 'handyman' for someone who does little bits of nothing? He turned at the sound of my entrance and read the accusation pouring from my eyes. His glance flicked down to the gun in his hand. Uneducated, yes, but he was not entirely lacking in common sense. He threw the gun to the ground and ran past me, his master, hurtling down the staircase. I pretended to pursue him, but I had more pressing matters to attend to."

"So you destroyed the note and called the cops?" Parker spoke to break the trance his telling had evoked and she found the sound of her own voice jarring after the singsong revelations of the madman. She knew she shouldn't push him if she wanted to buy time, but his cold-blooded account of his sister's death left her repulsed and impatient.

"I protected my family, yes." Not a shade of defensiveness in his tone.

"You protected yourself." Parker assumed the most disgusted expression she could muster. It wasn't hard under the circumstances.

"How much did you have to pay the ME to cover your tracks?" Tired of the imbalance of the situation, she resolved to provoke him to anger. Anything to gain some advantage while she formed a plan. She was certain she could hear a quiet groan close by. Steeling herself for sure conflict, she resisted the urge to cut a glance through the doorway of the adjoining room. *Skye, where are you?*

"How long had you been raping your little sister, Teddy?"

"I'm tired of talking now. Drink your coffee and I'll take you to see your friend."

Parker glanced down at the mug in her hand. All she could see was the glass of poison this man had driven his only sibling to drink. Teddy's hands were tucked under the table's edge and his stillness was unsettling. She had no doubt he was armed and was equally certain he had no intention of letting her live to reveal his sordid tale. She knew she had only seconds to act. Parker noted the steam as it wafted from the coffee mug and it inspired her. She drew the cup of coffee to her lips but at the last moment she wrenched it away and threw the heavy ceramic mug and its scalding contents at Teddy's head. He leapt from his seat, screaming in pain, as the liquid burned his eyes. Parker lunged across the table and knocked him to the floor with the entire weight of her body. She stepped on his wrist until he let loose his gun and she knocked it across the room. Fists whaling, she delivered the punishment she had wanted to administer since she caught him threatening Morgan weeks before. Unleashed, her rage drove her fists to strike him over and over again and she lost herself in revenge, for Morgan, for Camille, for countless other victims she had never been able to avenge.

A moan, louder now, broke her trance. Parker looked down at her own hands, bloody and broken, and shook her head as if to clear away the entire scene. Her mind cleared and she realized the sound wasn't coming from the man beneath her. She concentrated her every effort to focus. *Skye. I have to find Skye.* Parker winced as she grasped the arm of a chair for balance and stumbled across the room, following the sounds of Skye's pain.

Skye lay on the floor beside her bed. Her forehead was bleeding and her face was puffy from several well-landed blows. Her hands and legs were bound and it looked as though she had snaked her way out from under the bed before giving in to the pain of having been beaten. Parker bent to untie her and murmur words of comfort.

"Skye, baby. Look at me. You're going to be okay." Parker hurried to untie the cords wrapped tightly around Skye's wrists and ankles. Skye, hands now free, motioned for Parker to lean in. Parker moved in close, but could still barely make out Skye's labored words.

"I knew."

"Knew what?"

"Camille. Poisoned. I knew." Skye coughed and Parker motioned her to say no more. She didn't want to hear anymore because she didn't have the energy to absorb, let alone process, the revelation. Later. She would process things later. Right now, she knew she needed to call this in, but she needed to make sure Skye was okay first. Her face was almost unrecognizable. Once she freed Skye's bonds, Parker lifted her onto the bed and walked over to the bedside phone. She lifted the handset and started punching the numbers to bring help. Before she could finish, she heard a loud bump against the door frame and looked up into the eyes of the psychopath she thought she had rendered harmless. Teddy Burke leaned heavily against the door, weak from his beating, but drawing strength from the large handgun he trained on Skye. His eyes were mere pinpricks seated in swollen sockets, but his voice was clear and loud.

"Put the fucking phone down or I will kill you both."

Parker knew it was a lie. He planned to kill them both no matter what she did. She met his stare without waver, but she did not see him. Her mind was turned inward and all she saw was Morgan. All she could think of was how she would never be ever to tell Morgan she loved her beyond measure. She couldn't help it. She let loose a mirthless laugh at the irony of the revelation that surfaced too late.

"You think this is funny?" Teddy's hand shook as his rage consumed him.

Parker made a snap decision and she delivered her words on the run. "No, but I do think I'll have the last laugh." She was almost on him when the shot rang out.

❖

"Hey, Morgan, what are you doing back down here?" Ford was hunched over his desk in his office. From the doorway it looked like he was hard at work reviewing a file, but a closer examination revealed he was poring over a crossword puzzle.

"I'm not good at waiting alone. My students seem to have scattered to the wind so I thought I would bother you for a while. Any word?" Morgan spent the morning paralyzed. She could fine-tune her opening argument, but not knowing if she was going to need it robbed her of motivation. She had no idea where Dex was, and Gerald was the last person she wanted to see. Yolanda had sent her an e-mail letting her know Parker had dropped her class. Her e-mail, though terse, conveyed Yolanda's obvious anger at Morgan for letting her tryst with a student get so out of hand it affected the student's coursework. Morgan didn't blame Yolanda for being angry at her, but she had no idea how to resolve the situation. *I suppose it doesn't matter now. Parker seems to have found a resolution all on her own and she didn't need or want my help.* Morgan reached for the phone several times to call Parker, but hung up before dialing because she had no idea what she could say to bridge the gap that had formed between them.

"Let's go downstairs and bother young Valerie. She's bound to be all stressed out, and you'll feel much better if you can add to it."

"You know, I think you're right." She grabbed his hand and pulled him from his chair. "Let's go."

"Morgan."

"Yes?"

"Are you okay?" Ford asked. "I mean, I've never seen you get this stressed out working on a case. Excited, yes, but stressed, no. And, I couldn't help but notice you seem to have some sort of rift with Parker Casey."

Morgan started to deliver quick words of reassurance to let Ford know everything was fine in her world, but as she looked into his caring eyes, she knew she couldn't lie even if she couldn't bring herself to tell all. "I'm sure you're not the only one who noticed the 'rift' with Parker. There is something else going on, but I'm not ready to talk about it. Can we leave it at that?"

Ford locked arms with her and gave her a solid hug. "Of course we can. You know where to find me if you need to talk. Now, come on, let's go have some fun."

Ford and Morgan found Valerie Gibson hunched over her desk in the DA workroom, but she wasn't working on crossword puzzles, she was furiously examining her case file. Seated in a chair nearby was Detective Peterson, Skye's partner. He was nursing a cup of coffee but otherwise looked like he hadn't a care in the world. Morgan slide into the chair closest to Gibson's desk.

"Any news?"

Gibson growled her answer. "Not yet."

Morgan nodded at Peterson. "He seems to be hard at work looking for the suspect."

Peterson came out of his seat. "Look, lady, I've been out all night looking for Burke, and I'll likely be doing the same the rest of the day—all because of your stupid theories. Your client shot Camille Burke in the fucking face and no dirt you kick up suggests otherwise."

Gibson's hard stare forced the detective back into his chair, but it was obvious she felt the same way. Speaking to Morgan, she asked, "Is there some reason you stopped by?" Her tone was dismissive.

"Nothing specific. We're merely checking in, but I can see you have a lot to do so we'll leave you to it." Morgan rose and started to the door with Ford close behind. The ringing of a cell phone caused them both to pause and everyone in the room looked at their phones. Detective Peterson flipped his open. Morgan continued on toward the door, but she couldn't help but hear his side of the exchange.

"Peterson. What?…Yeah, that's Keaton's house…What hospital?…I'm on my way." Slamming his phone shut, Peterson started toward the door, tossing words at Gibson as he moved. "There's been a shooting at Skye's house. Two females are being transported to the ER at Memorial. I'll call you when I know more."

Morgan froze. Two females. She knew in her core Parker was one of them and she raced after the detective who was practically running down the hall. "Detective?"

He glanced back, but didn't slow his pace. "What?"

She cut to the question she needed answered the most. "How badly are they hurt?"

He shook his head and continued running.

❖

Morgan jumped from Ford's still moving pickup and ran to the doors of the ER while he went to find a place to park. On the drive over, Ford had contacted one of his police buddies and learned Teddy Burke had been arrested and Skye Keaton, along with another female, had been taken to Memorial with unspecified injuries. Morgan had just enough information to fuel an overactive imagination. Morgan had no idea how she was going to get more information from the nurses than she'd gotten from the detective, but she formed the beginning of a plan during the lightning drive across town. Rushing to the ER gatekeeper, she flashed her bar card.

"I came directly from the courthouse. I understand the detective on my case is being seen here." She hoped her authoritative tone would buy her entrance. "I'm meeting Detective Peterson here." All of her statements were true. The harried desk clerk pushed the button opening the automatic doors and waved her through. "She's in two C, on your right."

As Morgan walked through, she took a deep breath, steeling herself for whatever might greet her on the other side of the doors. She spied Peterson talking to a nurse in the hall and ducked past, her target straight ahead. She read the number on the door: 2C. Taking a deep breath, she pushed her way into the room.

❖

Parker refused to leave Skye's side. She knew her own body well enough to know she wasn't hurt badly, but Skye was a different story. Teddy made full use of the time before Parker arrived at Skye's house to administer a thorough beating and Parker was certain he had broken bones, at least in Skye's face.

"Parker." Skye's voice was faint.

"Don't try to talk. They are waiting on the x-rays and then you'll see a doctor. They'll fix you right up."

"We need to talk." Skye grabbed and held Parker's hand, willing her to listen to the words she forced from swollen lips. "Camille."

"Skye, you already told me. Let it rest. We'll talk about it later."

"You saved my life. I owe you the truth." Skye took a deep breath. "Crime scene techs recovered a glass from Camille's desk. The lab report showed it was loaded with strychnine. I got rid of it. ME was too lazy to do a tox screen and without the lab report, he didn't have a reason to. I thought I was doing the right thing. Didn't want it to mess up the conviction. I mean, Luis did shoot her even if the bullet wasn't what killed her."

Parker knew any guilt Skye was feeling now about her part in hiding the fact Camille Burke had been poisoned would skyrocket the moment she found out Teddy Burke, not Luis Chavez, had been the one who shot his dear sister in the face. Skye measured her worth by her ability to ferret out the truth. She knew Skye well enough to know the revelation would crush her self-confidence. Perhaps because she had her own beliefs shattered, Parker found herself wanting to protect her from the disillusionment of learning that no matter how hard you tried to get at the truth, you were limited by your inability to be omniscient. Having received a crippling dose of the same disillusionment herself, she wished its effects on no one else. Parker knew Skye's brush with death would mark an indelible change in her attitude about truth gathering. Skye had played fast and loose with the facts for the last time. Empathy drove Parker to lean in and speak gently in Skye's ear, delivering the words she knew Skye needed to hear. "I forgive you."

A sound at the door caused Parker to glance back. She expected to see either the nurse or doctor come to deliver news about the results of Skye's x-rays. Instead she saw the last person she expected to see in this place. Morgan Bradley was stunning even when she was wild-eyed and harried. Her hair looked as though she had been running her hands through it and her suit was in disarray. Parker was so absorbed by the intense craving she felt for Morgan, it took her a moment to realize Morgan seemed paralyzed. She stood transfixed, her hand still on the door, her eyes riveted on something in the room. Parker followed her stare and realized Morgan's sight was trained on her hand, firmly clasping Skye's. She was aware she was still leaning close to Skye and her face was mere inches from Skye's ear. She jerked upright, but not before Morgan turned as if to leave.

"Morgan, wait." Parker started toward the door.

"Sorry. I didn't mean to barge in. I wanted to make sure you were all right." Morgan refused to meet Parker's eyes though she remained rooted in place.

"I am."

"I heard there was a shooting. I was…I didn't know…" Morgan couldn't manage to speak her fears out loud.

Parker grabbed her hands and ducked to meet Morgan's gaze. "Teddy Burke is a bad shot. At least when he's shooting at the living."

Morgan shook her head. She didn't have the capacity at this moment to process anything other than the fact Parker was alive. The terror she felt the entire drive over washed away at the sight of Parker here and whole, leaving her feeling empty and out of place. Parker wasn't alone and she seemed fine, at least fine enough to hold and comfort Skye. Morgan felt her presence was superfluous and she started to walk away.

Parker slid her arm around Morgan's waist and moved her into the hall. Spying a storage closet, she steered them into the cramped space. "Morgan. Look at me. Please." Morgan's resistance collapsed against the strength of Parker's embrace. She turned her head and met a look from eyes so full of longing she shook from the impact. She started to speak, but Parker placed a finger across her lips and delivered words of her own.

"I love you." Parker had started to say more, but once those words left her mouth she knew no more were necessary.

Morgan pulled her closer and held her tight. Her words displayed an uncertainty her body did not possess. "Why are you telling me this?"

Parker's smile was slow and easy. "Because it's true and life's too short to be scared to embrace the truth when you discover it."

Morgan looked at her and noticed for the first time, the gash on her head and her bloody and bruised hands. Shots fired. She could have lost Parker to the bullet of a psychopath before she ever had a chance to admit her own feelings. Standing here, in her arms, she couldn't bring herself to care about all the things she once deemed so important: job, boundaries, propriety. All she cared about was the pulsing desire, the unwavering affection, and the limitless adoration she felt for the strong, sexy Parker who had softly spoken words of promise she deserved to hear spoken in return. "Parker, I love you too. I want to find a way past the obstacles. Can you be patient with me?"

"No." Parker let her response register before she continued. "Like I said, life's too short. I quit your class. In fact, I have enough hours to graduate without it at the end of this semester and that is precisely what

I'm going to do. This case is over. All your obstacles are gone. Be with me. If you say no to me now, your reasons are all your own."

Morgan registered Parker's gently worded ultimatum and knew she had this one opportunity to accept or reject Parker's offer of love, life, happiness. Control, mastered through years of work, was the one thing standing between her and promises offered. Even as she had the thought, she realized the extent to which her desire to be in control blocked her path to happiness. If she loved Parker, truly loved her, she should be able to shout it from the rooftops, let alone profess her feelings in front of one other person. And she did love Parker. She'd loved her from the very first time they stood in the alley and Parker provided what she wanted, what she needed, without a second thought. She had loved her since the day Parker introduced herself in class. And she couldn't have loved her more than the day she listened to the tale of hurt and betrayal this formidable hero faced from the ones she trusted the most. Morgan reached her arms around Parker's neck and pulled her in. She spoke the words she knew Parker needed to hear, words she meant with all her heart, words she had spoken to no other, words she wanted the whole world to hear.

"I'm yours."

CHAPTER TWENTY-ONE

I've never seen so many people show up for early graduation."
Yolanda surveyed herself in the mirror in her office. "We only
have ten students graduating and there are over a hundred people in the
audience."

Morgan straightened Yolanda's hood and made sure her doctoral
robe was squared on her shoulders. "Maybe some of your students are
very popular."

"You think?" Yolanda grinned. "Don't you want to go see her
instead of hanging out here with me?"

"I'd love to, but she has plenty of friends fussing over her right
now. They've all been here for her from the beginning. This is their
time." Morgan sighed. "Besides, who else would be back here with you
making sure you had your robe on straight?"

"If you are looking for volunteers…"

They turned at the sound of the male voice and Yolanda called out,
"Jim, get the hell out of here. I'm getting dressed."

Jim Spencer was undaunted by rejection. "Don't worry. You both
have on more layers than I care to fool with." He looked at Morgan.
"Our friend has quite the fan club out there. I bet you can't wait for her
to graduate."

"Matter of fact, I can't. I have more work lined up than I can handle
on my own." Morgan referred to the law office she'd opened several
weeks before. "She better pass the bar the first time out. I've already
had business cards made up." Morgan pulled Jim aside. "I want you to
know how much I appreciate whatever it was you said to Gerald."

"Not a problem. Gerald may think that because his father's a bigshot, he can throw his weight around, but I happen to know his father very well, and I urged him to have a talk with his wayward son. Gerald will be happy with whatever grade he truly deserves from you."

"Enough chatter, people. Let's get this show on the road." Yolanda clapped her hands and waved them out of her office. With Jim leading the way, they made their way to the small auditorium where the rest of the faculty and family and friends of the graduating students were assembled. Midyear graduations were normally small, intimate affairs with no more than a dozen or so well-wishers in attendance, but today the room was packed. Morgan recognized many of the faces and realized Parker was indeed popular. Quite a few law school students postponed leaving for the holiday to be present for this occasion, including Dex and several 1Ls. As she continued to scan the audience, Morgan noted several faces from the bar where she met Parker for the first time. Parker, however, was nowhere in sight and Morgan fought the urge to leave her colleagues to go looking for her.

❖

"Stand up straight. You can frame this one and hang it in your new office."

Parker shifted one last time as she waited for Kelsey to take her picture. As much as she wanted to take off the silly robe and run far away from all the pomp and circumstance, she knew this day meant as much to her friends who had always been there for her as it did to herself. At least the ceremony for early graduation was a smallish affair. Parker was ready to reenter the real world and swap solving hypothetical problems for championing genuine causes. Kelsey's next words killed her hopes about a modest, intimate affair.

"You should see all the people who are out there. I heard someone saying it's standing room only."

"Jeez. Think we can sneak out the back door?"

"Not on your life. I know of a certain woman in particular who would be very disappointed if you didn't walk across that stage." Kelsey paused. "And speaking of disappointed women, Skye's here."

"I saw her come in."

"Does it bother you that she's here?"

Parker shook her head. "No. It's okay. I'm okay. Skye doesn't

have the power to hurt me anymore. I think what happened with Teddy
Burke shook her to the core. She's resigned from the force and her only
involvement with the law will be to testify at his trial. He'll go away for
a long time for what he did to Skye."

"Not long enough. Too bad they can't prosecute him for murdering
Camille."

"Damn straight." Parker grabbed Kelsey's arm. "Walk me to my
seat?"

The ceremony itself was a blur. Because she was sitting in the
front row, Parker didn't register how many people were in attendance
until she walked across the stage. Irene must have closed the bar for
the day and required all her employees to attend. And, of course, there
was Dex, who had teased her unmercifully about graduating early. He
insisted she did it so she could win their competition to be top of the
class. Most surprising were all the other law students in attendance.

And there, in the front row of the faculty section, was her favorite
professor. As Parker crossed the stage, she flashed Morgan a smile full
of promise.

❖

"I thought I'd never get you alone." Morgan slipped her arms
inside Parker's gown and pulled her close.

"There are a hundred people about ten feet away. At some point
they're going to get tired of punch and cookies and go in search of more."
Despite her words, Parker didn't move out of Morgan's embrace.

"Scared they'll find us in a compromising position?" Morgan ran
her palm along Parker's breast and sighed at the shivered response.

Parker unzipped her gown and pulled Morgan all the way in.
"Maybe."

Morgan held her close. She didn't care who witnessed her passion.
This day was about celebration. Parker was graduating and she and
Morgan were poised to begin their new life together as lovers and
partners. She resisted the urge to shout her feelings, instead whispering
in Parker's ear, "Would you like to know the first thing I have planned
for us?" Morgan didn't wait for Parker's response, instead relying on
her demonstrative skills to make her case.

About the Author

Carsen works by day (and sometimes night) as a criminal defense attorney in Dallas, Texas. Though her day job is often stranger than fiction, she can't seem to get enough and spends much of her free time devouring other people's fiction and plotting her own. Her goal as an author is to spin tales with plot lines as interesting as the true, but often unbelievable, stories she encounters in her law practice. Her first stab at fiction, *truelesbianlove.com*, was a pure romance, released as one of the debut novels in the Bold Strokes Aeros eBook line. *It Should be a Crime*, Carsen's second novel, draws heavily on her experience in the courtroom.

Carsen is married (Canadian-style) and she and her spouse live near White Rock Lake in Dallas, where they enjoy cycling and walking the trails with their four-legged children.

Books Available From Bold Strokes Books

Erosistible by Gill McKnight. When Win Martin arrives at a luxurious Greek hotel for a much-anticipated week of sun and sex with her new girlfriend, she is stunned to find her ex-girlfriend, Benny, is the proprietor. Aeros Ebook. (978-1-60282-134-7)

Looking Glass Lives by Felice Picano. Cousins Roger and Alistair become lifelong friends and discover their sexuality amidst the backdrop of twentieth-century gay culture. (978-1-60282-089-0)

Breaking the Ice by Kim Baldwin. Nothing is easy about life above the Arctic Circle—except, perhaps, falling in love. At least that's what pilot Bryson Faulkner hopes when she meets Karla Edwards. (978-1-60282-087-6)

It Should Be a Crime by Carsen Taite. Two women fulfill their mutual desire with a night of passion, neither expecting more until law professor Morgan Bradley and student Parker Casey meet again…in the classroom. (978-1-60282-086-9)

Rough Trade edited by Todd Gregory. Top male erotica writers pen their own hot, sexy versions of the term "rough trade," producing some of the hottest, nastiest, and most dangerous fiction ever published. (978-1-60282-092-0)

The High Priest and the Idol by Jane Fletcher. Jemeryl and Tevi's relationship is put to the test when the Guardian sends Jemeryl on a mission that puts her not only in harm's way, but back into the sights of a previous lover. (978-1-60282-085-2)

Point of Ignition by Erin Dutton. Amid a blaze that threatens to consume them both, firefighter Kate Chambers and property owner Alexi Clark redefine love and trust. (978-1-60282-084-5)

Secrets in the Stone by Radclyffe. Reclusive sculptor Rooke Tyler suddenly finds herself the object of two very different women's affections, and choosing between them will change her life forever. (978-1-60282-083-8)

Dark Garden by Jennifer Fulton. Vienna Blake and Mason Cavender are sworn enemies—who can't resist each other. Something has to give. (978-1-60282-036-4)

Late in the Season by Felice Picano. Set on Fire Island, this is the story of an unlikely pair of friends—a gay composer in his late thirties and an eighteen-year-old schoolgirl. (978-1-60282-082-1)

Punishment with Kisses by Diane Anderson-Minshall. Will Megan find the answers she seeks about her sister Ashley's murder or will her growing relationship with one of Ash's exes blind her to the real truth? (978-1-60282-081-4)

September Canvas by Gun Brooke. When Deanna Moore meets TV personality Faythe she is reluctantly attracted to her, but will Faythe side with the people spreading rumors about Deanna? (978-1-60282-080-7)

No Leavin' Love by Larkin Rose. Beautiful, successful Mercedes Miller thinks she can resume her affair with ranch foreman Sydney Campbell, but the rules have changed. (978-1-60282-079-1)

Between the Lines by Bobbi Marolt. When romance writer Gail Prescott meets actress Tannen Albright, she develops feelings that she usually only experiences through her characters. (978-1-60282-078-4)

Blue Skies by Ali Vali. Commander Berkley Levine leads an elite group of pilots on missions ordered by her ex-lover Captain Aidan Sullivan and everything is on the line—including love. (978-1-60282-077-7)

The Lure by Felice Picano. When Noel Cummings is recruited by the police to go undercover to find a killer, his life will never be the same. (978-1-60282-076-0)

Death of a Dying Man by J.M. Redmann. Mickey Knight, Private Eye and partner of Dr. Cordelia James, doesn't need a drop-dead gorgeous assistant—not until nature steps in. (978-1-60282-075-3)

Justice for All by Radclyffe. Dell Mitchell goes undercover to expose a human traffic ring and ends up in the middle of an even deadlier conspiracy. (978-1-60282-074-6)

Sanctuary by I. Beacham. Cate Canton faces one major obstacle to her goal of crushing her business rival, Dita Newton—her uncontrollable attraction to Dita. (978-1-60282-055-5)

The Sublime and Spirited Voyage of Original Sin by Colette Moody. Pirate Gayle Malvern finds the presence of an abducted seamstress, Celia Pierce, a welcome distraction until the captive comes to mean more to her than is wise. (978-1-60282-054-8)

Suspect Passions by VK Powell. Can two women, a city attorney and a beat cop, put aside their differences long enough to see that they're perfect for each other? (978-1-60282-053-1)

Just Business by Julie Cannon. Two women who come together—each for her own selfish needs—discover that love can never be as simple as a business transaction. (978-1-60282-052-4)

Sistine Heresy by Justine Saracen. Adrianna Borgia, survivor of the Borgia court, presents Michelangelo with the greatest temptations of his life while struggling with soul-threatening desires for the painter Raphaela. (978-1-60282-051-7)

Radical Encounters by Radclyffe. An out-of-bounds, outside-the-lines collection of provocative, superheated erotica by award-winning romance and erotica author Radclyffe. (978-1-60282-050-0)

Thief of Always by Kim Baldwin & Xenia Alexiou. Stealing a diamond to save the world should be easy for Elite Operative Mishael Taylor, but she didn't figure on love getting in the way. (978-1-60282-049-4)

X by JD Glass. When X-hacker Charlie Riven is framed for a crime she didn't commit, she accepts help from an unlikely source—sexy Treasury Agent Elaine Harper. (978-1-60282-048-7)

The Middle of Somewhere by Clifford Henderson. Eadie T. Pratt sets out on a road trip in search of a new life and ends up in the middle of somewhere she never expected. (978-1-60282-047-0)

Paybacks by Gabrielle Goldsby. Cameron Howard wants to avoid her old nemesis Mackenzie Brandt but their high school reunion brings up more than just memories. (978-1-60282-046-3)

Uncross My Heart by Andrews & Austin. When a radio talk show diva sets out to interview a female priest, the two women end up at odds and neither heaven nor earth is safe from their feelings. (978-1-60282-045-6)

Fireside by Cate Culpepper. Mac, a therapist, and Abby, a nurse, fall in love against the backdrop of friendship, healing, and defending one's own within the Fireside shelter. (978-1-60282-044-9)

A Pirate's Heart by Catherine Friend. When rare book librarian Emma Boyd searches for a long-lost treasure map, she learns the hard way that pirates still exist in today's world—some modern pirates steal maps, others steal hearts. (978-1-60282-040-1)

Trails Merge by Rachel Spangler. Parker Riley escapes the high-powered world of politics to Campbell Carson's ski resort—and their mutual attraction produces anything but smooth running. (978-1-60282-039-5)

Dreams of Bali by C.J. Harte. Madison Barnes worships work, power, and success, and she's never allowed anyone to interfere—that is, until she runs into Karlie Henderson Stockard. Aeros EBook (978-1-60282-070-8)

The Limits of Justice by John Morgan Wilson. Benjamin Justice and reporter Alexandra Templeton search for a killer in a mysterious compound in the remote California desert. (978-1-60282-060-9)

Designed for Love by Erin Dutton. Jillian Sealy and Wil Johnson don't much like each other, but they do have to work together—and what they desire most is not what either of them had planned. (978-1-60282-038-8)

Calling the Dead by Ali Vali. Six months after Hurricane Katrina, NOLA Detective Sept Savoie is a cop who thinks making a relationship work is harder than catching a serial killer—but her current case may prove her wrong. (978-1-60282-037-1)

truelesbianlove.com by Carsen Taite. Mackenzie Lewis and Dr. Jordan Wagner have very different ideas about love, but they discover that truelesbianlove is closer than a click away. Aeros EBook (978-1-60282-069-2)